MW01529102

Omigod, had I been sleeping with a murderer? The pieces all fit together perfectly. And if they had her fingerprint in the victim's blood, what other explanation could there be? Wait a minute—I had shared a bed with this woman and she showed me tenderness like I'd never known. Could sheer evil and incredible tenderness exist in the same person?

Courting Death

by
Margie S. Schweitzer

Justice House Publishing, Inc.
Tacoma, Washington, USA
www.justicehouse.com

COURTING DEATH

Copyright © 2001 by Margie S. Schweitzer.

All Rights Reserved, including the right to reproduce this book, or
portions thereof, in any form whatsoever. For information contact
Justice House Publishing, Inc., 3902 South 56th St., Tacoma, WA
98409, USA.

Cover by R Paterson-Reed

Book Design by R Paterson-Reed

All characters and events in this book are fictitious. Names, characters, places and incidents are products of the author's imagination or
are used fictiously. Any resemblance to actual events or locales or
persons, living or dead, is entirely coincidental.

This is printed on acid-free paper. The typeface is Garramond, 11
point. The paper is Book Opaque.

ISBN 0970887450

Initial printing August 2002.

PRINTED IN THE USA

Dedication

I would like to dedicate this book to the memory of Joanna McNamara, a dear friend from whom I learned a lot about life, love and metamorphosis. I also dedicate this work to the love of my life, Nancy Langford, without whose support, gentle and constructive criticism, and patience; this work would not have been possible.

A Real Fixer-Upper

The party was pretty much like every other cocktail party I'd ever been to, with the usual assortment of buffalo wings, deviled eggs and weenie wraps, the latter an ironic choice for a mostly lesbian soirée. People were getting hammered and making polite chit-chat with strangers whose names would be forgotten moments after being spoken. I stood in the corner, propping up a potted palm, surveying the surreal social dance that emerges at such gatherings.

Then, *she* waltzed in. I noticed her immediately. Nearly six feet tall, she had a commanding presence and stately appearance. The way she carried herself conveyed an air of utter confidence, control, and effortless grace. I was completely mesmerized by this Amazonian beauty. As she moved in my direction, I felt my knees buckle slightly. For a moment, I thought I was going to nose-dive right into the Oriental rug. In my drinking days, this was a fairly common occurrence, but within the past 10 and-a-half years, carpet-diving was an event that I'd managed to remove from my list of party tricks. On this occasion, I somehow maintained an upright position, despite my buckled knees and the resulting loss of blood flow to my feet.

The co-hostess of the party, my best friend Samantha Devaraux, guided this gorgeous hunk of woman toward me, and I just stood there with a stupid grin on my face. No, not the *pleasant*, stupid grin that says "Hi, I'm terminally daft, but pleased to meet you anyway." Rather, the grin on my face was of the *crazed*, stupid grin variety, the one that says "I'm an ax murderer with a below average I.Q." It was just frozen there on my face. Try as I might, I couldn't manage to rearrange my facial expression into one that communicated any semblance of sentient, intelligent carbon-based life. Before I had time to dwell on this sudden onset of facial paralysis, the Amazon goddess was standing there in front of me. She seemed not to notice the idiotic grin plastered on my face, or perhaps she was just too polite to stare. Unfortunately, when my hormones take control, manners go out the window—I couldn't tear my eyes away from this magnificent beauty.

Sam said, "Sandy Garrett, I'd like you to meet my best friend, J.Z. Mackenzie." Sandy looked at me with genuine warmth in her eyes. With an alluring lilt in her voice, she said, "Nice to make your acquaintance, J.Z." After I stammered out a few "ums," "ers," and "uhs," I finally replied, "Likewise, I'm sure." That is what they say in all those high-class TV shows I'd watched through the years. I could tell at first glance, or, rather, at first leer, that Sandy Garrett was definitely high-class all the way.

For a moment, we said nothing, and I tried to take in all of her dazzling beauty at once. I allowed it to wash over me, and I could feel that familiar tingle on the back of my neck. The tingle that eventually works its way to southern parts of my anatomy. That sensation is an early warning system designed to communicate the following message: "Hey, wake up, stupid—you're about to go rushing headlong off a very steep cliff!" I always ignore that feature of the sensation, and enjoy it for its purely hedonistic, animal aspects. I have the bruised heart and ego to prove it. As I enjoyed the tingling on the back of my neck (and other places), my eyes wandered up and down this breathtaking creature in front of me, though I tried not to be obvious about it. She had wavy brown hair, the color of coffee, with just a hint of cream. It was thick and flowing, and fell just below her shoulders. Her eyes were a pale, icy green, the color of spring water on a cool morning, but much more inviting. These eyes revealed experience and worldliness beyond her years, which I guessed to be about 35. She was dark-complected, but I could tell that she came by it honestly, as her skin was flawless and looked as soft as my favorite velveteen pillow. I wanted to reach out and touch her lovely face, but I resisted the urge.

Sandy was dressed casually in tight-fitting black jeans, black leather ankle boots, a gray v-neck sweater that hung seductively off her oh-so-inviting shoulder, and a white tank top. Her only adornment was tiny silver hoop earrings. Simplicity at its finest. Sandy ran her fingers through her long hair and asked, "So tell me, what does 'J.Z.' stand for, anyway?"

I smiled, shook my head, and replied, "Well, that's one of the great mysteries of all time. Outside of my family, only Sam knows the answer to that one, and she's sworn to secrecy."

"That bad, huh?"

"Well, let's just say that it really doesn't suit me, that's all." Sandy smiled at me, and we grew silent for a few moments. But it wasn't that awkward silence you usually feel when you meet someone new. It was more like a long, comfortable pause, during which we both admired the scenery.

As I re-emerged from my brief lust-induced catatonia, I noticed that Sam had conveniently wandered off to mingle with other guests. But she kept trying to steal what she thought were surreptitious glances in our direction. Subtlety has never been Sam's strong suit. As I madly wracked the recesses of my brain for something witty to say, Sandy asked how long I had known Sam. I explained, with a modicum of nervous quaver in my voice, that I had known Sam since the fifth grade. About halfway into the school year, my parents moved the family from Portland, Oregon to Cloverdale, Oregon. On my first day at Cloverdale Elementary, Sam had taken me under her wing like a mother hen. We'd been best friends ever since, and she was still trying to look out for me. Some things never change.

"So, Sandy, how do you know Sam? She's never mentioned you."

Oh, that was smart. Now she's going to think that Sam is a heel for not telling me about her, and I'm a bigger heel for pointing it out.

"Oh, we've only just become acquainted quite recently. I'm new in town, and I've become involved with a couple of the same volunteer programs in which Sam participates. It was certainly nice of Sam to invite me to this party."

Nice, no; sneaky, yes. Now don't get me wrong—Sam is, without a doubt, the nicest, most generous, and most sincere person I know, or have ever known. But this invitation to Sandy had nothing to do with "nice" and everything to do with Sam's favorite pastime: fixing me up with women who, according to her, are my long-lost soul mates. The fact that there've been 30 or 40 (I've lost count) of these so-called "soul mates" does not dampen Sam's enthusiasm one bit. It's a crusade of epic proportions for her. It's like the search for the holy grail, and, like a rabid zealot, she will forge ahead with her altruistic mission until she can declare victory over the evil forces of the world which have conspired to keep me separated from my one true love. I have reminded Sam, on occasion, that warriors often meet with untimely ends, sometimes at the hands of those for whom they are fighting. Sam has never picked up on any of my veiled threats. Perhaps I need to be more forthright with her.

At any rate, joining me with a soul mate has been Sam's pet project for the past four years, ever since she met and fell in love with Nealy, a wonderful, earthy, free-spirited photographer, who was quickly cured of her wanderlust when she met Sam. Nealy does not approve of Sam's meddling in my love life, insisting that love is this Zen-like thing that happens only when the time is right; it can't be forced. Such counsel does not deter Sam: she was the kid who was stubbornly determined to force the square peg into the round hole, even if it required a sledgehammer to get the job done. When Sam is determined to make something happen, watch out. She can be irritatingly hardheaded. Contrary to popular belief, diamonds are not the world's hardest substance.

Sandy and I chatted for most of the evening, about nothing in particular. It was the most riveting discussion about "nothing" that I've ever engaged in. We didn't discuss much in the way of personal information, beyond some juvenile shenanigans that Sam and I had pulled in high school. Like the time we photocopied our asses and used them as the basis for an art project. By the time we painted them, poor Mr. Dittmeyer, our art teacher, didn't realize what they were. Sam got an "A" on the assignment, and when Dittmeyer remarked in class, "Nice use of space," the class cracked up, much to Dittmeyer's confusion and dismay. Because I only got a "B," Sam uses this as the basis for her assertion that she has a better ass. I know better than to argue with her.

As Sandy and I chatted about current events, new movies, good restaurants, and good books, we learned that we are both avid Atlanta Braves fans. This common bond consumed much of the conversation.

I never knew that an RBI could sound so sensuous. I listened with rapt attention as Sandy discussed the pros and cons of inter-league play and the limitations imposed by the designated hitter in the American League. As I listened, I struggled (in vain) to refrain from noticeably drooling down the front of my shirt. Even in the backwoods of Cloverdale, this is considered bad form on a first date, even a fix-me-up date. Anyway, it was Sam's new shirt and I didn't think she'd take kindly to having it returned with drool stains down the front. Throughout our conversation, I noticed Sam's watchful eyes upon us, and I couldn't miss that annoying, smug, self-satisfied look on her face. I think she was mentally running through the options of where to register Sandy and me for wedding gifts.

Shortly after midnight, as I was taking a gulp of my club soda, Sandy leaned close to me and whispered, à la Kathleen Turner, "Why don't we get out of here and go to my place." Needless to say, the club soda that I was in the process of swallowing as these words conjured up rather risqué imagery in my head did an impromptu, spirited water ballet in the back of my throat. Half of the club soda was sucked down my windpipe with Hoover-like force, while the other half spewed forth in a most unladylike fashion. I began coughing and gasping for air. *Very attractive, J.Z., not to mention smooth.* I was thankful that club soda did not erupt from my nostrils (Sam was witness to one such event; it was not pretty, and the carbonation was quite painful). Between hacking fits, I murmured, "I think I swallowed part of the lime." I didn't want my Amazon goddess to think that this little episode was precipitated by her suggestion that we adjourn to her place. I don't think she was fooled for a second. However, my display of poor party etiquette did not prompt Sandy to rescind her too-tempting-to-pass-up offer. I was encouraged and delighted by Sandy's willingness to overlook my rough edges, which are all too plentiful.

Before we made our getaway from the party, we located Sam and Nealy to thank them for the lovely evening. After pleasantries were exchanged, Sandy excused herself to use the powder room before we departed. I thought Sam was going to come unglued. She was actually jumping up and down—a 34 year-old woman jumping up and down, and only slightly inebriated. She would make a great game show contestant. Sam positively glowed with pride as she exclaimed, "I'm just so happy for you. I can't contain myself." Nealy looked on with disapproval, but remained silent. I replied, "Slow down—we're just going back to her place to talk. We're not picking out china patterns yet."

"I know, but something tells me that this is the one. I can just feel it in my bones."

"I think it might be the early onset of osteoporosis you're feeling in your bones. You better have that checked out. Look Sam, you do this every time you set me up with someone—you're planning the wedding before we've even gotten to know each other. And when it doesn't work out, you're more disappointed than me. Try to keep it all in perspective this time, will you?"

Sam just looked at me with a little glimmer in her eyes as she responded, "But this time is different." The little glimmer turned into a full-fledged gleam.

"Need I remind you that's what you said only two short weeks ago when you fixed me up with the psychotic taxidermist, Dede, who has more baggage than Samsonite? Apparently the baggage from this life is not sufficient, however, as she belongs to some Shirley MacLaine chat group that advocates past life regression therapy. She's convinced that she used to be Eleanor Roosevelt. I woke up in the middle of the night at her place and thought that the stuffed elk on the wall was trying to attack me."

Sam retorted, with a bit of hurt and defensiveness in her tone, "You're exaggerating as usual, J.Z. And anyway, Dede could not have been that bad, since you spent the night with her, which, by the way, is something you failed to mention during our date debriefing."

"Speaking of debriefings, I think *you* need a good debriefing, and I'm going to speak with Nealy about that soon. Listen, I *slept* at Dede's chamber of horrors—that's all. I didn't even want to do that, but I felt like one of her many trapped animals. Every time I tried to leave, she would start talking about something else and refill my drink. Then she'd look at me with those puppy dog eyes that you use on me when you need a favor. I finally gave up trying to escape and fell asleep on the couch. I think she was still talking about her past life as a chambermaid when I dozed off. You'd think if someone were going to imagine past lives, they'd at least come up with something more interesting than a chambermaid. Geez."

Again Sam looked up at me with that innocent expression she has and said, "J.Z., forget about the Dede debacle; this time is different. I just know it. Trust me." Famous last words. I quickly realized the futility of continuing this line of conversation with Sam while she was in the throes of a particularly virulent attack of terminal optimism.

Sam noticed Sandy approaching and said with a slight giggle, "By the way, nice imitation of a water fountain." My look told Sam that I was not amused, but I was thankful that she did not insist on telling the nostril/club soda tale. She'd wait for the third or fourth date before *completely* embarrassing me.

Sandy rejoined me and we bade farewell to our hostesses. As we approached the front door, I glanced over my shoulder to see Sam giving me the thumbs-up gesture; Nealy, ever the strong silent type, just rolled her eyes. For Sam's sake, I hoped this would work out.

Promises, Promises

I followed Sandy back to her place on the outskirts of our little hamlet. Despite its close proximity to town, it was surprisingly secluded and pleasingly quiet. It was a big rambling farmhouse surrounded by mammoth fir tress that must have been there for generations. The house itself was white with dark green shutters, complete with a whitewashed picket fence. The old, well-maintained house also featured a huge screened-in front porch that Sandy had filled with plants of every sort. By surveying this abundant, healthy plant life, I quickly surmised that Sandy would not be overly impressed with my mostly brown, wilted fern that my cats sometimes used as a hairball repository...or worse.

Inside, the place had beautiful hardwood floors and intricate crown molding. The living room contained a white stone fireplace and a mantle covered with what I assumed were family photos. The furniture and decor consisted primarily of earth tones, which gave the house a warm, inviting feeling, much like its current occupant. There was little artwork on the walls as yet. However, Sandy had hung two impressionist prints on one wall of the living room, somewhat reminiscent of Monet, but done in light earth tones. One piece depicted fall trees in the rain, very appropriate for the Northwest. The other piece, presumably by the same artist, illustrated a lake on a crisp fall morning, with heavy fog rolling off the lake.

As I was taking off my jacket, I said, "Wow, this is a great place, and so comfortable."

"Well, it's getting there. As you can see, the furnishings are rather sparse, since I haven't been here long. I love artwork. I think it adds character to a home and really personalizes it. But I'm kind of picky, so I'll take my time choosing what I think will accentuate the décor."

"Still, you've made a wonderful start."

"Well, thanks. Would you like something to drink? I think I have some brandy, and maybe some Merlot. Which would you prefer?"

"Actually, I'm quite fond of both. But, you see, AA, anal-retentive sticklers for sobriety that they are, frowns on any sort of imbibing. I've looked for some kind of loophole in the rules, but I can't find any."

"Oh, I'm sorry. I didn't know that you were in recovery. I just thought you liked club soda, especially when you tried to share it with everyone at the party." She flashed me a playful smile.

"Oh, you noticed that, did you? Spraying of the sacred club soda has been a ritual in Cloverdale for years. It dates back generations. By the way, what do you use to remove a club soda stain?"

She giggled as she tossed back her head and gently ran her fingers through her lush hair. There was something in the arch of her back, the sultry curve of her neck, and her slow, deliberate movements that I found intensely erotic. I wanted nothing more at that moment than to run over to her, gather her up in my arms, gently kiss the contours of her slim, Audrey Hepburn-like neck, and explore every inch of this glorious being. I've been that impetuous on a few occasions, I must admit. Okay, more than a few. But something stopped me this time. Dammit if it wasn't Sam! She was right: this time *was* different. Sandy was not a one-night-stand. I could feel that already. I mean, I didn't even know her, though I did have a pretty good idea of her favorite National League Baseball players, and I knew about her affinity for chili dogs with lots of onions and jalapeños. There was something between us. Call it chemistry or electricity, but it was definitely there. And it wasn't just her undeniable good looks that caught my attention. It was that nameless…*something* that we all look for in that certain someone. I just felt comfortable with her. Admittedly, her looks were a bit intimidating, but she didn't seem to be aware of her own beauty.

No, I wouldn't be impetuous this time. Instead, I would savor every attribute of this voluptuous, intelligent woman like a fine Godiva chocolate, filling my senses with her richness, appreciating every nuance and every hidden treasure. She deserved that. Certainly I was capable of exerting a modicum of control over my animal urges. Wasn't I?

As she finished stretching, Sandy turned toward me, her face illuminated in angelic fashion by the golden glow of a Stiffel lamp in the corner. "Well, why don't we wander into the kitchen and see what sort of AA-approved beverages I have on hand." As we made our way to the kitchen, we passed through the dining room, which held a solid oak dining set and a beautifully handcrafted china hutch, lined with fine china plates featuring a simple, yet striking, design of delicate lavender flowers.

I expected the kitchen to have some old, dilapidated stove, and maybe even an antique Norge refrigerator. Much to my surprise, it was a thoroughly modern kitchen with a gas stove, a Jenn-Aire grill, a huge refrigerator/freezer combo with a built-in ice maker, cabinets as far as the eye could see, and every smaller appliance known to the modern world. I gasped, and Sandy said, "Yes, I was just as shocked myself when I saw it for the first time. The former owner was a retired chef who still liked to spend his days creating new dishes. It's one of the reasons I bought this place. That and the privacy it offers. I love to cook. I find it uniquely relaxing."

Now was probably not the time to mention my culinary masterpiece: Chef Boyardee Surprise (Spaghettios, sliced Vienna sausages, a liberal sprinkling of parmesan cheese, and several dashes of hot sauce). The surprise happens the day after you eat it.

Rather than reveal my secret recipe, I replied, "Well, I'd be happy to allow you the honor of cooking for me anytime. It just so happens that I like eating. I find it uniquely relaxing. But I must warn you, I don't do anchovies or snails of any sort."

As I was admiring Sandy's impressive array of kitchen appliances, many of which I didn't recognize due to my culinary ineptness, I spotted *it* sitting there in the corner: the Barista 5000, the most sophisticated espresso machine on the planet. As I stood there in a state of wide-eyed wonder, an excited gurgle escaped from the back of my throat. Sandy looked at me with genuine concern registering on her delicate face, perhaps worrying that I was having a stroke. She asked, "Are you okay? Do you need some water or something?"

I whispered reverently, "You've got a Barista 5000" with disbelief and undisguised merriment in my tone.

Sandy responded, "Well, yes, I love espresso, and I believe in buying the best. If it wasn't so late, I'd make you a latte or cappuccino."

"Late? It's never too late for espresso, especially when it's made with a Barista 5000."

"Are you nuts? It's 12:30 in the morning. You want an espresso *now*?"

"Yes, ma'am. Anything with four shots will do."

"Well, all right. I'll make it for you, but I'm not taking responsibility if your heart starts to race uncontrollably."

"Too late."

She looked at me and blushed slightly—not much, just a hint of rosiness on her cheeks—though she quickly regained her composure and whipped me up the most exquisite cappuccino, with just the right amount of nutmeg and cinnamon on top of a thick layer of foam. She brewed herself some herbal tea and we adjourned to the living room.

"I could make a fire if you'd like."

"No, that's not necessary. Let's just sit and talk." We sat on the sofa, close enough to be cozy, but not too close. I took a sip of my cappuccino and turned to say something to Sandy, and she started laughing before I'd even opened my mouth. "What's so funny?" I asked, a bit defensively. She leaned over and brushed the cappuccino foam off my upper lip with her index finger and said, "You're not having much luck with your beverages tonight." We were just kind of frozen there on the sofa, leaning close together, for what seemed like an eternity. I broke the spell when I said, "The foam is running down your finger" and she said "Oh my" and licked the foam off her hand. Oh my was right. Did we really have to take this slowly? I mean, sometimes just plunging in right away is the best thing. No, no, no! I promised myself that I wouldn't rush this, and I was determined to keep that promise if it killed me.

I made a big production of clearing my throat and moved a few inches away from Sandy. I was trying, mightily, to look casual, but that scene from the movie *Body Heat* kept replaying itself in my head, the scene where Kathleen Turner spills a partially melted cherry snow cone down the front of her white dress and William Hurt offers to lick it off. However, in my version of the scene, William Hurt was nowhere to be found. In an effort to make the erotic imagery stop, I made myself think of dead kitties, Spam, and Howard Cosell, all at once. That seemed to do the trick.

With my raging hormones once again under control, at least temporarily, I said, "You know, we talked a lot at the party about baseball, food, books, and other stuff, but we never really got around to anything personal. I don't even know what you do for a living."

She shrugged and said, "Nothing much, I'm afraid. I got my money the old-fashioned way: I inherited it. My grandparents left me a modest inheritance, and I've made some good investments over the years. I spend quite a bit of my time managing my investments."

"So you're…rich."

"You don't have to say it like it's a dirty word. But no, I'm not what I would call rich by a long shot. I'm merely comfortable. I don't have to work, but I do have a budget that I must stick to. It's not like I can buy anything I want and travel around the world."

"Still, you must be some kind of financial wizard."

Sandy chuckled and said, "No, not at all. It's mostly common sense and luck. Plus, I do have good instincts when it comes to financial matters. I've made a few bad investments, but overall, I've done pretty well for myself."

"All that financial gobbeldy-gook gives me a headache. Do you really like investing?"

"If you mean do I find it fulfilling in some way, the answer is no. It can be challenging, to be sure. But for the most part, I manage my own financial affairs because I don't trust anyone else to do it properly. I know how hard my grandparents worked for that money. So, I think of investment management as a necessary evil."

Sandy looked wistful for a moment and continued. "What I really enjoy is writing. It's what I studied in college, and what I really have a passion for. I've had a few short stories and poems published, and when I lived in Kingston, I taught creative writing classes at the community college. I enjoyed that. It felt like I was doing something meaningful, you know? Inspiring others to be creative. And of course, I've always been involved in various volunteer programs in the community."

"It sounds like a pretty full life."

"Yeah, I have no complaints. But I've monopolized the floor long enough. Tell me about you. What do you do?"

"I'm a private investigator, a job that I dearly love. Though I'll never be rich. It's not all glitz and glamour like most people think, but it's rarely boring. I admit that I've had to do some things that are…well, kind of sleazy. You know, like hiding in the bushes with a high-powered telephoto lens taking pictures of some poor woman's husband doing the humpty-dance with his secretary. Unfortunately, those kinds of gigs usually pay the most, and I'm not in a position to turn down good money. But I've also been involved in investigations that uncovered criminal activities, and I've located missing persons, and so on. It's enjoyable, challenging work on the whole."

Sandy looked as if she was in awe of me and said, "How did you decide that you wanted to be a private investigator?"

"Well, after I punched my co-worker, another attorney, and found my belongings on the sidewalk, I thought it might be time for a career change."

The look of awe was replaced by one of carefully controlled fear. "Wait a minute…you were an attorney before becoming a P.I.? And you assaulted a co-worker?"

"Yeah. Boy, was going to law school a big mistake. I mean, some aspects of the practice of law are rewarding, but other aspects are so intolerable that it just wasn't worth it, at least not for me. All the assholes you have to deal with on a daily basis—partners and senior associates in your own firm, opposing counsel, and of course, clients who have unreasonable expectations and think that their case is the only one you're handling. Not to mention the total lack of ethics. No, it wasn't my thing. I went home every night feeling dirty and unappreciated."

"Um…you glossed over the assault thing."

I waved my hand as if swatting an annoying fly. "Oh, that. Well, it was kind of a mutual thing. I worked with this bitch-on-wheels attorney named Camilla Bitzburger, commonly referred to behind her back as 'Bitchburger,' who was a senior associate. She was always taking credit for my work, stabbing me in the back, and generally devising ways to make my professional life miserable. I don't even remember what we were fighting about on that particular day. Lord knows, we fought constantly. But somehow, we ended up rolling around on my office floor together, pulling each other's hair, scratching, biting, spitting, and engaging in other displays of unsportsmanlike conduct."

I cocked my head and stared off into the distance for a moment.

"Hmmm…come to think of it, if she wasn't such a bitch, I probably would have been turned on by the episode. Anyway, I quickly grew weary of the brawl and, in an effort to end it, I punched Camilla right in the nose. It started bleeding like crazy, and Camilla was screaming and carrying on like she was dying. Before I knew it, me and my stuff were tossed, unceremoniously, out the front door. I was history, just like that. In retrospect, they did me a favor."

"Did she press charges?"

"Bitchburger? Naw, she didn't have the guts. I kept a detailed log of every ethical rule she broke, just to cover my ass. She found a copy of it one day while rifling through my desk, and was smart enough to drop the whole thing."

Sandy sat there in silence for a few moments, before she said, "My, my, assault, blackmail, and spying on people doing, what was that charming term you used? Oh yes, the humpty-dance. What an impressive repertoire of borderline criminal skills you have."

"Well, I haven't had time to go to charm school. I do what I have to do in order to survive, and not all of it is pretty or genteel."

Sandy smiled and said, "I was only joking. Lighten up."

I inwardly relaxed and noticed that Sandy had moved a bit closer to me. My mouth suddenly got very dry, my heart rate increased, and I began to perspire. To make matters worse, my breathing sounded like that of an obscene caller. It was definitely time to get up and stretch. As I did so, Sandy looked at me with this mixture of hurt, confusion, and dejection, and she asked, "Is something wrong? You seem kind of nervous."

"It must be all that espresso I consumed. You warned me about that. I think I'll just sit over here on the footstool for a while."

Sandy momentarily pouted, but finally said, "If you insist, but I happen to know that the sofa is much more comfortable."

I could hardly argue as I sat in a grossly contorted position on a hard wooden affair that was almost big enough for one of my ass cheeks. But since she had no other living room furniture as yet, I really had no choice. So, I put on my best fake grin and said that I was fine on the footstool.

After a little more pouting, Sandy asked about my family. I told her that my father had been a welder and my mom was a secretary. Strictly lower middle class. But they had managed to scrimp and save, and had retired to Arizona. I explained that I see them once or twice a year for brief visits. I hate hot weather, so I rarely visit for more than two or three days. I also told her about my two brothers, with whom I have no contact. One is a right-wing religious freak who is sure that there is a special place in hell reserved for "queers." His name, appropriately, is Dick. I've told Dick to be careful about condemning people to hell, since most deities don't take kindly to open displays of hubris. He had to consult Webster's to figure out what I was talking about.

My other brother, Thad, I explained, is a worthless piece of white trash who belongs to some "white power" organization. He has never held a job a day in his life, and yet he can, with a straight face, cast aspersions on the "lazy" minorities who are dragging this country down. But don't look for Thad on the first of the month hoping to engage him in some heated debate about race relations—he's in line to get his food stamps. Not that Thad possesses enough of a vocabulary to actually engage in a heated debate of any sort.

Sandy sat there in awkward silence for a few moments before she replied, "Well…your folks sound nice."

"They are; they're good people. A little old-fashioned, but most people their age are. What about your family?"

She hesitated, with an embarrassed and sad look on her face, but she finally began telling me about her parents. She'd grown up in a small town in Indiana, and had, at least in her estimation, a very happy childhood, though she had no siblings to play with or confide in. Her father had owned and operated a small neighborhood butcher shop and her mom worked in retail, selling cosmetics, clothes, shoes, and the like. At first, times were hard, and they had to struggle and pinch pennies to get by. Gradually, the butcher shop operation expanded, with her dad opening up similar shops in other small towns in Indiana and Illinois. The shops were all successful, generating a healthy revenue. Eventually, her father sold the entire business to some big grocery store chain and became a very wealthy man.

Sandy grew quiet with a faraway look in her eyes. "Yeah, the money began coming in, but we all paid a price. Mom and I rarely saw Dad after he added the first new shops. He was always traveling from shop to shop to check on the operations and the profits. Mom didn't have to work then, and she fell into this depression that she never really emerged from."

"Are they still alive?"

"Mom died years ago. The doctor said it was her heart, but I think she died of loneliness and neglect. Dad hardly noticed. Last I heard, he had retired and moved to Florida, but that's been a while back. We fell out of touch, and neither of us was ever interested enough to try to locate the other."

I couldn't think of an appropriate response, and Sandy looked like she had more to say. So I just waited.

"I know it's hard to understand when you've never had money, but believe me, more often than not, it just messes everything up. My family was so happy in the beginning, with just the one small shop. After school and in the summertime, dad would let me help out in the shop, even when I was just a little thing. At first, it was just small stuff, like sweeping, and cleaning the display cases, but I loved being there with my dad. He had such a wonderful sense of humor, and he had a real zest for life. Between customers, he would enchant me with these incredible tales, and sometimes we'd play checkers, or just sit and talk. It was nice."

Sandy got up and walked over to the mantle and stared at an old photograph of three smiling faces. Then she continued.

"As I grew older, my role at the shop expanded. My dad taught me everything about the business, from how to grind sausage and cut a perfect New York strip, to how to get the best deals from all the vendors. I guess he thought I was going to follow in his footsteps. I did for a while, but when I left to go to college in California, he was absolutely furious. He asked me why I wanted to throw away a perfectly good trade for some, as he termed it, 'artsy-fartsy' vocation like writing. It's when I was away at college that my grandparents died in a house fire."

"How did you end up here in Oregon?"

"When I was in college, one of my friends persuaded me to come up here with her on break, to visit her family and friends. I loved Oregon the minute I saw it, and I promised myself that I would return when I was finished with school."

By this time I had returned to the sofa. I had no choice—there was no feeling remaining in my right ass cheek, and very little in the left one. I had that "pins and needles" feeling in my posterior, and not in a good way, which I very much wanted to alleviate. But everything I thought about doing to address the problem conjured up imagery of the family dog using his front paws to scoot his ass across the carpet in order to stop the itching in that oh-so-hard-to-reach place. Thus, I simply endured the discomfort.

Sandy, who had been gazing out at the night sky from her vantage point across the room, rejoined me on the sofa. She looked at me with kindness in her eyes as she said, "It's funny. I'm normally a very private person, and it's hard for me to open up and talk about personal matters. But there's just something about you. I don't exactly know what it is, but you're very easy to talk to." As she spoke these words, she reached over and gently took my hand in hers. She could sense my uneasiness, and she said, "You've been acting like a scared rabbit all night. What's wrong?"

I averted my eyes from her intense gaze and replied, "I just want to maintain my mystery and allure for a while. That's all."

Sandy replied in a breathless, taunting voice, "Do you think your mystery and allure will remain intact if I kiss you?"

After I started breathing again and was able to respond, I whispered in a weak, shaky voice, "I guess."

Since Sandy had been trying to get close to me all night, I expected her to lunge at me for this first kiss. But she didn't. Instead, she gently caressed the right side of my face and looked longingly at me for several heavenly moments. Then she leaned forward, ever so slowly, and tenderly kissed the side of my neck, my earlobe, and my cheek, before moving on to my lips. Her lips were so soft against mine, like angels' wings brushing up against me. Her movements were supremely sensuous, and I hoped that the kiss would never end. When it did, we were both breathing heavy, and we held each other. I breathed in her scent, which was a mixture of musk and vanilla. Sandy softly kissed my forehead and brushed the side of her face against mine. She kissed me again, this time with more fervor. I could tell that her entire body was becoming involved. She brushed my cheek with her hand, and her tongue playfully darted inside my mouth. She began pressing her writhing body closer to mine.

I gently pushed her away and said, "I think my mystery and allure are about to be severely compromised."

Once she could catch her breath, Sandy said, "You're looking more and more alluring to me every second. And pretty much everything is a mystery to me. I couldn't even figure out that stupid Rubik's Cube. Besides, mystery and allure are highly overrated traits."

"Well, it's not just the mystery and allure thing, to be honest. We are living in dangerous times, you know. I should really ask about your sexual history, just as a precaution."

"You're kidding, right?"

"No, I think it's the prudent thing to do. You can't be too careful these days."

After a few moments of thought, Sandy replied, "I guess it's a reasonable request. But how much of a history do you want? I mean, do you want a whole list, or what?"

I looked at her with renewed respect and said, "My, Sandy, you say that as though the list is quite extensive. About how many hours should we set aside for this little project?"

As a becoming shade of pink spread across her high cheekbones, Sandy said, "I didn't mean to imply that I'd been intimate with a vast array of people. I just meant...oh, never mind. Where would you like me to start?"

"The beginning is always a good place."

"Well, I got kind of a late start. When I was growing up in Greenburg, Indiana, population 18,523 and right smack dab in the middle of the Bible Belt, I was sure that if a sexual thought of any sort crept into my head, I was going straight to Hell. Somewhere in the back of my head, I knew I was different, but I didn't know how or why. I messed around with a few boys, nothing serious. When that didn't do it for me, I began thinking maybe I was frigid or somehow dysfunctional. I was in my early 20's when I went away to college, and still, these vague notions that I was different persisted, but hadn't congealed into anything specific."

At this point, Sandy rose from the sofa and paced the living room floor with a nostalgic expression on her youthful face. Her leather boots made a click clack sound on the hard, polished surface, the sound bouncing off the mostly bare living room walls. After a few moments, she continued. "Away from the oppressive, narrow-minded morality of Greenburg, those vague notions began to take shape. I met openly homosexual people, from all walks of life, and immediately felt a real kinship, yet guilt and shame prevented me from forming anything more than friendship with the lesbians I met. It was such a difficult, confusing time. I mean, I was definitely attracted to women, but the guilt I was feeling wouldn't allow me to explore, or even acknowledge that attraction. I might have continued in a state of sexual limbo for years, except..."

I waited patiently for Sandy to continue. When she didn't, I prompted her. "Except what?"

"It's kind of funny when I look back on it now—how it happened, so casually. My roommate, Rose, had a friend coming up from Southern California to visit for a week. About halfway through the week, Rose asked that I entertain her friend, Angie, for the evening. Rose had some prior commitment that she couldn't get out of, one that would keep her out of town until the following day. I thought Angie was a sweet girl, so I readily agreed to spend the evening with her. Angie and I decided to order some pizza, smoke a little pot, and listen to her new tapes. Angie was so easy-going, such a fun-loving, free spirit. And beautiful: long blonde hair, blue eyes the color of cornflowers, a deep tan, and legs that would put Tina Turner to shame. A real, honest-to-god 'California Girl' that the Beach Boys were always paying homage to. She had such a relaxed way about her. When she came into a room, I swear it was like a warm summer breeze followed her, calming everything in its wake."

Sandy returned to the sofa and sat with her back propped up against one end of the sofa, facing me. She seemed to be basking in that warm summer breeze, but when she returned from her reverie, she picked up the story. "We were both high, laughing uncontrollably about something or other. I was laughing so hard, my stomach began to hurt and I almost peed my pants. So, I laid back on the living room floor and Angie did the same. She rolled over onto her side and I turned to face her. Without thinking about it, without analyzing it, we moved toward each other and kissed. Somewhere during that first innocent kiss, the shackles of guilt and shame just fell away. Kissing her felt so *right*... I knew, immediately, that all the apprehension and confusion I had been experiencing were just a byproduct of the ridiculous, stifling morality of Greenburg.

"We made mad, impetuous love all night, and with Angie's easy, unassuming manner, I wasn't a bit nervous. I woke up the next day expecting to find her beside me, but she wasn't there. She left a note explaining that she had decided to visit some friends on the coast, and asking that I let Rose know. I found another note under my pillow. It said: 'Sweet Sandy, I will feel you every time the warm sun caresses my shoulders.' I never saw her again. And when I think about it now, that was probably best. Making love to a woman for the first time was a big step, and one that afterward, required some space and inward reflection. If she'd stayed, I probably would have convinced myself that I was in love with her or something."

"Didn't you ever try to see her again, even later?"

"No, I always wanted to remember her the way she was that night. Angie gave me something very special: the freedom to be myself. I knew from that moment on that I was going to be okay. I was completely at ease with my sexuality after that."

"Enough at ease to jump back in the saddle right away?"

"Well, I didn't run out that afternoon and hop into bed with someone, if that's what you mean. But during the remainder of my college days, there were some trysts and dalliances. I didn't get seriously involved with anyone until much later."

"*Some* trysts and dalliances? That's as much detail as I get? Can I at least get a ballpark figure?"

"You seem awfully preoccupied with numbers."

"Well, a preoccupation with numbers should be something you'd appreciate, given your financial wizardry."

"Let's just say it's a modest figure. A lady never reveals all of her secrets, right?" Sandy playfully batted her eyelashes at me and tried her best to look coy.

"All right, all right. But what about this 'serious involvement'? Can I at least get some details about that?"

"Oh, do we have to get into that? I liked what we were doing a few minutes ago." Sandy made a mock grab for me, but I ducked just out of her reach.

"A relationship you don't want to discuss, huh? Is it because you never got over her?"

"No, of course not. It's just so tedious and depressing. But, if it's details you want, details you shall have. I met Chris St. James after moving to Kingston. I chose Kingston because it was a beautiful, bustling city, with a small college well known for its writing program. I thought I had a pretty good chance of teaching some introductory level writing classes there."

"Wait a minute. I don't mean to interrupt you, but do you mean *the* Chris St. James, the hot-shot criminal defense attorney?"

With an air of sarcasm, Sandy said, "The one and only. Do you know her?"

My eyes grew wide and I exclaimed, "Only by reputation, but she's legendary among lawyers in Oregon. She once secured an acquittal for some guy caught at the scene of the crime, weapon in hand, covered in the victim's blood. The powder residue test was positive and the guy mumbled something about being guilty when the police arrived at the scene. Amazing!"

"Yes, well, excuse me if I'm not quite as enthusiastic about Chris's ability to put guilty, dangerous people back out on the streets. At any rate, Chris and I met at a fund-raising event for the local schools. We seemed to hit it off right from the start. She was not like any woman I had ever known, and to this day, I still can't pinpoint what it was about her that was different. Chris is a strong woman, and very aggressive, tools of the trade for a lawyer, I guess, particularly a criminal defense attorney. We dated for a while and within a few weeks, I moved into her place, a huge sprawling mansion, but a bit ostentatious for my tastes. I should have known it wasn't going to work. Chris and I were at different places in our lives. I was really just starting out, and she was in mid-career. And then there was the age difference: she was 41 and I was only 28."

Sandy got up and stretched at this point, trying to work some kinks out of her back. Then she sat down on the floor in front of the sofa, stretching out her long legs in front of her, propping herself up on her arms. Her face seemed to take on a somber expression, and her voice sounded somewhat weary as she continued. "It was nice in the beginning, as most relationships are. But, as often happens, we grew apart. The relationship was dead in the water long before I moved out. For all intents and purposes, we were total strangers by then."

"How long were you together?"

After a long period of silence, I said "Sandy?"

"We were together for eight years. Eight *very* long years."

I did some math in my head and asked, "Excuse me for being nosy, but how old are you, anyway?"

Sandy brushed her hand in front of her mouth and mumbled something.

"Excuse me? I didn't catch that."

"I'm 36, okay?"

Again, I hurriedly did the math in my head; math has never been my strong suit. In fact, I went to law school simply because math was not a part of the curriculum. After I had completed the calculations, I asked, "Well, how long have you and Chris been apart?"

Again I got the hand-across-the-mouth-and-mumble routine. After I pointedly stared at Sandy for some moments, she answered, "A month."

I jumped up and exclaimed, "What? You've only been single for a month?"

"Calm down. I told you the relationship has been over for ages. I was even sleeping in a different room by the end. A terminal case of LBD…lesbian bed death, in case you're wondering."

"A month?"

Sandy rose from the floor and gently placed her hands on my shoulders to calm me. In her most soothing voice, she asked, "What's wrong? Are you afraid that I still have feelings for Chris?"

"Well, that did enter my mind. I mean, you haven't been away from her long enough to know if you still have feelings for her. Plus, if your ex was Chris St. James, I have some pretty big shoes to fill."

"I swear to you, I'm not harboring any amorous feelings for Chris. That's over, and has been for a long time. I don't know what you mean by 'big shoes to fill'."

"Like I said, I only know Chris St. James by reputation. I know that she does everything with flourish and style. I can only imagine that this flourish and style spills over into her personal life."

Sandy looked perplexed for a moment, and then began to laugh. When she regained her composure, she said, "I think I catch your drift. If you're worried that you won't be able to fill Chris's 'shoes' sexually speaking, don't. I can assure you that you have nothing to worry about on that score. In fact, the kisses we shared earlier were more passionate than anything Chris and I ever shared. Chris was all show, with no substance."

"Then why did you stay for so long?"

"Good question. Habit, I guess. Chris kept promising me that things between us would change, and I wanted *so* badly to believe it. I put everything I had into that relationship. But I guess, in the end, it just wasn't enough. The weeks turn into months and the months turn into years, and you don't notice the time slipping away. Inertia can be a powerful force."

At that moment, Sandy looked at me with those pale green eyes, a look of such intense lust and desire I thought I would melt right there on the spot. She ran her hands through my long brown hair and then drew me closer to her. She kissed my neck tenderly and then held me tight. Her desire was palpable, a strong sexual current electrifying me. The world seemed to stop. I felt safe and content in her embrace, and I thought I could probably stay there forever.

Just then, my beeper went off, intruding upon the solitude we had found in each other's arms.

Sandy sighed and asked, "Who would be calling you at this hour?"

"Such is the life of a private investigator. People get into trouble at all hours, unfortunately. I better return this call. Can I use your phone?"

"Sure, it's over there next to the sofa. I'm just gonna go get myself some more tea while you make your call."

I didn't tell Sandy that the number that came up on my beeper belonged to Sam. I quickly dialed her number and she answered on the first ring, as I expected. In an excited and breathless voice, Sam asked, "What took you so long?"

"Why are you calling me so early in the morning? Don't you believe in sleeping?"

"We had some diehards at the party. In fact, the last guests just left a few minutes ago. Remind me never to serve crab puffs at a party again. Rae Swanson can't leave until the last crab puff has been consumed. And her date, gender indeterminate by the way, kept making googly eyes at me all night. Anyway, I tried to call you at home, and when I got no answer I surmised that you and Sandy must have hit it off."

"So you just thought you'd interrupt?"

"Look, I know patience is a virtue, but I haven't been a virtuous woman for a long time. I just couldn't wait to find out how it went. So shoot me."

"Believe me, I've considered it. And remember, I'm licensed to carry. Anyway, it went…" Before I could finish the thought, Sandy walked back into the room. I cleared my throat and continued. "Well, I think you better sit tight and wait for me. This sounds serious."

"Oh, I get it, Sandy just walked back into the room. But why are you going to leave? Oh no, it didn't go well? I felt so sure this time. Damn!"

"Don't get excited. The situation isn't as dire as you think. But I feel strongly that we should proceed with caution. Just do as I say and everything will be fine."

"Now I'm really confused. Did it go well or not? Look, if you're leaving her house, you better haul your ass over here and give me the low-down, or else!"

"Yes, that seems like the prudent course of action. I'll be there right away." With that, I hung up the phone and turned to Sandy. A look of deep disappointment had spread across her soft features and her shoulders were slumping forward. I walked over to her and said, "I'm sorry, but it really is an emergency. I can't provide you with any details. You know, client confidentiality and all. I wouldn't go if I didn't have to. You understand, don't you?"

"Yes, of course I understand, but I'm still disappointed." She brightened and said, "Maybe you could come back for dinner tonight? I'd love to cook for you."

In the back of my head I was thinking that it might be better if we went out to eat, someplace well-lit and very public. Maybe someplace with lots of screaming children and computerized singing rodents. It would make the promise I had made to myself a lot easier to keep. But I relented and agreed to come back for dinner.

As I was heading out the front door, Sandy asked, "Oh, what should I make for dinner?"

I turned back and said, "Surprise me…I love surprises." I winked at her and jumped into my van. As I drove away in the soft morning light, I saw her seductive outline in the doorway. This was one promise that would be hard to keep.

Full Disclosure

I drove home in the eerie, surreal light that exists between night and day, thinking about my time with the enchanting Sandy Garrett. For the first time in a long while, I felt as though I had truly connected with another human being. Sandy was intelligent, engaging, witty, sexy, and warm, all the attributes I look for in a woman. If I wasn't careful, I could wind up with a broken heart.

I was still deep in thought when I pulled into the driveway of my small brick home. I live on a quiet, tree-lined street, just two short blocks from Sam and Nealy. Most everyone on this street is a long-time resident of Cloverdale and we all know each other by name. Well, everyone except my next-door neighbor, Ethel Hale. Ethel is 75, but has the energy and vigor of someone half her age. She also has Alzheimer's Disease. This used to be a source of great frustration for both Ethel and her family, at least when Ethel's youngest daughter, Darlene, was looking after Ethel. Darlene got upset when Ethel couldn't remember anyone's name, not to mention any other details of her daily life—like the fact that it's best to wear underwear on the inside of your pants. Darlene finally told the family that she didn't have the patience to deal with Ethel anymore, and Ethel's eldest daughter, Cecelia, took over Ethel's care.

Cecelia decided it was easier to go with the flow. So, if Ethel wants to call Cecelia some other name, or insists that meatloaf is ham, Cecelia goes along with it, and encourages everyone else to do the same. I take this approach with Ethel as well, and as a result I've carried on long conversations with Ethel where she was certain that I was either her old friend Ruby, her sister Edna, her grade school teacher Mrs. Phipps, or her hairdresser Rita. One day, Ethel was sure that I was Earl, her deceased husband—I was wearing a pair of overalls and a baseball hat for an investigation I was working. I was relieved that Ethel did not request that I perform my marital duties on that occasion. I'm willing to play along, but I have my limits. In truth, it's kind of fun being all those different people for Ethel.

I walked up the drive and noticed that the dahlias and pansies needed watering. As I opened my front door, I saw an airborne feline zeroing in on her target. But when the target heard the door open, she moved to greet me, and the airborne feline crashed, face first, into the hallway carpeting, wounding only her pride. It's some kind of kitty ritual that my two cats practice together: one perches on the stairs and waits for the other one to linger in the hallway below, and then, BAM! Kamikaze Kitty strikes again.

I greeted Tasha, my gray tabby, with a scratch behind the ears, her idea of kitty heaven. We tried not to notice as Corey, a white and brown Himalayan Lynx, extricated herself from the carpeting, shook herself off, and rearranged her ample fur. Cats can be *so* sensitive.

Corey, all her fur back in place, ambled over for her morning attention and I obliged with a vigorous tummy rub. I looked at them both, shook my head, and asked, in my best motherly voice, "When are you two going to tire of the airborne routine?" I knew the answer to that question without asking, since they'd been practicing their dive-bomber skills together for over two years now, with no sign of a cease-fire on the horizon.

While they usually looked at each other with disdain and contempt, I suspected that each felt a certain level of affection for the other. It was some kind of twisted love/hate thing, far too complex for a mere human to fully grasp. I often caught them sleeping close together on my bed or playing amiably together in the backyard. But then on occasion, one would walk over to the other and, for no apparent reason, land a solid kitty punch to the head. I gave up trying to understand the intricacies of their relationship long ago.

I went into my office, where I conduct my investigation business, and checked my phone messages. Nothing pressing: one offer to replace my windshield (which wasn't broken), a sales pitch for Sears home siding, a wrong number, and a message from Dede, asking when we could get together again. I thought maybe Dede and I could get together again as soon as that elk on her living room wall sprouted legs and ran away.

I wandered into the kitchen to grab something to eat before heading down to Sam and Nealy's place. Corey and Tasha promptly assumed their normal station in front of the cabinet next to the refrigerator. Corey looked at the cabinet, looked at me, and began meowing in this pathetic kitty voice. Corey is the appointed spokesperson for the duo, since Tasha never meows unless someone steps on her tail. She continued this well-rehearsed routine until I relented and opened the cabinet to give them each a few tuna crunchies. As they crunched away happily, I perused the ingredient list on the back of the tuna treat bag. I'm certain there's some form of kitty opiates in these things. As someone in recovery, I readily recognize the monkey-on-my-back syndrome, and these two had a couple of giant gorillas on their furry backs.

As soon as Corey had polished off her crunchies, she did a 360 around the perimeter of the kitchen as fast as her short legs would carry her, zipped into the living room, returned to the kitchen, and came to a skidding stop only inches from where she had started. Tasha and I looked at each other and shrugged…at least I did. We have yet to determine the impetus for Corey's spirited sprints. They occurred at all hours and ended as quickly as they began. Maybe Corey is like that kid in *The Sixth Sense*. She sees dead cats, walking around like regular cats. Or maybe she's just nuts.

I grabbed a package of Pop Tarts (brown sugar and cinnamon, of course) and ran into the bathroom to splash some cold water on my face. Imprudently, I glanced in the mirror. At 34, it's really not wise to stay up all night. Every lost moment of sleep makes itself known in dark bags, sags, and weary lines. *Face it, J.Z., you're not a kid anymore.*

My furry friends were disappointed to see me head for the door rather than up the stairs to the bedroom. They loved nothing more than whiling away the hours with me in our king-sized bed. I tried to ignore their looks of disappointment as I locked the door behind me.

I walked the two blocks to Sam and Nealy's place slowly, both because I wanted to enjoy the crisp morning air on this lovely April day and because I wanted to finish my Pop Tarts before arriving. I knew that Sam would not be patient enough to allow me to finish my nutritious breakfast before launching a barrage of questions about my evening with Sandy. I had polished off the last few crumbs as I reached the front door.

Before I could ring the doorbell, Sam jerked the door open and pulled me inside. She put her arm though mine and led me into her bedroom while squealing, "I want to know everything. Don't leave out any details." Nealy was in bed reading the newspaper and glanced up at me as I entered the room. Her look conveyed pity and great sympathy: she knew I was about to be Samonized—interrogated mercilessly until I crumpled into a shaking heap on the floor, too weak to even crawl away. If the FBI even found out about Sam's amazing interrogation skills, she would be silently whisked away in the middle of the night.

A stranger meeting Sam for the first time would have great difficulty reconciling Sam's Gestapo-like tactics with her innocent good looks and down home charm. She bears an uncanny resemblance to Tawny Kitaen. You know—the redhead who did the splits on the hood of a sports car in those Whitesnake videos. She has auburn hair, brown eyes, fair skin with lots of freckles, and a smile that can light up any room. She's about an inch shorter than me, and very slim. In other words, she's gorgeous. Her looks could be intimidating, but Sam has an unassuming way about her, a casual elegance that puts everyone at ease. And that's the trap: once she has you at ease with her all-American good looks, perky smile, and soft, expressive eyes, she zooms in for the kill!

Sam hopped into bed, patted the spot between her and Nealy and said, "Get your bony ass in here and start talking." I wisely did as I was told. After having painstakingly relayed every detail and nuance of the evening to Sam, and after I had answered all of her questions, Sam turned to me and said, with an air of superiority in her voice, "I told you this time was different."

"Yes, I know you did. But please, don't get carried away. As I said, I'm trying to take this slowly. And it's not as if I'm miserable being single, you know. I have a great career, two loving cats, wonderful friends, and a full set of presidential steak knives from Ralph's Union

76. Oh, I almost forgot—a complete set of Cameron Diaz videos. What more could a girl want?"

"Someone to make her clutch the bed sheets tightly, scream out 'Oh God' in a ragged, breathless voice while covered in a sheen of perspiration, with a spasm of ecstasy rippling through her body."

I glanced at Nealy with a look of genuine respect and said, "It's always the quiet ones."

Nealy smirked and said, "Practice makes perfect."

I chuckled and said, "You braggart." I turned to Sam and remarked, "If I turn out the lights and sit close enough to the TV while watching a Cameron Diaz movie, I experience some of the same effects you just mentioned."

Sam shook her head, bounded out of bed and announced, "I'm too excited to sleep. I'm going to whip us up some waffles." With that, she was off.

"Doesn't Sam have to open up the store today? Saturday is her busiest day."

"No, she talked Kit into opening up the store today, knowing that the party would take its toll."

Sam owns and operates a new and used bookstore that sells only murder mysteries, called Murder by Numbers. It's become the chic hangout in Cloverdale, with its overstuffed chairs, stacks of radical and mainstream newspapers, and espresso bar. Adding to the mystique and allure of the place was Kinsey, resident cat of Murder by Numbers. Sam dubbed the cat "Kinsey" in homage to her favorite mystery character, Kinsey Millhone, and because when Sam found her, the cat looked like someone had cut her hair with fingernail scissors.

One of Sam's employees is Kit, Sam's much younger cousin. Kit is a quirky, radical nut, on a different crusade every week. Recently, Kit had been involved in the following causes: Save the Snail Darter, Save the Earth, Save the Whales, and Save Our Ears (a small movement seeking to prevent the release of Kathie Lee Gifford's new music CD). She even started something called "Save the Greenhouse Effect" when she heard that scientists were trying to minimize it. Kit theorized that because greenhouses are nice places where plants grow, the greenhouse effect must be a good thing. In short, Kit flitted from one wacky cause to another, a pattern that repeated itself in her love life. She left a trail of human carnage in her wake, oblivious to the pain she was causing to the young men she toyed with on a regular basis. Kit had a well-established reputation as a heart-breaker, but one look at her, and guys threw caution to the wind. If Kit could ever manage to channel her energy into one cause, and one person, she might make some kind of useful contribution to society. I wasn't going to hold my breath.

While Kit marched, protested, picketed, and boycotted to save this or that, Sam tried to save Kit. Kit was the only child of Sam's favorite aunt, Gertie, who had died almost two years before from breast cancer. When Gertie died, Sam promised to look after Kit, who was only nineteen at the time. Sam always kept her promises, and she refused to fire Kit, even though Kit sometimes failed to show up for work, or was late when she did show, habits which were bad for employee morale. Just as disturbing, Kit sometimes alienated customers with her acerbic rhetoric.

I tried to convince Sam that maybe what Kit needed was a dose of reality, like a trip to the unemployment line. Even though Sam knew I was right, her love for Gertie prevented her from taking this step.

I turned to Nealy, who was still reading the paper, and asked, "How do you do it?"

With a perplexed look, Nealy asked, "Do what?"

"Live with someone who is so damn cheerful all the time, and is determined to make everyone else just as happy."

"I meditate a lot. And, of course, there's always sex. By the way, Sam's not on a mission to make all of her friends happy—just you."

"Lucky me."

"You? You've got the easy part in all of this. Do you know what it's like to go grocery shopping with a woman who finds a way to strike up a conversation with every marginally attractive woman in the store?"

"Well, actually I do—my most recent ex was very adept at that sort of thing, though she didn't restrict herself to grocery stores."

"I'm serious. It's embarrassing. After she's determined that they're single, she starts in on the 'well, have I got a friend for you' routine. Last week, we were at the Shop 'n Save in the produce section, and Sam had struck up a conversation with an attractive redhead. The woman indicated that she was single, and Sam said 'In that case, I've got a real treat for you.' Unfortunately, Sam was clutching a very large cucumber when she said these words. The woman misunderstood and ran screaming from the store. We've been banished from some of the better supermarkets in the tri-state area."

"Just how attractive was the redhead? Are we talkin' more like Julia Roberts attractive, Debra Messing attractive, or what?"

Nealy hit me with her pillow and said, "You're just as exasperating as Sam. No wonder you've been best friends for so long."

Sam reappeared in the doorway, looking far too good for someone who hadn't gotten a wink of sleep. Wielding some sort of kitchen utensil that I probably should have been familiar with, she asked, "Anybody up for a sugar rush?" Considering her audience, it was a rhetorical question.

We stuffed ourselves with waffles topped with sliced strawberries and mounds of whipped cream. With a full tummy, the fatigue really began to take over. I got up to waddle home and noticed that Sam and Nealy were making goo-goo eyes at each other. I guessed that some serious bed sheet clutching action would soon be underway.

As I made my way home, I realized with a bit of shame that I was somewhat envious of the relationship Sam and Nealy share. There was a real bond between them, and an uncanny ability to communicate without words. They truly cared for each other, with a depth of emotion that many rarely achieve. They were soul mates, predestined to be together. Would I ever find my soul mate?

As I neared my humble abode, it was daylight and Ethel was already in her front yard tending to her precious roses. I greeted her as I passed and she squinted her eyes to get a better look at me. She ambled over to the edge of her yard and said, "Ruby, I never have forgiven you for kissing my beau, Johnny Ray, at the spring dance."

I was really too weary to humor Ethel, but I managed a quick response. "Yes, I know. That was an awful thing for one friend to do to another. I'm truly sorry, Ethel."

"Well you should be, Ruby Jean McHenry! It was disgraceful!"

"I was the one who was disgraced, Ethel."

"How do you mean?"

"Johnny Ray told me that compared to you, I kissed like a dead mackerel."

Ethel visibly swelled up with pride and announced, "Johnny Ray always did know a good thing when he saw it. I forgive you, Ruby."

"I'm glad. Now, if you'll excuse me, I have to go inside and arrange for some kissing lessons." I dragged myself inside and trudged upstairs. The cats were already waiting for me in their designated spots on the bed. I didn't even bother to undress. I just fell onto the bed and into a very deep sleep.

I awoke several hours later with one cat perched on my head and the other one burrowing into my sock drawer.

"What's with you two? Your allotment of tuna crunchies is about to be drastically reduced." As if they understood my words, they both got down on the floor and assumed their best innocent kitty poses.

It was probably good that they had awakened me, since it was afternoon. I had some paperwork to get to that I'd been putting off. Plus, I needed to call Sandy and ask what time I should come over for dinner. She had given me her number last night and I quickly retrieved it from my wallet. She picked up on the third ring.

"Hello?"

"Hi, Sandy, it's J.Z. I was just wondering what time I should come over for dinner tonight."

"Oh, I think around 7:00 should be fine. I'm really looking forward to it."

"Me too. So, what kind of gourmet delight are you whipping up for this evening's fare?"

"Oh no, you told me to surprise you, so that's what I'm doing. You'll find out what we're having when you get here, not before."

"Sassy, I like that. Okay, have it your way. I'll be there at 7:00 with bells on."

"You don't have to wear bells, or anything else, if you don't want to."

After a brief period of silence and some heavy breathing from the other end of the phone, I said, "Last time I dined naked there was a terrible incident with hot gravy. I still have nightmares. If it's all the same to you, I think I'll show up fully dressed."

"I have no objection to you *showing up* fully dressed, Ms. Mackenzie." After a brief pause, Sandy said, "Something is boiling on the stove, so I think I better go. See you later."

Something's boiling, all right. How was I going to get through another night of grope-and-dodge? At some point, Sandy and I would need to have a serious talk. But right now, I had invoices to prepare, reports to type, and paperwork to file. Ah yes, the exciting life of a modern-day private investigator.

I fired up the computer and filled in all the information for Mrs. Johnson's invoice, soon to be the ex-Mrs. Johnson. I had some good shots of Mr. Johnson, minister of the Cloverdale First Baptist Church on Elm Street, doing the old slap-and-tickle with Peggy Sue Parker, a local girl young enough to be the good Reverend's daughter. Perhaps this was some sort of religious exercise I had immortalized on celluloid, designed to thrust the demons out of Peggy Sue's soul. After all, Peggy Sue did scream "Oh God" several times during the evening. So perhaps the religious exercise had been a success. After all, the Reverend Johnson had seemed quite pleased with the results.

Typically, a divorce lawyer engages my services for these delicate matters. But Mrs. Johnson was a greedy ol' bird, and she didn't want to pay an attorney to do something she could do on her own: squeeze every last penny out of her snake-in-the-grass husband. The Reverend Johnson, ironically, had written a couple of books about how to enrich the bonds of holy matrimony, and they had sold well, and, in fact, were still selling well. Mrs. Johnson had finally tired of the Reverend's cheating ways, and realized that a few incriminating photos could topple both her husband's ministry and his stature as an expert on the subject of marriage. She knew that he would immediately realize this as well, and, as a result, fork over the money he'd been hoarding all these years. A divorce, after all, would be far less scandalous than an affair with a young woman. To cinch the deal, Mrs. Johnson had taken the best photograph I had obtained, one in which the Reverend looked particularly pious, and with her computer, scanner, and her graphics software, created a very eye-catching flyer. Below the photograph was the following caption: *The Reverend Johnson, seen here exercising his little johnson with 18-year-old Peggy Sue Parker on their recent outing to the Brownsville Motel 6.* Mrs. Johnson planned to use the flyer merely as an incentive to ensure the Reverend's generosity. If the flyer was made public, Reverend Johnson had more to fear than his loss of livelihood; Peggy Sue's father, Butch, a former boxer and rabid NRA member, was very protective of his little girl.

Once my administrative duties were completed, it was time to get ready for my dinner with Sandy. I agonized over what to wear, as usual, finally selecting my most comfortable jeans, a lavender polo shirt, and brown leather loafers. I stood in front of the full-length mirror in my bedroom to examine the finished product. Not bad. I like to think I have no delusions about my looks. I mean, I know I'm no beauty queen. But on the other hand, people don't run away in horror when they first meet me. I guess, like most people, I'm average looking, and that's okay. I can live with it. One of my pet peeves is beautiful women who constantly talk about how big their asses or their thighs are. Please!

Personally, I've never spent much time staring at my ass, for many reasons. First, you have to get into an awkward, contorted position to see your own ass, and second, I'd rather look at someone else's. Anyway, I suppose my ass is average, just like the rest of me. I'm just a smidgen over 5'6", and the last time I weighed, I was about 135 pounds. I've been told that my best features are my eyes and my smile. My eyes are dark brown, almost black, and very intense. Sam tells me that my eyes remind her of Patricia Charbonneau's eyes in *Desert Hearts*, all dark, mysterious, and romantic. I'm in pretty good shape, though I despise exercise. I figure that walking to the store for ice cream should count for something, right?

With butterflies in my stomach, I bade farewell to my feline companions and headed out the door. En route to Sandy's place, I stopped off for some flowers. My mother always told me never to show up empty-handed on a lady's doorstep. Actually, she told my brothers this, but I figured it was good advice for me, too. By now, it felt like those butterflies had tripled in size and were doing a rumba inside my stomach. If I managed not to toss my cookies, it would be a very pleasant evening.

Hot & Spicy

I arrived at Sandy's place right on time. She heard me drive up and greeted me at the front door, wearing khakis, a very tight-fitting chocolate silk pullover with a high neck, a light beige sweater, and expensive-looking leather slip-ons. Her hair was pulled back into a chignon, revealing even more of her sensuous neck and accentuating the simple pair of tiny pearl earrings she wore.

She smiled warmly as she greeted me and thanked me for the flowers. As I handed them to her, she planted a quick kiss on my lips and led me inside. The house was filled with this wonderful, mouth-watering aroma.

"Mmmmm, what smells so good?"

"It's my own version of curried chicken. It's big chunks of chicken, garbanzo beans, potatoes and carrots, and golden raisins smothered in a thick curry sauce, seasoned with coriander and a touch of cumin. We'll have it over rice accompanied by homemade naan. For dessert I made lemon cheesecake, and if you play your cards right, there will be espresso."

I got quiet, my eyes glazed over, and my breathing became shallow, prompting Sandy to ask, "Are you okay?"

"Huh? Oh yeah, I'm fine. I was just a little overcome there for a moment. How did you know that Indian food is my favorite?"

"I cheated. I called Sam. She told me that you love spicy food, especially Indian and Mexican, the hotter the better."

"Sam knows me well."

While enjoying the fresh air on the deck attached to the rear of the house, we chatted about our day, my cats, and the weather as we waited for the food to finish cooking. As we did so, we sipped tall glasses of iced tea flavored with mint sprigs. It was easy being around Sandy, and if it was possible, I was even more attracted to her tonight than I had been the night before.

Since it was a warm evening, we ate dinner outside at a small table on the deck while strains of Etta James, Billie Holliday, and Patsy Cline filled the night air. The candlelight heightened Sandy's beauty, casting her striking features in a warm amber glow. We ate slowly, enjoying each other's company. I didn't think it would be polite to have thirds, so I stopped with two servings of Sandy's spicy concoction.

I helped her tidy up, and then we retired to the living room with our espresso. We talked more about our respective backgrounds, and Sandy asked about my prior relationships. "I've been in love three times, and all of them ended badly. The last was a few years ago. I guess at that point I made an unconscious decision to forget about living happily ever after with someone. It just hurt too much to try. After that, my attitude was, well, if I can't have quality, then I'll have quantity. In other words, I slept with a lot of women, trying to find some kind of fulfillment that way. Of course, it didn't work. Sam convinced me that the quest for Ms. Right was worth it in the long run, and I began opening up to that possibility a while back. I must admit, things have been looking up recently."

Sandy looked at me with a mixture of lust, admiration and hope. She slid over next to me on the sofa and put her hand on my thigh. Then, she leaned forward and kissed me with a kind of passion I'd never felt before. She kissed me again and again, and then whispered in my ear, "I want to make love to you."

The feeling was mutual, a fact attested to by my racing heart and butterfly-ridden stomach. Looking at Sandy's soft features, I was overcome by an undeniably strong feeling of attraction, almost a physical need to feel my body entwined with hers. I hid my face in the curve of Sandy's neck so that she couldn't see this raw lust. I nuzzled her neck and gently kissed her rosy cheek. With my eyes averted from hers, I whispered, "I don't think that's a good idea."

Sandy slowly rose from the sofa and walked over to the window to look out at the starry night. I waited for her to say something, and when she didn't, I said, "Sandy?"

Still no response. I went to her and saw that tears were sliding down her beautiful face. She quickly wiped the tears away and said in a shaky voice, "If you're not attracted to me, just say so."

"Sandy, you know I'm attracted to you. We can both feel the attraction. It's nothing like that."

"What, then?"

"When I came home with you from the party, I was ready to go to bed with you. But I promised myself that I'd get to know you first. Don't get me wrong—I love sex, probably a little too much. But let's face it, good sex muddies the waters. It's easy to confuse good sex with love. People do it all the time. And there's something very special about that first part of a relationship before sex comes into the picture. The build-up, the waiting, the anticipation. It's like an extended version of foreplay. Once you cross the line, once you sleep with the other person, you can't go back to that stage. You've entered the next stage of the relationship."

It grew quiet for a moment, and Sandy continued to stare out at the night sky, an impassive look on her tear-streaked face. I sighed and continued. "Look, I really like you and I feel a connection with you. I haven't felt that in a long time, and I was beginning to wonder if I ever would. I just don't want to blow it by rushing things."

Sandy turned away from me and walked slowly to the other side of the room. When she reached the rounded archway separating the living room from the dining room, she spun around and looked at me with a pained expression. "I didn't tell you everything about my relationship with Chris."

I didn't know what her relationship with Chris St. James had to do with this, but I waited patiently for her to enlighten me. Sandy looked down at the floor and said, "This is difficult to talk about. It's just so embarrassing."

"Whatever it is, you can tell me. I won't judge you."

After a few moments and some heavy sighs, she looked up at me and continued. "I was very attracted to Chris right from the beginning. But every time things got a little steamy between us, Chris would slam on the brakes. She had a million excuses: she'd had bad experiences in the past, she had a headache, she had to get up early the next day, you name it. Finally, she sensed my growing impatience and we made it to the bedroom. She made love to me, but when I tried to make love to her, she stopped me. She said she just wasn't ready, and asked that I be patient with her. Eight years later, she was still asking that I be patient."

"Wait a minute. You mean that Chris never let you make love to her? Not even once in eight years?"

Sandy looked at the floor and muttered, "That's right."

"So that's why you're so upset with my hesitancy to make love with you tonight?"

"Yes. Can you blame me?"

"Look, I don't know what kinds of problems Chris had. But I'm not Chris. You have to understand that. And believe me, you'd never have that kind of problem with me. Not in a million years. This is a totally different situation."

"It doesn't feel different. Once again, someone is asking me to be patient, to wait. Well, I'm sick and tired of waiting, goddammit! It's been over eight years since I've made love to a woman. Eight years!"

Sandy leaned up against the archway and began to sob. I ran to her and held her tightly. I could feel her heart beating against mine, and I could feel her sobs subside. We kissed again. She grabbed me and forcefully pressed my body against hers. Her body was writhing against mine and I could sense the intensity of her pent-up sexual energy and tension. She pulled away from me, took me by the hand, and led me up the stairway off the front entryway. As we climbed the stairs, I couldn't take my eyes off the shapely derriere swinging back and forth just inches from my face.

She guided me into her bedroom and immediately began unzipping my pants. She slipped my shirt over my head and began caressing my breasts through the black lace bra I had worn. With expert hands, Sandy unfastened my bra, letting it fall to the floor. She tenderly kissed my breasts and playfully flicked her tongue across my nipples, and a shiver of ecstasy ran through me. Pleased with the effect, she pulled me close and kissed the side of my neck, stopping to nibble on my earlobe, and then her tongue darted inside my ear. A second shiver rocked me.

Slowly, she backed me over to her bed and gently pushed me down.

In a whisper, Sandy asked me to lie down and she removed my shoes, socks and jeans, revealing my matching black lace panties. She crawled on top of me, kissed me hard and then tenderly kissed her way down to my panties. She stroked and kissed my inner thighs and then kissed my crotch through the lace panties, which were now moist with my excitement. She deftly removed my panties and then crossed the room to light a candle. In a breathless voice she said, "I don't want to miss anything."

I got up and removed her sweater. I wasn't prepared for what lay beneath. Muscles bulged from her clingy, short sleeve pullover. I gasped and stroked her biceps, amazed at this wondrous mix of strength and femininity. I looked at her and said, "You big strong woman, you."

She laughed and flexed her muscles in an exaggerated manner. Her laughter quickly turned to heavy breathing as I unfastened her belt and unzipped her pants. I plunged my hands inside her silky underwear and firmly grabbed her behind, pulling her close to me. She slipped off her shoes, and I yanked her socks and pants off. I kissed her deeply and then slipped her top over her head. I could see by the soft glow of the candlelight that Sandy was wearing a lavender silk bra and matching panties. I caressed her breasts and felt her nipples harden. I quickly removed her silky underthings and held her in my arms, fully aware of how good her soft, full breasts felt against mine.

Sandy guided me back to the bed and again climbed on top of me. She kissed me hard and passionately while exploring the contours of my breasts. Her hand made its way down to my crotch and within minutes, spasms of pleasure had overtaken my body. She held me for a few moments and then slid on top of me and ground her crotch into mine. I grabbed her shapely ass and pressed her against me harder, and we writhed together until moans of pleasure filled the room.

She briefly nuzzled my neck and then made her way down to my breasts, which she expertly stroked, kissed and licked. She then slid the tip of her tongue down the length of my stomach and I involuntarily shivered. Sandy slipped between my legs and I could feel her tongue gently moving against me, a rhythm that I matched with my body movements. The pressure of her tongue increased and her rhythm quickened, as did my own. Soon, my entire body was quivering.

Sandy climbed back to the head of the bed, kissed my cheek, and brushed the hair off my forehead. I turned to her and said, "I think it's safe to say that your sexual hiatus did not diminish your prowess in the boudoir."

She giggled and said, "It's easy to make love to you."

In a mock angry voice I said, "Are you calling me easy?" and I slid on top of her and made love to her with the same tenderness, passion, and fervor she had shown me. We made love for hours and then talked until we fell asleep in each other's arms. For the first time in a long while, my dreams paled in comparison to the reality slumbering next to me.

A Visit from the Grim Reaper

I woke up late the next morning with Sandy sleeping soundly next to me. For several minutes, I just lay there quietly admiring her beauty, the morning sunlight dancing across her striking features. Teasingly, I lightly ran my fingers up and down her flat stomach. She wiggled and squirmed and then rolled over and began tickling me mercilessly. I begged her to stop and the tickles turned into loving strokes and tender kisses. Soon, we were well on our way to a repeat of the previous night.

After the morning wake-up call, we showered and ate leftover curried chicken. With regret I said, "I've got to drive over to the coast today and follow up on some leads in a missing persons case I'm working. Sunday is the only day I can meet with the people I'm interviewing. Then tonight, I've got to do some stakeout work over in Lakeville. Apparently, the only night the two adulterous lovebirds get together is on Sunday night. I feel like a heel, making love with you, eating your food, and then flying out of here. I wish I could spend the rest of the day with you, but I really can't. Will you forgive me?"

Sandy smiled and replied, "There's nothing to forgive. I understand that you have to work. I'd love to spend the day with you as well, but I can keep myself busy with some projects around here. In fact, I've been meaning to get around to cleaning up the mess in the garage. The previous owner left behind a lot of junk out there, and the shelving is falling down. I need to haul the junk away and replace the shelves. That should keep me busy for most of the day."

We kissed for several minutes and then I said, "I gotta go, but I'll call you later tonight." With that, I was gone, but I could still feel her loving embrace and exuberant kisses, and thoughts of the pleasures we had recently shared made me warm and giddy.

I stopped by my place and gathered up my files on the two cases and other necessary supplies, including a nice assortment of munchies. My favorites are the pink Snoballs—the ones with the chocolate cake and creme filling, covered in a gelatinous marshmallowy substance. A couple of those babies and a thermos of coffee and you're good for the duration. Plus, I once used the marshmallow part to reattach a broken rear view mirror. NASA and Hostess should get together; I think that stuff could be used to secure the tiles that keep falling off the space shuttle.

Before leaving, I checked my answering machine and noticed that I had about 86 messages from Sam, each more desperate-sounding. I vowed to call her during the drive. Once everything was in order, I headed out for the coastal town of Pacific View, which should take no more than two hours, assuming I didn't run into any traffic snafus. En route, I called my interviewees and arranged for a meeting place and time. After that, I called Sam to fill her in on recent developments. Her squeals of excitement nearly deafened me. I think she was pleased.

The interviews were not as helpful as I had hoped, but I did pick up a few tidbits of useful information. Knowing that the drive to Lakeville was about an hour, I decided to take a walk on the beach. It was about 5 p.m., and the subject lovebirds did not typically rendezvous until about 8 p.m., so I had a couple of hours to kill. I figured I might as well kill them on a scenic stretch of beach. Before meandering down to the beach, I tried Sandy's number again. I let the phone ring several times, but she didn't pick up. She told me she hated answering machines and refused to get one, so I decided to try later. She was most likely still busy in the garage, which was not attached to the house, so she probably couldn't hear the phone ringing out there.

Walking on the beach has a way of putting things in perspective. On occasion, we all tend to get self-involved, but a visit to the ocean reveals the utter folly of such thinking. Standing there in front of the vastness and power of an enormous body of water that disappears into the horizon, how can a tiny speck on the shore amount to much in the grand scheme of things? I pondered this with my jeans rolled up just below my knees, barefoot with the wet sand gushing between my toes and the ocean foam lapping at my ankles. I also thought about Sandy. Making love with her was incredible, as intense and erotic as the sex scene in *Desert Hearts*. As thoughts of our intimate moments rushed through my mind, making the hair on the back of my neck stand up, I silently warned myself to slow down, not to rush this. But I knew I wouldn't listen.

After getting lost for a time in the solitude and beauty of the ocean, I reluctantly trudged back to my van. I always hate leaving the ocean. On impulse, I tried Sandy's number again. Still no answer. I sighed and headed out for Lakeville, munching on some Fritos along the way. I found the sleazy motel the lovebirds always used and waited. My patience was richly rewarded. You'd think adulterers would make sure that the curtains were closed all the way. Oh well, their stupidity was my gain.

With my stomach aching from all the junk food I'd consumed during the stakeout, I began the trek home. Once again, I called Sandy's number, and still got no answer. I was beginning to get worried now, since it was going on 10 p.m. What if she tripped over something in the garage and hit her head? This was silly. She probably just went out for dinner, maybe ran into some of the people she knew from her volunteer work. Surely that was it.

I ran into an accident on the way home, and it was after midnight when I finally rolled into Cloverdale. I decided to drive by Sandy's place, since I still hadn't been able to reach her. Her car wasn't in the driveway, nor was it in the garage. It looked as though Sandy's garage project was about halfway done. I knocked on the front door but she didn't answer, and the place was completely dark. Disappointed and extremely worried at this point, I went home.

I always have a hard time falling asleep, but when I'm worried about something, it's nearly impossible. I tossed and turned for most of the night. I wanted to keep calling her, but I didn't want to seem needy, or worse yet, like a stalker. So, I decided to wait until a decent hour in the morning to try her again.

At a little after 8 a.m., I finally got an answer. When Sandy answered the phone, she sounded groggy, upset and edgy. With genuine concern I asked, "What's wrong? You sound…different."

"Oh, I just didn't get much sleep."

"Where were you yesterday? I tried calling, and even stopped by when I got back."

There was a long, awkward pause, and then Sandy replied, "I had to go out of town to visit a friend…a sick friend."

"Oh, I hope it's nothing serious."

"Me too. Look, I don't feel so good. I think I need to go back to bed and rest. I'll talk to you later."

I offered to come over and take care of her, but she abruptly refused.

One skill that's indispensable to a good private investigator is the ability to read another person. To put it bluntly, you have to be able to tell when someone is feeding you a line of crap. While I was talking to Sandy, my expert crap-o-meter was going off like crazy. I could tell by the tone of her voice and her abruptness that she was either lying to me, or not telling me everything. But why? I could only think of one reason that made any sense: she was seeing someone else last night. *Maybe she's a player and I just fell for it. Or maybe I'm just being paranoid.*

Well, I couldn't lie around all day and ponder this. I had work to do, as well as a number of household chores. But first I'd treat myself to a bowl of Lucky Charms and the morning paper. I like to stay on top of current events. I retrieved the paper from the doorstep and tossed it on the dining room table. With breakfast in hand, I glanced down at the front page of the paper, and my Lucky Charms promptly clattered to the floor. Chris St. James had been murdered last night.

A Shock to the System

Holy shit! Obviously, Sandy hadn't heard the news yet, otherwise she would surely have mentioned it to me on the phone. How would she take this?

I scanned the story for details, but few were provided, since the police were actively investigating the crime. I immediately called my old friend Cathy Lockhart, an officer with the Kingston Police Department. Cathy and I had weathered the first year of law school together. She had done better than I in terms of grades during that first year, but she just decided that she didn't want to be a lawyer, and she left law school to attend the police academy. We had stayed in touch through e-mail and an occasional phone call.

As soon as I got Cathy on the line, I said, "Okay, spill it. I want all the details on the St. James murder."

"You *know* I can't give you any information. It's an active investigation. My ass would be grass if I got caught."

"So don't get caught. Look, Cathy, I wouldn't compromise your job. It's just that someone close to me is going to be affected by this, and I'd like to be in the loop on this one."

After several moments of silence, Cathy sighed and said, "There are lots of people milling around in here. Let me call you back in a few minutes on my cell phone."

I waited right by the phone, and when it finally rang, I jumped about a foot off the floor, startling Corey and Tasha, who had just recovered from the flying Lucky Charms. In hushed tones, Cathy said, "I'm just outside of the department, so I have to keep my voice down. Here's what I know so far. The vic was murdered with a very large meat cleaver, and whoever did it must be pretty strong, since St. James was almost decapitated. No signs of forced entry, so the perp is probably someone St. James knew. There was one hell of a struggle. I don't think this will be an open case for long, since the perp left behind a fingerprint in blood, presumably the vic's, as well as a partial shoe print, also in blood. And I think one or two long strands of hair were found near St. James, who had short hair. The perp may also have left behind some tire tracks. Someone peeled out of the driveway fast enough to burn rubber, and the tracks weren't there yesterday afternoon, at least according to the gardener."

"Shit! Sounds like somebody was royally pissed at St. James. Is the evidence being processed now?"

"Yeah. So we just have to wait and see if the owner of that fingerprint is in the system. If so, we should be able to make an arrest real soon. In the meantime, the usual interviews with neighbors, friends and co-workers are progressing."

"Do you guys have a time of death yet?"

"Doc Winston tentatively puts the time of death between 6 and 8 p.m."

"How and when was the body discovered?"

"One of the neighbors called it in around 11 p.m. The neighbor was driving home from the movies and noticed that St. James's front door was standing wide open. He went to investigate and found the body. He was hysterical when the uniforms arrived on the scene."

"No chance that the prints belong to the neighbor?"

"He says no. As soon as he saw the body lying there in all that blood with the head barely attached, he ran out of the house screaming, puked in the front yard, and called us on his cell phone. Claims that he didn't touch anything or get close to the body."

I thanked Cathy profusely for the information and hung up the phone. What an incredibly grisly crime. It would be standard procedure for the cops to interview Sandy, since she was close to the victim. I wondered when that would happen. I didn't want to be the one to tell her about the murder, but it would probably be better coming from me than some cop. I called her and when she answered the phone I could tell she was crying. She already knew—the cops were there interviewing her now. I told her to call me when they left and she agreed.

I decided to stick close to the phone, not knowing when Sandy would call, so I worked on some bookkeeping and did some more filing to pass the time. Around 11 a.m., she finally called. She was very agitated, so I asked if I could come over, thinking maybe I could hold her and calm her down. She fought me on the issue briefly, but then relented. I got over there as quickly as I could.

I didn't think it was possible, but Sandy looked like hell, her eyes all puffy and red, fatigue evident on her face and in her movements. I made her some tea and held her until she seemed reasonably calm. Finally, she said, "It's all so horrible. I can't believe this happened. It seems kind of surreal, you know? Like it isn't really true. It's hard for the brain to accept death."

"I know what you mean. I've lost some family members and a couple of friends. But it takes a while for the reality of it to sink in. I mean, I must have picked up the phone to call Sarah, a friend who died in a skiing accident, a dozen times after she died. As I was dialing the numbers, I remembered she wasn't there anymore. I guess this difficulty with death is the brain's way of protecting us, part of our built-in defense system. I don't know."

"Yeah, maybe." After a few moments, Sandy spoke again. "The reality of Chris's death is bad enough, but then the cops interrogated me like they think I did it. Like I'm a…murderer."

"Oh, don't fall for that. They treat everybody that way, for good reason. First, everybody *is* a suspect until positively ruled out. Second, sometimes the cops get lucky with their strong-arm tactics and the guilty party confesses, relieving the cops of a lot of work. Don't worry about it."

But she looked worried, very worried. I didn't know what else I could say, though. After a while she looked at me and stammered, "It's just that I…I, well, oh god…oh, never mind. It's nothing." Sandy had broken out in a sweat, even though the interior of the house was rather cool. She was shaking.

I looked at her intently and asked, "What is it? Is there something you want to tell me?"

The color drained from her face and she replied, "No, there's nothing to say."

Uh oh. Crap-o-meter on full alert. "Sandy, if there's something you know about this, you should tell me. Or the police."

"No, no, no. There's nothing to tell."

I tried to get her to open up to me, but it didn't work. There was definitely something Sandy wasn't telling me. I couldn't imagine what it might be. I spent the night with her, just holding her and telling her that it was going to be okay. I tried to get her to eat something, but she refused, insisting that she wasn't hungry, even though she hadn't eaten in hours.

I had to leave about 8 a.m. the next morning to meet with a client, but I told Sandy that I'd stop by later with some lunch. A little after noon, I kept my promise and stopped by her place with burgers, not wanting to engender further trauma with some of my cooking. But Sandy wasn't there. Odd, since I told her I'd be coming by with lunch. I waited for some time, but finally went home. I found a message on my answering machine from Cathy Lockhart: "Tell your friend not to worry. We've made an arrest in the St. James murder. Looks like St. James was whacked by her long-time mate, Sandy Garrett. Talk to you later."

I made it to the bathroom just in time to toss my burgers. I sat there for a long time, my head resting on the porcelain god. Could it be true? Was Sandy a cold-blooded murderer?

Sleeping with the Enemy

The cold porcelain finally brought me to my senses and synapses started firing, light bulbs appeared over my head, and puzzle pieces began snapping into place. St. James was murdered with a meat cleaver...Sandy was presumably adept with meat cleavers, skilled at slicing through bone and marrow. Ugh! The killer was strong. Sandy was built like a brick shithouse. Sandy knew St. James, and so she would readily allow Sandy access to her home, especially since it had been Sandy's home until recently. Obviously, the fingerprint left at the scene belonged to Sandy, since the cops arrested her so quickly. Did she have a criminal background? When I tried calling Sandy at 5:00 p.m. yesterday, there was no answer. It was a three-hour drive to Kingston from Cloverdale. Assuming Sandy left before 5:00 p.m., she had time to drive to Kingston and do the dirty deed, at least according to the medical examiner's estimated time of death as it currently stood. That would explain why she got home so late—she had to stop somewhere and clean up. Wash away all that...blood.

Then there's the nature of the crime. When someone gets whacked with a meat cleaver to the neck, with such force that the victim's head is nearly severed from her body, it suggests two possible scenarios: 1) it's the work of a crazed lunatic; or 2) it's the work of someone driven by sheer, deep-seated hatred for the victim. Sandy had spent eight years with St. James, patiently waiting for things to get better, waiting for her lover to finally say 'yes.' There had to be some bitterness on Sandy's part that the waiting was all in vain, and that she had wasted eight years of her life with this woman. Was it enough bitterness to propel that meat cleaver with bone-splitting force?

Plus, she was extremely upset, and the officers' interrogation yesterday had certainly struck fear in her heart. I could tell last night that there was something she wasn't telling me. But murder?

Omigod, had I been sleeping with a murderer? The pieces all fit together perfectly. And if they had her fingerprint in the victim's blood, what other explanation could there be? Wait a minute—I had shared a bed with this woman and she showed me tenderness like I'd never known. Could sheer evil and incredible tenderness exist in the same person?

When she had talked about St. James, I'd noticed some regret in her tone, and a hint of bitterness and resentment. But certainly not the level of resentment evidenced by this crime. Then again, lust had a way of interfering with my instincts, blinding me to things I didn't want to see.

If Sandy did this, what set her off? This was clearly not a premeditated murder. No, this was clearly a murder committed in the heat of passion, on the spur of the moment. Sandy had seemed calm when I'd left her early Sunday afternoon. What could have sent her into a rage so quickly?

God, I was so confused. I felt stupid for not seeing all of this sooner, and guilty for thinking any of it. How could I think that someone I was beginning to have feelings for could be a murderer? But in the face of such overwhelming evidence, how could I think otherwise. I felt like my head was going to explode from the force of these competing emotions.

Corey and Tasha were now sitting in the bathroom doorway eyeing me warily. I could tell by their quizzical expressions that they wanted to know what I was doing clutching their water cooler. With some effort, I pulled myself off the floor and took a very long, hot shower, attempting to wash away the shock of the recent events. When I realized that it wasn't going to work, I got out and pulled on some clean clothes. It was time to pay a visit to the person responsible for all of my misery.

I strode into Murder By Numbers like a woman on a mission,

which I was. Kit was behind the counter and when she saw me approaching, she let out a blood-curdling scream. I jumped and looked to see if an ax murderer was behind me with an ax poised to slice and dice me, the imagery courtesy of recent events. No one there, except a blur of fur, presumably Kinsey running for cover. I looked at Kit like she was crazy, which she undoubtedly was, and asked, "What the hell's the matter with you?"

She looked down at my feet in horror and merely pointed to them. I looked down and saw two perfectly normal tennis shoe clad feet, then I looked back at Kit, her face still wracked with horror, and asked simply, "What?"

"Your shoes."

"They're Nike high tops. I know they're old and somewhat beat up, but there's really no call for screaming."

Kit looked at me like I was some kind of alien pod creature with three heads and said in a superior tone, "Haven't you heard of the sweatshop conditions associated with the manufacture of Nike products? Aren't you aware of the low wages and poor treatment foreign workers endure, just so elitist Americans, like yourself, can proudly display the Nike Swoosh on their feet? Don't you care that…"

I interrupted Kit before she really got going. "Kit, I don't have time for your theatrics today. I just need to see Sam. Where is she?"

Again, the pod creature look, and Kit picked up her socially conscious soliloquy where she had left off. I shouted, "Kit, where is Sam?"

With hurt and anger in her eyes, Kit responded, "We were getting low on milk, so she went down to the corner market to pick some up. Don't get your panties in a bunch. She'll be right back."

An uncomfortable silence descended upon us. I noticed that Kit was wearing her power suit: army boots, camouflage pants, an old t-shirt, and lots of tacky bracelets and love beads. Upon closer inspection, I could see that the old faded t-shirt had some words on the front: Free Minnesota. I decided not to ask.

At that moment, Sam breezed in, milk in hand and a perky smile on her face. The smile faded as I grabbed her by the arm and led her into the back room. In a sharp tone, I asked, "You heard about the St. James murder?"

"Yes, I saw it in yesterday's newspaper. I remember you telling me that she was Sandy's ex. She must be devastated—how is she?"

Heavy on the sarcasm, I responded, "Not so good. She's been arrested for the murder."

Sam just sat there with a stunned look on her face. Finally, she said, "Well, there must be some mistake. A sweet woman like that can't be guilty of murder. She wears Liz Claiborne, for chrissake."

I didn't even try to figure out Sam's logic. I didn't have time to follow that twisted path. Instead, I said, "The police don't arrest people on a whim, you know. There's some pretty strong evidence that Sandy did it."

"That just can't be. I don't believe it for one second."

"It doesn't really matter what you believe."

"Why are you angry with *me*?"

It was my turn to give Sam the pod creature look. "Correct me if I'm mistaken, but wasn't it you who set me up with a murderer? Let's face it, Sam, you're not cut out to be a matchmaker. I mean, setting me up with a murderer is the capper, but your other matches haven't been much better. Of course, there's Dede. And before her…who was it? Oh yeah, Margaret, how could I forget. I've been meaning to write to the power company about her, because if they could somehow harness all the gas floating around in her, we'd have no more energy shortages. Everything gave that woman gas! And before her, there was Shannon, the music lover. She'd take things I would say during casual conversation and, at random, make them into country songs right on the spot. Do you know how annoying that is?"

Sam sat in the corner with her head down, looking ashamed and hurt, like some errant student. I continued, "And before that, Erin. She wanted to mother me and take care of me 24/7. How could you think that kind of treatment would be appealing to me? Don't you know me after all these years?"

No reaction from the errant student, so I continued with my litany of ill-fated romances. "And before Erin, there was Inez, the soap opera queen. She couldn't tell you the name of the vice-president, but she sure can tell you the twists and turns in the life of Erica Kane, and she can name every member of the illustrious Quartermaine family."

"All right, all right. I get the picture."

"Do you?"

"Yes. But isn't it possible that you're being just a bit too picky? I mean, just because a woman has a slight gastrointestinal problem, or has an unusual interest in music, doesn't mean she couldn't be your soul mate."

"And how 'bout if she's a murderer? Huh? Can she still be my soul mate then?"

Again Sam looked down at the floor. I shook my head and said, "Look, I don't need any more of your help, thank you very much. I've been trying for months now to drop some subtle hints. But I guess the time for subtlety is over. From now on, just butt the hell out of my love life and mind your own damn business!" With those words ringing in the air, I marched out of Sam's store as her eyes welled up with tears. Well, good. Maybe she finally got the message.

By the time I got home, I felt more than a little guilty. Sam's my best friend, and I know she means well. My outburst was uncalled for and childish. I vowed to stop by her place later and apologize. With that thought in mind, I slouched into my office to check my messages. Mostly junk, but the last one was from Sandy. In a shaky, tearful voice she said, "They told me I could call a lawyer, and, well, you're a lawyer. I know it looks bad, J.Z., but I didn't do it. I swear I didn't. Please come here and let me explain. I need your help. Please."

Some nerve she has, asking *me* for help. But the detective in me couldn't resist—I had to hear this "explanation" she mentioned. It should at least provide some entertainment value. So, I climbed in my trusty van and headed off to Kingston. I stopped along the way to replenish the tossed burgers. It was about 6:00 p.m. when I rolled into the Kingston Police Department parking lot. As expected, I found Officer Lockhart putting in some overtime hours. She'd always been a workaholic.

"I love a woman in uniform."

Cathy looked up from her desk, clearly surprised to see me. A big smile spread across her pleasant face and she rushed over to hug me. After a few moments of hugging, she asked, "What are you doing here?"

"It's the St. James thing. Remember the friend I said would be affected by this?" Cathy nodded. "That friend is Sandy Garrett."

She tilted her head and in a stern voice asked, "Did you have any reason to think that Garrett was a viable suspect when you weaseled information out of me?"

"Absolutely not. I was completely in the dark."

Cathy got a little glimmer in her eyes and asked, "You're not the lawyer Garrett called, are you?"

"Yeah, that's me."

"You're not seriously thinking of representing her, are you?"

"Hell no. I gave up that gig a long time ago, as you well know. Besides, I never practiced criminal law. But, I *am* a lawyer and she did call me. So, technically, I have a right to see my client."

"Take it easy, Perry Mason, you can see her. But I should tell you that it looks bad for your *client*. We got a match on the fingerprint and the partial shoe print. We'll probably get a match on the tire tracks in the driveway. And, of course, there's the will the crime scene unit found in the vic's desk."

"The will?"

"Yeah. It seems that St. James's original will left everything to various charities. But she drafted a new one about six weeks ago, leaving everything to Garrett. If she beats the rap, she'll be a very wealthy woman."

My stomach started to churn again. As I labored to keep the second batch of burgers down, I asked, "The prints...how did you match her fingerprints?"

"Garrett taught some writing classes at the community college. That particular college requires that perspective teachers pass a background check, which includes a criminal check. You probably remember reading about the big lawsuit against the college a while back. The idiots hired a convicted rapist to teach a class in women's studies. Ironic, huh? Since then, the college does extensive checks, which includes fingerprinting. Garrett, like other teachers, was fingerprinted for that, so we had her prints in the system. With the print match, we got an arrest warrant and the detectives who searched Garrett's place found the shoe with the vic's blood on the sole. Pretty incriminating stuff. I mean, she has an explanation of sorts, but it contradicts what she told the officers who interviewed her yesterday morning."

"Yeah, you're right. It looks pretty bad. I guess I should go talk to her now."

"She's next door in the temporary holding facility. We'll hold her there until after her arraignment day after tomorrow. I'll call over and tell them you're coming."

"Thanks, Cathy. I owe you one."

"No problem. Hey, you're not thinking of driving back to Cloverdale tonight, are you?"

"That was my plan."

"We've been having some pretty severe storm warnings. Been listening to them for the past hour. Why don't you just crash with me?"

"No, I don't want to intrude."

"You wouldn't be intruding. You want to hear a confession? I hate thunder and lightning."

"The big, bad police officer afeared of a little thunder and lightning?"

Cathy playfully punched me on my shoulder, and with a look of chagrin, said, "Shut up! I didn't say I was *afraid*. It just makes me a little…uneasy. Anyway, why don't you stay with me and we'll rent movies, stuff ourselves with pizza, and talk trash about everyone we went to law school with?"

"An offer I can't refuse." I agreed to meet Cathy at her place after I was done talking to Sandy. My plans for the night set, I reluctantly made my way over to the jail. This was one rendezvous I wasn't looking forward to.

Jailhouse Blues

Sandy looked like hell. For a moment, she flashed a feeble smile, which quickly melted from her face. "I can tell by looking in your eyes, you think I did it."

I shrugged and said, "The evidence is pretty overwhelming. It seems to be shaping up into an airtight case."

"Not when you hear my side of it. Look, I admit I was there, but I didn't kill Chris. I swear that I didn't kill her. She was dead when I got there."

"Why were you there?"

"Chris called me around 4:00 on Sunday. She was frantic. She said someone had been harassing and threatening her. I asked her what the police were doing about it, and she said that she hadn't called the police, that she couldn't. I pressed for more information, but she said we needed to talk in person. There was something she needed to tell me."

"Did Chris say what kind of threats this person was making, or who this person was?"

"Chris said she couldn't tell me anything about this person over the phone, because she needed to explain it to me face to face. She was adamant about that. Chris did say that the person was getting more agitated and reckless, and that she feared for her life. She thought maybe I might be in danger."

"What else did she say?"

"That was really all I could persuade her to tell me on the phone. I felt that I had no choice but to go. I mean, we did spend eight years together. I owed her that. Chris was revered by many, but she really didn't have any friends. She never learned how to open up to people. She rarely opened up to me."

"Do you have any idea what Chris wanted to tell you, or who would want to harm you?"

"No on both counts. As you might guess, though, Chris had a lot of enemies: prosecutors that she humiliated, victims and their families who felt like Chris cheated them out of justice, the occasional disappointed defendant, associates that she stepped on to get to the top. The list goes on and on."

"But why would any of them want to harm you?"

"I have no idea. Maybe Chris was exaggerating to get me to come. I don't know."

"Okay, if what you say is true, why did you run? Why didn't you just call the cops?"

"You have to understand how shaken up I was. I mean, when I saw Chris lying there in all that blood...so much blood...with her head...oh god! I just panicked and ran out of there as fast as I could. It was sheer panic. I'm surprised that I didn't have an accident—I was driving like a maniac. After a bit, I pulled over to call the police from a pay phone. But then I thought to myself, what if the police don't believe me? What if they think I'm involved somehow? Chris was dead. It's not like a phone call to the police was going to help her. So, I decided to pretend my trip never happened."

"Bad plan. By the way, how did you get Chris's blood on your hand? And how did you get into the house?"

"The door was ajar when I got there. As for the blood on my hand, I dropped my car keys when I saw Chris and they landed in some of the...blood. And I guess I must have stepped in some too. It all happened so fast. It's a blur now. I don't remember touching anything after picking up my keys, but I guess I did. Nor do I remember stepping in any blood, and had no idea until the police told me today. Had I known, I obviously would have called the police from that pay phone."

Sandy started to sob and the color drained from her face. Part of me wanted to run over to her and hold her, protect her from all that was happening. But another part of me cautioned that I'd better stay on my toes, with my crap-o-meter finely tuned. I allowed Sandy to regain her composure before continuing. "What can you tell me about Chris's background, her family and where she grew up?"

"Surprisingly, not much after eight years together. Chris was always so private, almost secretive. When we met, she told me that she was an only child, and her parents had died years ago in some horrible accident, which she never wanted to discuss. She said she considered herself to be from both the East Coast and Midwest, since she'd moved around a lot. She'd frittered away a few years after college, trying to decide what she wanted to do with her life."

"Where did she go to undergrad?"

"I asked her once, but she said it was some small college on the east coast that no one has ever heard of. Odd, but I didn't push it. She went to law school in Oregon, at Lewis and Clark College. I'm embarrassed to say that's about all I know."

"You're kidding. After eight years, that's it?"

"I guess the sad truth is, Chris didn't want to share *anything* with me. Wait…there is one other thing. It's probably nothing, and I'm a bit embarrassed to even bring it up. But, at some point fairly early in our relationship, I got fed up with Chris's secrets, and I was curious about what she might be hiding. She had an office at home, and she asked that I never go in there, because she had a lot of confidential client information lying about. One day, I just couldn't stop myself. I knew if Chris had any personal papers or effects that would give me any clues about her background, they would be in her office. I found a locked drawer in her desk, and searched everywhere for the key. I finally found it, but the drawer didn't contain much, just a picture of a couple I assumed were Chris's parents, a picture of a young woman, and an old newspaper clipping."

Sandy paused as if she was trying to remember something. I finally nudged her. "Yes, go on."

"Oh, I was just thinking about the picture of the couple. There was a third person in that picture, but Chris, or someone else, had cut out that part of the picture."

"Could you tell anything about that person? Was the person male or female, young or old?"

"Not really. I got the feeling that it was a man, because what was left of the shoulder looked like a sports coat. But I'm not sure."

"What do you remember about the newspaper clipping?"

"That was odd too. It looked like a picture had been attached to it at one time, but it was gone. The article was about the son of a prominent family from Springfield, Pennsylvania. Their last name was Hollingsworth. That stuck in my mind because growing up, our next-door neighbors were named Hollingsworth, but they were far from prominent. Anyway, the young man had been piloting his plane when it went down at sea. The wreckage of the plane was recovered, but his body was never found. I assumed the young man had been one of Chris's friends."

"What about the other picture, of the young woman?"

She looked up, her brow furrowed, as she tried to recall the image. "The picture quality was poor, and the woman seemed nondescript. I recall long brown hair and glasses, but that's about it."

I thought for a moment and said, "Tell me about the will."

A pained expression ran across Sandy's face and her skin flushed. She rested her head in her hands and looked down at the scuffed metal table between us. In a moment, she shook her head and responded, "I told Chris not to do that. She told me three or four years ago that she intended to leave everything to charity, and I thought that was great. Then, about six weeks ago, after we'd decided it was best to part, Chris said she was changing her will. She thought that I deserved something for putting up with her for so many years. I insisted that she leave her will as it was. I told her that I have enough of my own money to live comfortably, and that's all I need. I have no desire for that much money, and anyway, I wouldn't know what to do with it. I thought that I'd convinced her to leave her will as it was, but I found out otherwise today."

"Anything else you want to tell me?"

"No, I don't think so." After a long pause, Sandy asked, "Do you believe me?"

"I can't give you a definitive answer. I'd be lying if I did. I want to believe you, that's for sure."

Sandy looked down at the gray concrete floor, a dejected expression on her face. I hoped she wouldn't cry again. Before she could, I said, "Look, you have more important things to worry about than what I believe. You're being arraigned day after tomorrow. You need to have an attorney present for that. Surely you know lots of criminal defense attorneys in Kingston."

"Oh sure, and they all worshiped Chris. Who among them will step forward to defend Chris's alleged killer? I need your help in finding someone."

"I don't know many attorneys here, especially criminal defense attorneys. But I know one who might be able to help. I'll call her tonight."

"I'd really appreciate that. But I think I might also need a good investigator. How 'bout it? But before you answer, understand that I would expect to be billed just like all your other clients."

"I'm flattered that you repose such trust in my abilities. However, I may not be the best person for the job. I mean, we have been intimate, and that tends to cloud a person's judgment and objectivity."

"Are you willing to keep an open mind with regard to my guilt or innocence?"

"Yes, of course."

"Do you want me to be innocent?"

"More than anything."

"Well then, I think you're perfect for the job."

I drummed my fingers on the table and sighed heavily. Sandy was looking at me with expectation and a hint of desperation in her eyes. "If the attorney I'm calling later decides to represent you, I'll discuss the matter with her. It's really her decision to make, and I trust her judgment."

We chatted for a bit, though it was pretty superficial. I told her I'd have someone water her plants and pick up her mail and such. I figured that I probably wasn't the best person for the plant-tending job, since the only plant I have is brown. She didn't want me to leave, but the guard outside the door was getting antsy and we really had nothing left to say. As I sat with her, I tried not to think about how it felt to have her warm, shapely body pressing up against mine, but I had little success on that score. At the same time, I struggled to take the emotions I had started to feel for Sandy and bury them deep inside my subconscious, again with little success. We parted awkwardly, with me promising to let her know as soon as possible about the attorney.

When I arrived at Cathy's home, she had already rented a couple of action-packed flicks. Cops, go figure. We decided on barbecue chicken pizza with extra garlic and cheese. We made ourselves comfortable on Cathy's overstuffed sofa. She popped the first movie into the VCR, and we waited for the pizza to arrive. Then, Cathy asked, "Are you doin' the nasty with that Garrett woman?"

I chuckled and said, "Why, Cathy, you've always had such a way with words."

Cathy grinned and said with an air of triumph, "My finely honed cop intuition tells me that the answer is yes. Next question. Are you nuts, Mackenzie?"

I opened my mouth to defend my sanity, but then changed my mind. Instead, I said, "Since you're a cop, and there's a chance I might become involved in this case, we probably should refrain from discussing anything even remotely related to Sandy Garrett or the St. James murder."

Cathy stuck out her lower lip in a convincing pout and said, "You take all the fun out of everything."

"No, we can talk about you. Who are you doin' the nasty with these days?"

Cathy rolled her eyes and responded, "Men are all dogs. I'm never having sex again."

It was my turn to roll my eyeballs, and then I said, "It seems to me that I've heard that somewhere before, and not that long ago if memory serves." I paused, an evil grin on my face, and said, "You could always switch teams."

"Naw. On your team, I'd get stuck on the bench a lot, being a rookie and all. On my team, I'm a position player."

I leered and said, "Oh really? What position?"

Again I received a shoulder punch. Before our conversation could degenerate any further, the phone rang. It was Mavis Weathers, known to her friends as "Slick," the attorney I had left a message for earlier. We caught up on old times briefly, and then Slick said, "I assume this isn't a social call."

"No, it isn't. I've got a proposition for you, Slick."

There was a pause on the other end of the line, and a brief hacking fit. Slick has never taken the Surgeon General's warning seriously. "Babe, I appreciate the offer, but I'm old and tired. Maybe some other time."

"Funny, Slick. I'll meet you at your office first thing in the morning, if that will work for you."

She agreed and I returned to watching some futuristic shoot 'em up with Cathy. I readily lost interest and my thoughts drifted to Sandy. I already knew that if Slick agreed to take the case and wanted me on it, I wouldn't hesitate. But I was still conflicted: did she or didn't she? I had to know.

Law and Disorder

I was waiting at Slick's office in downtown Kingston when she arrived a little after 8:00 a.m. I watched from the lobby with amusement as she climbed out of her cherished Buick Skylark, which she stubbornly refused to replace, even though the old heap was reluctant to get going on most mornings. But then, so was Slick. As she stepped into the building, I sensed right off that she hadn't changed. There was the ubiquitous cigarette dangling perilously from her lips, which were streaked with a hideous shade of neon magenta lipstick. As expected, Slick was clad in an old, worn-out dress at least 20 years out of fashion. Her hair was a bit grayer than the last time I saw her, but worn in the same "style": sticking out in places, flat in others, with a liberal dose of hair spray. I silently mused that Slick's hairdo was actually in vogue these days. Who would have guessed that Slick would be a trend-setter?

Now, don't get me wrong. It's not as though Slick is poor. She's actually pretty well off, now in the twilight of a very successful criminal defense practice. And it's not as though she's cheap. It's just that the only thing Slick has ever seen fit to focus any real energy on is her work.

Slick bustled over to me, beaming as she said in her gravelly voice, "How's it goin', kid?" We hugged briefly and Slick took my arm and led me to her office. As we walked down the hallway lined with Slick's diplomas and awards, she hollered over her shoulder, "Irma, bring us some coffee, will you? Make it extra strong." Irma was almost as old as Slick (early 60's), and had been Slick's assistant from day one, though Irma had slowed considerably in the last few years. Age seemed to make Slick accelerate, as if she knew her days on this planet were growing shorter. But no matter how much Irma slowed down, Slick would never fire her. Slick was fiercely loyal and eternally grateful to those who helped her get where she was. Slick had offered Irma a generous retirement package, but Irma was from the old school: she believed in working for her money. Besides, Irma loved being in the trenches, and would probably take her last breath in front of her old Smith-Corona.

Slick was the same way. She was a crusty, curmudgeonly old bird, set in her ways. Other lawyers called her "Slick" because of her incredibly effective courtroom theatrics and the down-to-earth way in which she related to juries. She didn't look like some expensive mouthpiece. She looked like one of them, one of the community, and they loved her. For the hell of it, I'd sat in on some of her shorter trials. What a show! I remember one trial where I counted 9 of the 12 jurors openly sobbing during her closing arguments for a criminal defendant who had undoubtedly butchered his father during a heated argument. The prosecuting attorney couldn't do anything but shake his head and kick himself in the ass for not cutting a deal. Slick was as much of a legend in Oregon as Chris St. James, but there were vast differences in their styles. St. James looked very much the part of a typical lawyer: expensive, well-tailored suits, hand-tooled leather briefcase, Rolex watch, and all the other requisite accoutrements. Slick, on the other hand, looked like a truck stop waitress with bad fashion sense. She inevitably stumbled into court looking like she just rolled out of bed, papers hanging out of her shoddy briefcase (held together by masking tape and wire), pencils stuck in her wild, gray hair. Out-of-town attorneys unacquainted with Slick (not many anymore) interpreted Slick's unkempt, chaotic appearance to mean that she was unprepared or in over her head. Soon enough, their self-satisfied, holier-than-thou grins were replaced with shell-shocked expressions as Slick dipped into her bottomless bag o' litigation tricks. Like St. James, Slick rarely lost. But unlike St. James, Slick treated opposing counsel with respect, courtesy, and dignity.

I met Slick a few years ago when she taught a particularly enlightening CLE (continuing legal education) course on evidence. We chatted at length after her presentation and became fast friends. Now, I occasionally did investigative work for her, which allowed us to keep in touch.

After we'd settled into her office, a firetrap with its mountains of case files, stray papers, stacks of books, and general clutter, Slick looked at me with an earnest expression and asked, "Ok, what's the proposition?" Good ol' Slick—right to the point.

"Well, you've no doubt heard about the St. James murder."

"Heard about it? Honey, I'm old, not dead."

"I'm…um…uh…acquainted with the woman who's been arrested for the murder, Sandy Garrett."

Slick furrowed her brow for a moment, then said, "I remember Sandy. Nice gal, and cute as a bug's ear. And sweetie, I think I can guess what you mean by 'acquainted.' What, you think you're gonna shock me? Please. At my age, I've seen it all."

I tilted my head and rolled my eyes. "Anyway, she's being arraigned tomorrow and she needs an attorney. I promised to help her find one. She can certainly afford you, and she needs the best."

Irma ambled in with our coffee, which Slick belted down greedily. After a brief hacking fit, Slick said, "Yes, I've heard that the case against her is as tight as a sixteen year-old's ass. But I suppose *you* think she's innocent."

I sighed heavily, and a heavy mantle of guilt settled on my shoulders. I replied, "Slick, I don't really know what to think." At this point, I filled Slick in on everything Sandy had told me, as well as everything I was able to weasel out of Cathy. I also told her how Sandy and I had met, and the ensuing fledgling relationship. After I was done, Slick eased back into her big leather chair and said, "Holy shit."

"My sentiments exactly. It looks bleak. But we've got one thing going for us—St. James had a lot of enemies, ones that truly despised her."

Slick cackled and nodded her head. "That's an understatement. St. James was revered, feared, and hated, all at the same time."

"What did you think of her?"

Slick ruminated for a moment, and then replied, "She was one hell of an attorney. Knew her stuff, all right. But she was ruthless. Very unpopular with prosecutors, needless to say."

"But aren't most criminal defense attorneys?"

"Not like this. Criminal trials are dramatic productions, and part of the show is making the jury believe that you are outraged and incensed with the other side. It's all for show. When the curtain comes down on our little production, whatever the outcome, defense attorneys and prosecutors go out afterwards and swill down a few beers. There's an atmosphere of mutual respect. Cases and defendants come and go, but lawyers interact with these same people in the legal profession over and over. We grow to either like or tolerate each other, like dogs tolerate fleas."

Slick grew silent for a moment, thinking, then continued. "But with St. James, the contempt for the other side was real. She wanted nothing to do with prosecutors, and took every opportunity to humiliate them in court. She was a cold bitch, even in social settings. I never even noticed any warmth between her and Sandy."

I flashed her a surprised look, and Slick said, "Yeah, maybe that sounds strange coming from me, an old spinster. And don't think that I haven't heard all the speculation about *my* sexual preference. Why, I've even heard rumors about me and Irma. Can you imagine?"

Actually, I had imagined, since Irma was also a spinster, but I kept this to myself.

"My sexual preference is just as much a mystery to me as it is to everybody else. I haven't had the time or inclination to give it much thought. Maybe in another 10 years, I'll retire and ponder it."

A bald-faced lie, and she knew it. Slick took another hearty slug of Irma's thick coffee-like concoction and said, "Anyway, I get the distinct impression that you perceive some involvement for yourself in this case."

With a sheepish look, I said, "Well, that's entirely up to you. That is, if you decide to take the case. Sandy wants me to be the investigator, but I don't know if that's wise, given my involvement with her."

"Normally, I'd have to agree with you. But you seem to have a healthy skepticism. You don't just automatically assume that Sandy's innocent simply because you've been doing the horizontal mambo with her. Under the circumstances, I see no problem with you being the investigator."

I smiled and asked, "Does that mean you'll take the case?"

Slick cocked her head to one side in a coy manner and said, "Let me see…a wealthy, well-known criminal defense attorney murdered in her own home. The alleged murderer is the victim's longtime, but recently estranged, lover. The evidence against her is solid. Things look dismal for the accused. Almost no chance of pulling a win out of this one." A few moments of dramatic silence. "Hell, yes, I'll take it! This is the kind of white-knuckle, nail-biting case I live for, baby."

Slick and I hunkered down for the next hour or so, mapping out a strategy. She wanted me to start digging into St. James's background, which might take some time, given the sketchy details Sandy provided. She also asked that I begin interviewing St. James's former co-workers, disgruntled clients, and victims and families of victims who were particularly upset with St. James's winning ways in the courtroom. A very long list, no doubt.

In the meantime, Slick would meet with Sandy for a more detailed interview. Then, she would ask the state for "discovery," the legal version of "I'll show you mine if you show me yours." The discovery process requires each side to provide the other with certain categories of evidence. At the same time, Slick would begin the inevitable volley of motions, attempting to get some or all of the charges dropped or some of the evidence suppressed, meaning that it couldn't be used at trial.

I decided to stay in town for Sandy's arraignment, not that I was needed. I just thought it might be nice for Sandy to see a friendly face as she was entering her plea of "not guilty" and asking the court to be released on bail. Despite my "healthy skepticism," I hoped that Sandy was granted bail. She looked awful when I had gone to see her, and I didn't know if she would survive inside a jail cell until this matter could run its course through the justice system.

Of course, Cathy insisted that I stay at her place again. I agreed, and to show my gratitude, I took her out to dinner at a nice little bistro. The atmosphere was warm and inviting and the food was delicious. Cathy drank a little too much petit sirah and became chatty and doe-eyed with our waiter, Antonio. As we left the bistro, Cathy slyly passed Antonio a cocktail napkin with her telephone number written in lipstick. She was positively swooning for the rest of the evening. Finally, I said in an accusatory tone, "I thought you said men were all dogs, and you're never having sex again."

Cathy blushed slightly and replied, "That was just a bit of creative hyperbole. I never meant it to be taken seriously."

"Well, I'm sure Antonio will be glad to hear that. He's pretty cute...for a guy."

At this point, the conversation degenerated into a discussion (well, more like a soliloquy) of Antonio's obvious sexual prowess and his many physical attributes and social charms ("Oooooh, did you see the way his nose curved just a bit, and how soft his hair looked....and the way his ass filled out those chinos..."). I couldn't get as excited about all this as Cathy, but I grunted and nodded at appropriate points in feigned excitement. Cathy appreciated the effort, even though she knew it was total B.S. on my part. Finished extolling the many virtues of Antonio, Cathy said, "You know, the great thing about lesbian friends is that they'll never steal your quarry. But the bad side is that you guys never really appreciate a hot male bod when you see it." Cathy thought for a moment and then continued, "All in all, I'll take lesbian friends any day."

The wine had made Cathy tired and she hit the sack pretty early. I couldn't sleep. I was worried about the bail issue, and my mind kept racing with the events of the past few days. I used the time to make notes about the things I wanted to find out about St. James, and the people I wanted to talk to. Uncovering the truth in this case would be difficult, I suspected. And there was no guarantee that at the end of the legal process we would be any closer to the truth. A verdict of "not guilty" doesn't mean that the person is innocent. It simply means that the jury wasn't satisfied with the evidence presented by the state. What would I do if I couldn't uncover the identity of the killer (assuming it wasn't Sandy), and Slick worked her typical razzle dazzle in the courtroom? What would I do if Sandy was found not guilty, but I wasn't convinced of her innocence? Damn. So many questions, and not enough answers. Maybe this would make me work harder to uncover the truth.

Arraignments begin at 8:30 a.m. in the Kingston Correctional Facility, a drab, depressing-looking standard issue government building. Slick and I sat on the hard, unyielding benches waiting for Sandy's case to be called. At 9:10, Sandy was led to the small, bullet-proof enclosure where defendants appear with prison guards at their sides. The district attorney assigned to Sandy's case, Amy Witherspoon, asked that the judge deny bail, since Sandy had ample funds with which to flee the court's jurisdiction, and because of the viciousness of the crime. Slick responded that Sandy had no prior criminal history and was an upstanding member of society. Yadda, yadda. Witherspoon outlined the strength of the evidence against Sandy, and Slick tried to poke holes in it, but the judge wasn't biting. Bail was denied and Sandy was led out of the courtroom looking like a whipped puppy. Before she left, she glanced at me with an expression of desperation I had never before seen on any human being.

Slick and I walked outside together. She shook her head somberly and said, "As soon as I found out that Witherspoon was on the case, I knew we wouldn't get bail. She is as tough as nails. The best D.A. I've ever been up against. Damn smart and driven. She also has political aspirations, and you can bet that she will use this high-profile case as a vehicle for those aspirations. The good news is that she's ethical and plays by the rules. Even so, this is going to be an uphill battle all the way."

I told Slick how I intended to start the investigation and I promised to call as soon as I found out anything useful. With that, I was off to Cloverdale.

Catching Up
with Old Friends

I strode into my home to find two very perturbed cats sitting in the entryway. Upon seeing me, they simultaneously turned their backs on me and assumed their best "screw you" postures. They were always pissed when I was away overnight, even though I had an arrangement with Cecelia to come over and see to their needs when I'm gone overnight. Ethel would always come with her and shower the cats with affection, but they still acted like I had abandoned them when I returned each time.

"Ok, girls, how long will my punishment last this time? Aren't you tired of this little game? You know I adore you both. And besides, I'm making tuna salad for lunch." As soon as they heard the can opener and detected the scent of tuna fish, their little noses began to twitch and they pranced happily about the kitchen. Once again, they both gazed at me with looks of adoration. The little tuna whores. If only human moods could be altered so swiftly.

Once the three of us were sufficiently fortified with yummy tuna salad, I ambled into my office. I knew that the investigation for Sandy would monopolize my time. So, I farmed out a lot of my projects to investigator friends, keeping only a few that would require limited investments of time. I then tied up a few loose ends: returning phone calls and correspondence, preparing invoices for completed projects, and finalizing reports. It was late afternoon by the time I'd finished and I remembered that I still owed Sam an apology.

I walked down the street to the corner florist and purchased a bouquet of purple and lavender irises. I scampered back to Sam and Nealy's place and knocked on the door. Sam opened the door with a contrite look on her face, and we both said "I'm sorry" at the same time. I shook my head and said, "No, you have nothing to be sorry for. I acted like an ass and I'm really sorry, Sam."

"No, your response was justified. I've been butting into your personal life way too much."

"I can't argue with that. But still, I know you mean well, and I had no cause to lash out at you like that. It won't happen again."

The mea culpas continued briefly, then we hugged and all was right with the world once more. I had to admit, the making up process with the cats was much easier. If only Sam's body shook with excitement at the mere sight of a tuna can. Oh well, we rarely argued.

I filled her in on the status of Sandy's criminal matter and my role in her defense. "Oooooh, this is so exciting!"

"Sam, I'm not appearing on *Who Wants to be a Millionaire*. This is serious business. Sandy's life is at stake."

"I know, but it's still exciting. You get to be a part of vindicating someone, righting a wrong, securing justice."

Oh brother. Sam watches way too many TV shows. Law and Order *is her favorite. I hate watching it with her because she jumps up during the courtroom scenes and objects, as if she's on the show. I try to explain to her that it's not an interactive television show, but she just ignores me.* "Yeah, I guess it seems exciting, but it's really pretty tedious. There's a lot of legwork, tons of phone calls and interviews, and computer checks. It's pretty mundane stuff. It only gets exciting if you are lucky enough to unearth something useful, and that doesn't always happen."

"But you'll do it. I know you will. You have to—Sandy's innocent."

I wished that I could be so sure. Sam and I chatted for a while longer and I poked my head into Nealy's basement studio to say hi. Then I headed home, once again feeling guilty for doubting Sandy's innocence. The best way to counteract that guilt was to plunge into the investigative tasks that awaited me. It was too late in the day to interview the person at the top of my list, so I sat in my office and thought about questions to ask my first interviewee.

After having confirmed with legal assistant extraordinaire Ann

Boyd that my quarry would be in the office the following day, I was on the road back to Kingston by 6:00 a.m., espresso firmly in hand. God, I hated mornings. But this would be fun. I arrived at the prestigious law firm of Cooper, Langley, Hayden, and Dowd at a little after 9:00 a.m. I checked in with the receptionist and said that I had an appointment with Ann, who appeared moments later to greet me. Ann beamed at me and said, "It's been a while, J.Z. How have you been?"

"Real good. But why is someone like you still working for Bitchburger…and why is someone of her low caliber and dubious ethics working for a chic firm like this?" Cooper Langley was perhaps the largest and most prestigious law firm in the state, which is why Chris St. James had been a member of the firm.

Ann pulled me into the little conference room off the reception area and said, "Well, as you know, Bitchburger was quietly asked to leave Dunkel, Dean, Curtis, and Stuart after some, shall we say, 'issues,' with prescription drug use arose." This was the firm where Bitchburger and I had worked together, though not amicably. Ann cleared her throat and continued. "Next thing I know, she calls me and begs me to come over here and be her assistant. I was floored! Naturally, I wondered how she managed to land a job at this posh firm, but I didn't ask. I mean, how do ask someone 'hey, how did a lunkhead like you land such a cush job' without sounding gauche? But anyway, she told me that she could get me a 30% increase and all these added benefits. With my bills, I couldn't possibly say no."

"But how do you put up with her crap?"

Ann chuckled and responded, "Over the years, I've learned to dish her shit right back at her. As long as I keep her in line, things run smoothly. I mean, let's face it, I've saved her ass from malpractice suits more times than I can count. She needs me, and she knows it. That puts me in the catbird seat. I hear that her search for an assistant was somewhat reminiscent of Murphy Brown, a new contender everyday or so. Nobody wanted to deal with her tantrums and blame-placing. For the money I'm making here, hell, I'll deal with it."

"Did you ever find out how she got offered a job here?"

Ann hesitated, but then said, "Well, there have been some rumors…and some googly-eyed looks exchanged between Bitchburger and one of the senior partners, Rich Bailey. He's a horndog if there ever was one. Your classic dirty old man."

"She slept her way to the top. How original. Well, I've been looking forward to the fun at hand all morning. I think it's time to pop in for a little visit with the Bitchburger. Thanks, Ann. You've been great as usual. We'll get together for dinner one of the nights I'm in town."

"That would be great. And hey, you can always count me in when it comes to creating grief and misery for the Big B."

Ann pointed the way to the Big B's office and I entered without knocking. Startled, Bitchburger looked up, and when she realized it was me, she shot me a look of pure evil and said, "Get the hell out of here before I call security."

"Now, now, don't get your pretty lace panties in a bunch. I'm not here for another slugfest. After all, you weren't much competition. I merely need your assistance on a matter I'm investigating."

She let loose with one of her ear-splitting, annoying laughs, throwing her head back in the process. "Fuck you! What makes you think I would ever lift a finger to help you with anything?"

"Look Bitchburger, we both know that I have the goods on you. I'm sure the Bar would be very anxious to hear about your sexual escapades with at least two of your clients, one of whom bought you very expensive gifts while going through bankruptcy. Interesting. I know about the drugs, the drinking, the gambling, and all the other seedy stuff. You read about it all in my little black book. You really should cut down on the substance abuse—you have a tendency to get quite chatty when you're high."

Bitchburger, who had jumped out of her chair when I entered her office, slumped back down into her seat with a defeated look on her face. She brightened for a moment and said, "You can't prove any of it."

"I don't have to prove it. The Bar will climb so far up your ass, they'll be able to tell what you had for breakfast last year. You'll be under a microscope for months. They're very adept at uncovering the truth."

"Shit. What the hell do you want from me, anyway?"

"Just some information. I'm looking into the St. James murder. So naturally I need to find out about her clients, especially ones that were unhappy with their representation. I need to know about prosecutors and victims who hated St. James, and co-workers who resented her. Basically, I want to know who her enemies were. And I want to know about any background information you have on St. James."

Bitchburger looked stunned and said, "You're kidding, right?"

"Do I look like I'm kidding?"

"You obviously didn't know Chris. She had tons of enemies. It would take months for me to dig up that kind of information."

"You've got two days to get me some names to start with. I'll expect the rest of the names in a week."

"Are you fucking nuts? I have clients to attend to."

"Well, your clients will just have to be serviced by someone else. If I don't get what I want when I want it, you'll be very sorry."

"You're a shit, J.Z. I've always felt that way. I used to wonder why I was the only one who saw the *real* you. Then it hit me: it's not politically correct to dislike our gay and lesbian co-workers. People feel compelled to like you because of it. But not me, dammit! I don't trust a woman who can't appreciate a huge stiff prick. It's just not normal."

I shook my head and said, "Yeah well, it's not politically correct to dislike our mentally disturbed co-workers either, but it never stopped me from disliking you." I paused for a moment and then continued with an edge of contempt in my voice. "And where do you get off talking about trust! You'd sell your own mother down the river if the price was right. Look, I don't have all day to chit-chat with you. Just get me some names, and fast." With that, I stormed out of Bitchburger's office. I wasn't watching were I was going, and almost ran into Ann.

"I take it things went well with you and the Big B?"

"I hate that woman! She's intolerable!"

"That's why I get paid the big bucks."

Ann took my arm and led me into a quiet corner of the library. "I was thinking. You should talk to Chris's secretary...well, former secretary. Her name is Kara Welsh. She can probably give you lots of information about Chris, since they worked together for quite a while."

"That's a great idea. Is she here today?"

"No. I guess Chris's death hit her pretty hard. It's not like they were close or anything. But even so, it can be overwhelming when someone you see everyday gets murdered, so she's taking a few days off to regroup."

"Do you think she'd mind if I showed up on her doorstep to ask her a few questions?"

"Let's find out. Why don't you wait up in the reception area and I'll give her a call. If she says it's okay, I'll get directions to her place."

I dutifully walked back to the reception area and took a seat. This place reeked of money. Real leather chairs and a couch, mahogany tables, carpet so thick you could lose a shoe in it, and very tasteful artwork everywhere. But the most amazing thing was the new magazines, from this month even. I couldn't believe it. Typically, a review of magazines in most waiting rooms was like a history lesson, albeit fairly recent history. But this was no ordinary waiting room. This was a waiting room designed for attorneys who bill $200-300 an hour. Maybe I'd been too hasty in my decision to leave the practice of law. At that moment, one of the inner-office doors flew open, and a harried attorney ran down the hall. I could see the bottles of Maalox lined up on his bookcase through the open door. Naw, I guess I made the right decision after all.

Ann tapped me on the shoulder and startled me out of my brief reverie. "Sorry, didn't mean to sneak up on you. Kara says you can come right over. Here are directions to her house."

"Great. Ann, you're an incredible woman. Will you marry me?"

The receptionist raised her eyebrows, but kept typing. Ann giggled and said, "Ask me in another 20 years when sex isn't a big issue for me anymore."

"Not that again. Damn…I keep running into that same problem. Well, if you won't marry me, how 'bout dinner sometime?"

"You got it. Give me a call and we'll set something up."

Ann and I hugged and I was off to Kara Welsh's place. It was easy to find and I was there in just a few minutes. It was a quaint home, white with pale yellow trim and a matching fence. Kara was obviously an avid gardener, as flowers bloomed in every available nook and cranny. The grass was a perfect shade of emerald green, with not a weed in sight. The overall effect was inviting. I made my way up the sidewalk and was greeted by an obese black and white tabby. The cat lumbered over to me and sniffed my pant leg, obviously picking up the scent of my two critters. I reached down to pet the overstuffed feline and the door opened.

"Hi, I'm Kara Welsh. You must be J.Z. Come on in."

I followed Kara inside and it was like walking back in time. The place was filled with antiques, old photographs, rows of tattered books, and so on. There was nothing new in the place, at least not that I could see. It was nice and homey, kind of like going to grammy's house, but somewhat disconcerting in a way.

Kara noticed my stares and said, "My folks own an antique store on the other side of town. They insisted on furnishing this place for me. I didn't have the heart to say no. Besides, the old stuff kind of grows on you."

I wanted to say "Yeah, kind of like mold," but I thought better of it. Kara, unlike her cat, was skinny as a rail. If a good wind came along, she might be swept away unless she held onto the cat to anchor her down. We settled into a couple of well-preserved velvet wing chairs in the living room and I responded, "It's nice, really. It's just a bit surprising that someone so young would have this many antiques, that's all."

"Yeah, that's what I tried to tell my folks, but they wouldn't listen. Anyway, Ann tells me you're looking into Chris's…murder. I still can't believe it. I mean, we get our share of crime here in Kingston, but you never expect it to happen to someone you know."

"I know what you mean. It's a sobering thing to have someone you know get killed." I gave Kara a rundown of the kind of information I was looking for and she began thinking.

"Well, as you probably already know, Chris had her share of enemies, but a few do stand out from the rest, at least in my mind. About a year ago, Chris defended this guy who was accused of raping and murdering a woman while her husband was out of town. He made the two small kids watch, and then he sodomized them. They guy was definitely guilty, but Chris managed to persuade the jury otherwise and the guy went free. The husband was, understandably, outraged. He threatened Chris's life and was caught stalking her on a few occasions. He went bonkers and lost his job, and his kids were sent to live with relatives. His name is Blaine Darrow, and his wife's name was Kitty. I haven't heard anything about him in the last five or six months, but you never know. That kind of grief and rage can last forever."

As Kara talked, I wrote down all the pertinent information in the trusty little notebook I always carry with me. Kara told me that Darrow lived in Kingston at the time of the trial, but may have moved. Kara thought some more and continued. "A couple of years ago, Chris defended a man who wiped out an entire family, the parents and four kids, when he was driving drunk. Chris got a lot of the evidence tossed out, and the State couldn't make the case stick. The woman's parents were just devastated, as you can imagine. You could see the hatred in their eyes for Chris. A couple of days after the trial, Chris got a letter from them. It said 'One day, when you least expect it, you'll get what you deserve.' It was eerie. Let me think…their names were Bill and Jackie Freeman, I think. I believe they lived over in Copperville at the time."

Kara excused herself to get us some lemonade. I was quickly realizing how daunting my job might be, since it appeared that Chris was not well-liked. Kara returned with the lemonade and after we had a few sips, she said, "And there are a couple of prosecutors who really hated Chris. Nobody likes to lose, but some people take it harder than others. Chris had lots of run-ins with Will Beaton, one of the Assistant District Attorneys. Their rivalry was well-known and highly publicized. Chris made Beaton look like a fool on several occasions. She just didn't like him, for some reason. She pummeled him into the ground more than once right in the middle of trial. It was like watching Perry Mason and…what was his name? Oh yeah, Mr. Burger. You wondered why Burger kept showing up for trial, when he knew that Perry Mason was going to kick his ass. I wondered the same thing about Beaton."

"Any other prosecutors feel the same way?"

"Oh yeah—Michelle Knight, another ADA. She was determined to beat Chris, even if it meant bending the rules. Chris caught Knight destroying evidence and brought it to the court's attention. Rather than face disciplinary proceedings, Knight left the practice of law. I hear she now sells insurance downtown."

"How 'bout any clients who were upset with Chris?"

"Well, not many, since Chris usually helped them out of jams. But even Chris lost once in a while. As you probably know, she defended Wilson Torrington, the serial killer. God himself could have testified on behalf of Torrington and it wouldn't have helped. Torrington's brother, who had quite a rap sheet himself, vowed revenge against Chris. I think his name was Daryl Torrington, and if I remember correctly, he worked for some construction company in Lincoln."

Kara took another sip of lemonade and stared at the floor for a few moments. She looked up, embarrassed by the silence, and said, "I'm sorry. I was just thinking about Chris. It's kind of ironic that she was so despised simply because she did her job well. I understand why people hated her, but it just doesn't seem fair somehow."

"I know, and I appreciate your helping me out like this. I don't mean to push, but are there other clients who had it in for Chris?"

"A few. Two or three years ago, Chris began representing certain members of organized crime."

"The mob? In Oregon?"

"Yes, the mob, but not in Oregon. This was down in Los Angeles. Chris was also admitted to practice in California. Much to the dismay of the firm, she started representing crime bosses accused of money laundering, murder, illegal gambling schemes, racketeering, mail fraud, tax evasion…you name it. She got good results. But when you're working for the mob, they expect better than 'good.' I think they expected her to do whatever it took to win, including jury tampering, destroying evidence, and so on. Chris wasn't the most ethical lawyer, but she had her limits. She'd finally had enough about two months ago, and told the mob they'd have to find another mouthpiece. You probably saw Chris on TV about that time, when she got a 'not guilty' verdict for Sammy 'The Knife' Capano. That got national TV coverage. Capano was accused of offing the head of the notorious Ransicco crime family. Apparently, he'd become very unpopular. Capano and his thugs executed Frankie Ransicco, and Capano took his place at the head of the family. It was all over television and the newspapers."

"Yeah, I remember seeing something about that. How did the mob take it when Chris dropped her bombshell?"

"You can't ever just walk away from the mob. It doesn't work like that. They kept hounding her and threatening her, and I think eventually she would have given in. But I guess now we'll never know."

"Why do you think Chris decided to represent organized crime?"

"I assumed it was for the challenge, and the money, of course. Chris billed twice her normal rate when she did work for them, and they gladly paid it. But…there were rumors that Chris was somehow mixed up with the mob. You know, taking a small percentage from some of their illegal operations as an incentive to keep up the good work. The rumors were rampant, but nothing was ever substantiated, and frankly, I don't believe any of it."

"How well did you know Chris, I mean, personally?"

"Nobody really *knew* Chris. She never let anybody get that close. We had an amicable working relationship, but she never thought of me as a friend. I wish she would have." Kara tilted her head to the side, and with a faraway look in her eyes, spoke again. "I did go out with Chris for drinks one time. Well, we didn't really go out for drinks. I stopped by The Chambers, a local watering hole for attorneys, and Chris was there. She motioned me over to her booth. I could tell she'd had a few already. We drank for a while and chatted. I did most of the talking. I remember telling her about my childhood and the small, provincial town I had grown up in. She looked like she was going to cry and started rambling about her past. None of it made any sense. I chalked it up to inebriation. I can't remember any details now. The one thing I recall is that she started to tell me where she was from. She slurred the name of the town, but I'm sure it began with 'Spring.' The state was Pennsylvania. I asked her to repeat the name of the town, and she got this startled look on her face and said she had to go. She lit out of there like nobody's business. The next day she acted odd and uncomfortable around me."

"Did you ever ask her about her background again?"

"Oh no, I could see that was a touchy subject. I was curious, so I looked at a map of Pennsylvania. I found a city named 'Springfield' and I assumed that's where Chris was from. But something didn't seem right. I looked in Chris's personnel file one night when I was working late. She had listed Chicago as her hometown. I thought that was strange. I guess she could have moved to Chicago later."

If I remembered correctly, Springfield was the name of the town mentioned in that newspaper clipping Sandy had found in Chris's office. "Hmmm…that is kind of weird. I wonder why she was so secretive about her background?"

"Who knows? Some people are just naturally private. Then again, maybe she was trying to outrun a past that was upsetting or embarrassing to her. Maybe she came from a poor family that she was ashamed of. It could be anything."

Kara and I chatted for a few more minutes, and then I thanked her for her time. I gave her my card and asked that she call me if she thought of anything else.

As I drove around the city searching for someplace to eat lunch, I couldn't help but wonder what Chris St. James was hiding from the rest of the world.

Burgers, Fries, and Alibis

As I munched on a sinfully greasy bacon cheeseburger and fries, I could almost hear my arteries clogging. Yes, Al Honecker, of Al's Diner fame, still knew how to cook up a mouth-watering, taste-tempting, grease-dripping burger. Al and I weren't personally acquainted, but his homely mug was plastered on the back of the diner menu. And, being a private investigator and all, I deduced that the guy frying up the burgers was none other than Al himself.

You can't get one of these burgers at a fast food joint. No sir, you can only get this kind of real deal burger at the little hole-in-the-wall diners across America, the kind that have Formica tables, old vinyl booths cleverly repaired with masking tape, checkered tile floors, and a giant grill right behind the counter. Mmmmm…real cheese, a grilled sesame bun bigger than your head, thick tomato slices, pickles, red onions, lettuce, thick slabs of peppered bacon, and glorious beef. I was in burger heaven.

The aroma of grease hung heavy in the air as my thoughts drifted back to the case. It seemed like the list of Chris's enemies was endless, and I was just beginning to scratch the surface. How was I ever going to figure out which one of them wanted Chris dead more than the rest? At that moment, my cell phone rang. It was Slick. "Hey kid, where are you?"

"I'm in town. I was chatting with some of Chris's co-workers, and now I'm just finishing lunch."

"Well, shake a leg and meet me at my office. I've got some news."

"Okay, I'll be right there." I scarfed down the last few morsels on my plate and trudged out of Al's with a longing backward glance at the lemon cream pie. Oh well, maybe some other time.

I arrived at Slick's office a few minutes later and Irma told me Slick was waiting for me. I went in, hoping that the news was good. "What's up?"

"I was just downtown talking to Witherspoon, the D.A. The cops have been scouring St. James's phone records. There's no record of any call from St. James to Sandy on the day of the murder. They've checked both her home and work records, and nothing."

"Well, what about a cell phone?"

"St. James must be the only attorney in America who refused to carry a cell phone. She had one for a while, but didn't like all the interruptions, so she tossed it. She liked to use her travel time devising trial strategies and going over opening and closing arguments, not talking to people on the phone."

"Well, did they check Sandy's incoming calls for that day?"

Slick nodded hear head and answered, "Yeah. There's a record of a call from a pay phone in Kingston to Sandy's number around the time Sandy claims St. James called her. But there's no way to verify that it was St. James."

"So have you told Sandy about this?"

"No, I thought maybe you'd want to go with me."

"Sure. Right now?"

"Yeah. There's more, though. When the cops were searching St. James's home, they found a wall safe in her office. They almost missed it since it was behind a painting. It had a lot of the usual stuff in it, stocks and bonds, her will, jewelry, that sort of thing. But there was also a shoe box with some rather unusual items in it." Slick opened her dilapidated briefcase and pulled out a thin sheaf of papers. She slid them across the desk to me. The hair on the back of my neck stood up and my stomach churned.

"A rat?"

"Yeah. Apparently, someone left a dead rat in St. James's mailbox. A little note pieced out of newspaper type came with it: 'It takes one to know one.' St. James took a picture of the rat and kept it with the note. She wrote down when she received it and how."

"According to her note, it was just about six weeks ago. And look at this. It's a mutilated Barbie doll." The head was snapped off and someone had cut off the breasts and the pubic area (not that Barbie really has a pubic area). The note that came with it said 'You can't fool everyone, especially not me. I might reveal your secret to the world with glee. Aw, pretty baby, don't lose your head. Soon enough, you'll be dead.' A regular budding Shakespeare. "This one was sent about a month ago."

"Yeah, St. James kept the doll itself. I got a look at it. I'd say somebody followed through on their promise."

"Either that or somebody knew about the threats and wanted to make it look like the author of these notes did the dirty deed."

"That's possible. Look at the other note. It came by itself about seven weeks ago."

Another newspaper-print note, like the others. It just said 'Freak' in big bold letters, nothing else. "Interesting. Maybe Sandy knows something about these."

"Another reason why we should mosey on over to the Big House and chat with her. You game?"

"Sure, but I'm driving."

"Chicken."

"Naw, I'd just like to live long enough to eat another one of Al's Diner's burgers before I cash in, that's all."

"If you keep eating Al's burgers, you'll be cashing in before your time. I have defended Al against quite a few health code violations."

I gave Slick a nasty look and said, "Now why did you have to go and ruin it for me like that? You know I won't be able to eat there anymore, now." I paused and said, "Aren't health code violations a little out of your area of specialty?"

"Yes, but Irma used to be sweet on him."

Silently wondering what sort of mutant strain of bacteria I had ingested at lunch, I cruised toward our destination, Slick bitching the entire way. "Can't this heap go any faster? And how 'bout some air conditioning? Don't tell me your spy mobile doesn't have air conditioning. Turn the radio up."

"Look, old lady, you better zip it or I just might leave you at the jail. You might get a chance to explore your sexuality sooner than you think. I'm sure there's some big-boned felon named 'Queenie' just dyin' to make you her love slave."

Slick gave me a look that said she got the message and was surprisingly quiet the rest of the way there. We meandered into the jail and endured the security checks. Slick showed her Oregon State Bar card and we were granted a private audience with Sandy. She looked a little better than last time, but not much. I had agreed to let Slick do most of the talking.

"How are you holding up, kid?"

"Ok, I guess. I hope you have some good news for me."

"Well, not exactly. I was talking to the D.A. this morning and she told me that the cops had checked St. James's phone records, and there's no record of any call to you on the day she was murdered."

Sandy visibly shrank before us. She looked at the floor for a long while, then said, "I do remember hearing some traffic noises when she called me. I thought it was odd. Maybe she was calling from a pay phone. She didn't carry a cell phone, you know."

"Well, why didn't you mention the background noises to the police, or us when we talked about it?"

"I don't know. I didn't think *where* Chris was calling from mattered. It just didn't occur to me to mention it."

Sandy looked at me with pleading in her eyes. She wanted for me to believe in her innocence so badly. So did I. Slick told Sandy about the threatening notes we had just looked at. Sandy brightened and said, "Those must have been the threats Chris was talking about when she called me. She also mentioned something about threatening phone calls, but she didn't give me any details. Those threats prove something, don't they? They prove that I'm telling the truth."

Slick and I exchanged glances and then Slick responded, "I wouldn't pin my hopes on those notes. If we introduce them into evidence, the D.A. will suggest that you left them for Chris to find, or that you found out about them and killed St. James in an attempt to mimic the notes to throw the cops off. Some of these things were sent while you were still living with St. James. Didn't she mention them to you?"

Sandy shook her head and said, "No, but then, that doesn't surprise me. Chris liked to keep things to herself."

I took advantage of the lull in the conversation and asked, "Did you get the impression that Chris knew who was leaving these threats for her?"

Sandy looked at me with those puppy dog eyes before saying, "Yes, I did. When she called me, I asked her a couple of times if she knew who was threatening her. Both times, there was a long pause, and then she said, 'I just need for you to come here now.' She knew who was doing it, but she just couldn't tell me over the phone, for some reason."

"Did you get any impression of whether the person making these threats was male or female?"

"No, none. I wish I had more information, but I don't."

"Who usually checked the mail?"

"Chris always did. She went to work at the crack of dawn everyday. She'd meet with clients in the morning usually, and then court appearances were typically in the late morning and early afternoon, I think. She'd come home late in the afternoon and would pick up the mail then before I got home. Then she would go to her office and work. She preferred the solitude of working at home when she could. Her schedule varied, of course, if she had a trial to attend or depositions to take."

We all sat in silence for a while, staring into the distance. Sandy looked from me to Slick, and back again. "I'm innocent. I swear it. You've got to believe me."

I opened my mouth to speak, but Slick beat me to the punch. "Honey, it doesn't matter one hairy iota what I think. It only matters what a jury thinks. Hell, I try not to even think about my client's guilt or innocence. Strange as it may sound, it just doesn't matter. I go to the plate swinging for a home run every time, no matter what I think about my client, or their guilt or innocence. I promise you, I'll give this my all. Now try and keep a positive attitude, and for god's sake, stay away from the meatloaf."

After I'd exchanged a few awkward smiles with Sandy, Slick and I departed. As we were exiting the jail, I turned to Slick and asked, "What the hell is a 'hairy iota' anyway?"

"How the hell should I know? Ask Irma. She used that term a lot when she was seeing Al. She used to say 'I wish that man would stop trying to show me his hairy iota.' Maybe it's a special breed of dog."

"Yeah, something like that."

I drove Slick back to her office with images of hairy iotas dancing in my head. I just couldn't turn off those damn images. Now I was sure that I could never eat another burger at Al's. As Slick was ambling into her office, I called Officer Cathy on my cell phone. "Hey, Cathy. How's it goin'?"

"Fantastic! I have a date with Antonio this weekend. Can you believe it?"

"No, I can't. I thought your attractive hunchback and that clubfoot would turn him off. But some guys are into those sort of things."

"Very funny. What do you need?"

"Am I that transparent? Perhaps I just called to tell you what a wonderful friend you are, or what dreamy brown eyes you have."

"What do you need?"

"Ok, ok. I need to know the name of St. James's neighbor. The one that found the body."

"His name's Barry Cole. He lives in the house just beyond St. James's on the same side of the street."

"Thanks, Cathy. And don't forget the condoms."

I called Mr. Cole to make sure he was home, and he agreed to talk to me. I hadn't been to that part of Kingston before, and I was amazed. These weren't homes—they were palaces. Damn! With my sense of direction, I'd get lost going from the kitchen to the bathroom. The St. James place was especially breathtaking. It was huge and elegant, with pillars and a circular drive. The grounds were lush and well tended. There was even a marble fountain that sprayed water several feet into the air.

I continued down the road and located Barry Cole's home. It was about half the size of the St. James place, but still huge and quite lovely, just less "showy." It was brick with white double doors in the front entryway. The grounds boasted lots of fir trees, flowering shrubs, ivy, and well-placed islands of perennials. A dog was barking in the backyard and I could smell something cooking on the grill. Unlike most of the homes in this area, this house looked and felt like real people lived here. As I was walking up the steps to the front door, a man popped his head over the back fence and said, "Come on back." I did as instructed, and when I reached the backyard, I was greeted enthusiastically by a big bear of a man. "I'm Barry Cole. Nice to meet you, Ms. Mackenzie."

Barry shook my hand and I said, "Please, call me J.Z."

"J.Z. it is, then. You can call me Barry. Come on over and take a load off, and help yourself to some iced tea."

I poured myself a giant glass of iced tea and added one of the lemon slices next to the pitcher. Mmmm…just the right amount of sugar. I walked over to the grill area and saw the most humongous ribs I'd ever seen in my life. They were slathered in thick barbecue sauce, and even though I was still full from the burger, they made my mouth water. "Those smell wonderful."

"Thanks. Me and the missus are going to a birthday party later, and I promised to bring the ribs." At that moment, a German Shepherd wandered over and began gazing longingly at the massive ribs. He started whimpering and sniffing the air wildly, thumping his tail on the ground. I could relate. "Barney, behave yourself. We've got company. You know I'll give you some when they're done. Now go lay down." Barney bowed his head and dutifully lumbered toward his doghouse and fell into a defeated heap in a patch of sunshine. Could I get some ribs if I followed suit?

"Now, you say you want to talk about Chris St. James?"

"Yes, I'm investigating her murder."

"I've already talked to the cops. Didn't have much to tell them, I'm afraid."

"I'm not a cop."

"Oh, so you're probably working for Sandy, huh?"

"I can't really say, since that's confidential information."

"Yeah, I get it. Well, I can tell you one thing: Sandy didn't kill Chris. She simply could not have committed a crime like that. Such a gentle soul."

"How well did you know Chris St. James?"

"Not well. Me and Elizabeth—that's my wife—are very social people. We're always inviting neighbors over for barbecues and the like. Sandy would often stop in, but Chris rarely did. She was an odd one, and I should know. I'm a psychologist, so I see my share of odd ducks." He coated the ribs with more piquant-smelling sauce and continued. "I went over to their place one night to borrow some ice. Chris answered the door, and I could tell right away that she'd been crying. I asked her what was wrong, and she tried to downplay whatever was bothering her. I was persistent, but the only thing I got out of her was a cryptic statement: 'I don't fit in…not in either world.' I asked her to explain, but she wouldn't. There was something about Chris that was off, somehow. But I could never put my finger on it."

"Something was off?"

"I guess that's not a very helpful description, especially for someone in the metal health field. I don't know how to describe it. There was just something about her persona that was jarring in some way." Barry grimaced momentarily, brightened, and then said, "Have you ever had someone put a plate of food in front of you, and it looks absolutely delicious? You dig in, and the flavor is not at all what you expected. Maybe it's still good, but it's just different from the flavor you expected. You ever had that happen?"

"Sure, lots of times."

"Well, that was Chris. There was something about the way she looked that just didn't jive with how she acted, and how she came across to people. That's about as descriptive as I can get."

"I appreciate a good food metaphor."

Barry chuckled and said, "I knew you would. I saw you salivating over the ribs. If you can hang around for another twenty minutes or so, you can help me sample them."

"Oh, no, I couldn't." Yes, I could.

"Sure you can. I can't serve these ribs at a party without getting an honest opinion as to their quality. Barney's not too discriminating, you see."

"Well, maybe just a little sample, for the sake of the party guests." Now my mouth was really beginning to water. I hoped that my supply of Alka-Seltzer was intact. The last time I left the box out on the bathroom counter, the cats knocked the whole thing into the toilet. By the time I got home, the toilet resembled some rabid beast from the netherworld. The girls were quite pleased with themselves, as usual. "If it's not too difficult, can you tell me about the night you found Chris?"

Barry darkened and said, "Not much to tell, really. Elizabeth and I were returning from the movies a few minutes before 11, and as we drove by I noticed that Chris's front door was standing wide open. I immediately found that odd, since she is…was…a real security freak. I went inside my own home to get Barney to take him for a walk. As Barney and I were passing Chris's home, I noticed that the door was still open. We walked up the driveway and I told Barney to stay in the front yard. Chris hated animals. I called for Chris at the front door, but no one answered, so I went in. Before I went too far, I saw her. She was lying on the living room floor in a huge pool of blood. I could see that she was dead. No question about that. It was horrible! I ran out of there as fast as I could and called the police."

Barry was shaking slightly, so I decided not to ask anything further about the crime scene for now. "What did you think of Sandy?"

Barry relaxed and said in a wistful voice, "Sandy...what a truly wonderful and delightful person. So sincere and genuine. I really respected and admired her. I couldn't for the life of me understand why she was with Chris. They just didn't seem like a good match, you know? And they didn't seem very happy together, either. I was glad to see Sandy move on with her life, even though I was sorry to see her leave the neighborhood. Believe me, she didn't do this. No way."

A wave of guilt washed over me again. "Did St. James ever have many visitors at her place?"

"Almost never. I don't think she had any friends to speak of, which is why I tried to reach out to her on a couple of occasions. But she just pushed me away, like she did everybody else."

Barry and I chatted for a while longer. He hadn't noticed anything unusual next door in the past few weeks, no strange vehicles or people lurking about. But then, you couldn't see the St. James place from Barry's home. You had to walk down the street a little ways to catch a glimpse of it. I hadn't learned anything useful, but I couldn't say that the trip was a waste of my time, not with a steaming plate of ribs in front of me. If this was a little "sample," I'd hate to see the Cole family's Alka-Seltzer bill. No wonder Barry was a big guy. The sauce was spicy and sweet at the same time, and the meat just fell off the bones and melted in my mouth. *Sorry, Al, you've been replaced by a new guy.* "Oh my god, Barry, these are simply orgasmic. Why are you wasting your time psychoanalyzing people when you could be creating delicacies like this? I'm convinced that clinical depression is caused by a lack of good food. Hey, you could open a combination counseling center and restaurant. When someone comes in with a problem, just serve them a giant plate of yum and watch their depression melt away. No one could be depressed eating these ribs."

Barry let out a large, hearty laugh and said, "If only it were that easy. But you might be on to something, J. Z. I'll have to give it some thought."

Barney finished his share and fell over on his side and let out a contented groan. I felt like doing the same, but thought it would be unladylike. I helped Barry gather up our dishes and we went inside. I thanked him for the information and the ribs, especially the ribs. As I was leaving, he shoved a doggy bag of ribs in my hands. I tried to refuse, but he insisted. What could I do? "You need anything else, just let me know. And if you're in the area, feel free to stop by. This time of year, I'm almost always home by late afternoon cooking up something on the grill. Swing by if you want. We'd be glad to have you."

What a great guy, and I think he really meant that last part. Everybody says it, but I think Barry really meant it. As I was driving away, trying to undo the top button on my pants, I was overwhelmed with the enormity of the job ahead of me. St. James had so many enemies, and she was so private. How was I ever going to learn anything about her that might give me a clue as to who would want to kill her? I had a few tidbits of information, but that was it. Damn. What next?

Leavin' on
a Jet Plane

"Maybe this sounds impetuous, Slick, but I follow my instincts on a job. And right now my instincts are telling me, loud and clear, to hop a plane to Springfield, Pennsylvania. I have to learn something about St. James's background. I have to know what made her tick if I'm going to find out who killed her."

Slick looked skeptical as she reclined in her office chair. "Look, I'm not about to tell you how to do your job. And it's not as though the expense is going to be an issue. But I just don't see what you hope to learn there. I mean, St. James hasn't lived there in decades—if that's where she was from. Her secretary could be wrong. How could anything that remote in time be of any value? Especially when you have so many leads to look into here."

"For someone who doesn't want to tell me how to do my job, you're certainly not being shy about giving me your opinion."

"You know I don't have a shy bone in my body. But I wasn't trying to be bossy. I was just, as you said, offering you my opinion. You don't have to agree with it."

"Sorry. I'm just feeling a bit overwhelmed by all of this. How do you do this every day? How do you hold someone's freedom, their life, in your hands and not feel completely overwhelmed by the enormous responsibility?"

"Are you shittin' me? I do feel overwhelmed. All the time. But that's what keeps me going. When I first started out, all this responsibility felt like a burden. Now I thrive on it. You get used to it, kid."

"I don't know. Maybe I'm more suited to catching careless adulterers in the act."

"Your tune will change when we win this and you see what an incredible adrenaline rush it is. Just wait."

I hoped Slick was right about us winning, at least I thought so. I just hoped that when we won, I knew for sure who committed this murder. If there was any doubt, I knew there could be no future for me and Sandy. On that positive note, I drove home to make reservations for the next available flight to Springfield, Pennsylvania.

As I entered my humble abode, I sensed something was wrong. The cats did not greet me at the door as they usually did. I stealthily crept from room to room looking for something amiss. I saw nothing out of place, nor did I see any cats. A formidable lump formed in my throat and my heart began to race. I silently crept up the stairs, the tiny hairs on the back of my neck standing at attention. As I entered my bedroom, I relaxed. There was Tasha cowering in the corner, that fretful look on her furry face. Corey was perched in front of her playing the bully. Every time Tasha would try to move, Corey let out a throaty growl and edged closer to her quarry.

"Corey! Your sister has enough self-esteem issues without you bullying her. Behave yourself!" Corey looked somewhat contrite, though only momentarily. She scampered over to me with that "give me treats" gleam in her eyes. Out of spite, I ignored her and walked over to Tahsa, who was still shaking in the corner. I scooped her up in my arms and rubbed her face against mine. "And you, young lady, need to learn how to defend yourself." I silently wondered if cats could get ulcers or have irritable bowel syndrome. I hoped not, for both our sakes.

After a liberal dose of pets and treats, I set about making airline reservations. There was a connector flight leaving the next morning at 10 a.m. from Kingston. Cloverdale had a small airport, but no commercial flights serviced the airport. You could catch a private puddle jumper to the Kingston Airport, but personally, I didn't like to experience nausea unnecessarily. I arranged for the airport shuttle to pick me up in the morning and drop me off at the airport in plenty of time to check in for my flight.

I spent the rest of the evening packing a few things and returning phone calls, mostly from investigators who were now handling various matters for me while I was working full-time on Sandy's case. I answered their questions and packed a small overnight carry-on bag. I didn't expect to be in Springfield for more than a day, but I packed enough for two days just in case. As I was finishing, the phone rang. It was Sam, as I suspected. She invited me over for dinner and even though I was still stuffed, I accepted. Being full is no reason to turn down a perfectly good, not to mention free, meal.

On the way down to Sam and Nealy's, I stopped by Ethel's place to let Cecelia know I would be out of town for a day or two. Ethel answered the door and promptly pulled me inside. For an old bird, she sure was strong. "Helga, you've got to stop doin' what you're doin', and I mean pronto, girl!" Helga was Ethel's long time next-door neighbor. In fact, she lived in my house for much of her life, until she died a few years back. I had no idea what "doings" Ethel was referring to, but I decided to play along.

"Hey, it's my life, you know."

"And that's exactly my point. Why don't you take control of the situation?"

"What situation are you referring to, Ethel?"

"Oh, don't play dumb with me. I didn't just fall off the turnip truck, you know. I've got eyes. I can see what's goin' on right next door. The rumors are spreading like wildfire. It won't take long until Roy catches wind of it."

Roy was Helga's husband. I think they divorced at some point. Roy must have caught wind of "it," whatever "it" was. "I don't think there's any danger of that."

"Don't be a fool, woman! He may already know."

"Know? What's there to know, anyway?"

Ethel looked at me like I had a third eye growing out of my forehead. "Well, what the hell do you think we've been talkin' about, you nitwit! Your exploits with Earlene Milstead—that's what there is to know."

"Exploits?"

"Yes, that's right. Don't bother denying it, girl. I know all about it.

It's not like I was trying to be nosey, either. You leave your drapes wide open and I can see right in from my window. I saw you and Earlene groping each other."

"And you think we should stop, is that it?"

"No, not if that's what you want. But I do think you need to make a choice between Roy and Earlene. It's not right to carry on with both of them like that. Someone's gonna get hurt. And whatever choice you make, I'll support it."

Well, well. Now I knew how Ethel felt about my sexuality. I guess I had always assumed that she would be shocked, given her age. I now realized what an unfair generalization that was. "I guess you're right. But in the meantime, how 'bout you and me go out for a night on the town?"

Ethel laughed heartily and when she caught her breath, she said in a wistful tone, "Helga, you are barkin' up the wrong tree, my dear. Earl has the biggest schlong I've ever seen and—"

"Momma!" Cecelia came to a screeching halt in the living room upon hearing Ethel's words. Rosy patches instantly appeared on Cecelia's plump cheeks. She turned to Ethel and said, "Momma, I do not think that's an appropriate topic of conversation."

Ethel shook her head and looked at Cecelia with concern. "Ruby Jean, why are you always calling me Momma? I am not your Momma. I'm only one year older than you, and you know it. And don't tell me what I can and can't talk about in my own home. If I want to talk about Earl's giant trouser snake, I will. So there!" With that, Ethel turned on her heel and left the room in a huff.

Cecelia turned toward me, still quite mortified by the news that her father had a giant trouser snake. Who wouldn't be? "I'm sorry about that. She just gets carried away sometimes. She's like a kid in many ways. You never know what's gonna pop out of her mouth. We were at the grocery store a couple days ago and she pulled a big package of Depends off the shelf, turned toward me, and said in a booming voice, 'Ruby Jean, these might help with that leakage problem you've been having lately.' I thought I was gonna die right there on the spot."

"Well, you don't need to apologize to me. I think she's delightful. But then, I don't have to go grocery shopping with her." I told Cecelia that I would be out of town for the next day or two, and she agreed to check on the kitties for me. She would anyway, but I thought it was polite to ask. Every time I came home from a short trip, I found a new kitty toy in their stash of goodies. They tried to bury it on the bottom of the heap, so that I would think they were ignored or mistreated while I was gone. I knew better.

I made my way down the street to Sam and Nealy's place in the crisp evening air. The sounds of televisions, laughter, barking dogs, and clinking dishes filled the night air in this cozy little town. I couldn't imagine living someplace where I didn't know my neighbors. Now, I admit that I knew a little bit more about some of them than I wanted to. Like the fact that Ted and Bessie Russell had sex every Sunday night at 8 p.m., just like clockwork. Ted was known to shout out "yehaw" at the crucial moment—which usually occurred at 8:09 p.m. I also knew that Maudie Feldman, a 93-year old firecracker, was known to answer the door in her birthday suit on occasion, like when an unsuspecting delivery boy showed up on her doorstep. Yes, there was a downside to knowing my neighbors. But all in all, the good outweighed the bad.

As I expected, Sam opened her front door and immediately unleashed a barrage of questions about the investigation. Nealy interceded before I had a chance to protest. "Honey, give J.Z. a chance to catch her breath before you interrogate her. Come on in, J.Z. We're making vegetarian lasagna and garlic bread for dinner. About another 15 or 20 minutes should do it. In the meantime, can I get you some strawberry lemonade or something else to drink?"

"Yeah, a strawberry lemonade sounds great. It smells wonderful in here." And it did, too. Suddenly, I wasn't full anymore. Funny how that happens.

Sam tapped her foot in annoyance and completed her impatient look with a hand on her hip. "Ok, enough of the niceties already. I'm going to gag if I have to put up with much more of this. Tell me what you've found out, and don't give me any of that 'it's confidential' crap, either."

It's a good thing Sam never had her heart set on a career in the diplomatic arena. "I've only just begun the investigation, you know. So, I haven't really learned that much yet. All I know is that Chris St. James was not well-liked, and she was an extremely private person. Both of those things combine to make this a very difficult case."

"Oh, come on. Surely you know more than that." Sam gave me her best pout and looked at me expectantly.

"Well, apparently St. James had some mob connections. She was doing some legal work for some crime bosses and there were rumors that she was taking a cut of some of the action, but those rumors have not been substantiated."

Sam screeched, "The mob! Well, that's it, then. Of course! That explains the brutality of this crime. The mob was sending a message to other people they have dealings with—not to get too greedy, or overstep their bounds. That makes perfect sense."

"Well, I guess that's a wrap. I'll call the D.A. right now and demand Sandy's release. Thanks so much, Sherlock, for your intuitive powers and deductive logic. How could I have done it without you?"

"Okay, smart ass, you've made your point. I'm just saying that this mob angle seems to make sense. If they'll put a horse's head in bed with someone, they're capable of this kind of brutality."

Oh brother. "Sam, the horse's head thing happened in a movie. It wasn't real. You do understand the difference, don't you?"

An impertinent look spread across Sam's face as she said, "I have to go check on the lasagna." And with that, Sam disappeared in an exaggerated huff.

Nealy watched Sam's exit with raised eyebrows. "Sam's gonna be just like Ethel when she's older. Only, Sam will relive episodes from books she's read or TV shows she's watched."

"Well, it should be entertaining for you, if nothing else."

The lasagna was wonderful, as is just about everything that Sam and Nealy cook. I can think of only one exception. It was some kind of strange eggplant and tofu concoction that had a pudding-like consistency and almost no taste (which was lucky, because what little taste there was in the dish was bad). That's the great thing about close friends—you can tell them when their cooking tastes like shit, and you're still friends.

During dinner, I filled them in on the other details of the investigation, what few details there were. After dinner, we had chocolate chip cookie dough ice cream and homemade white chocolate chunk cookies. As I was finishing plowing through my trough of goodies, I explained that I was flying to Pennsylvania in the morning to see if I could uncover any information about St. James's past. Sam crinkled her nose and said, "What could you learn in Pennsylvania that would be of any use to the investigation?"

I sighed and, in a level voice, said, "You sound just like Slick. I don't know. It just bothers me that St. James was so secretive. It suggests to me that she had something big to hide, maybe something that got her killed. Maybe she was being blackmailed by someone from her past. Blackmail and secrets go hand in hand. Maybe the person threatening St. James was from her past. After all, the threats did mention secrets. And there's something about that newspaper clipping that Sandy found. I don't know what it means, but there's something there. I just have to do this, that's all I know."

Nealy shook her head in agreement. "I'm a big believer in instincts. If you listen to that little voice inside, it will usually lead you where you need to go. It's worked for you on several occasions."

"Yes, in the professional arena, anyway. Sometimes that little voice fails me in matters of the heart."

"No, it doesn't. You just tune out the little voice and listen to the booming voice coming from your crotch, that's all. That voice is hardly ever right."

"No, but it sure knows how to have a damn good time!" We all laughed and then chatted for a while longer. When we ran out of things to say, I promised to call if I stayed in Pennsylvania for more than a day. They were both such mother hens at times. It's good to be loved.

I went home and crawled into bed, hoping that I wouldn't have to wait too long for sleep to overtake me. But sleep didn't come easy. The events of the past few days were swirling around in my head at a maddening speed. What could be such a big deal that St. James felt she had to keep it secret, even from Sandy? Everyone knew she was gay. What was "bigger" than that? I didn't feel like any of the puzzle pieces were snapping into place, but I hoped that would change in Pennsylvania. But maybe this trip would be a boondoggle, as Slick and Sam predicted. Even so, I had to do it.

I was up early the next morning, fixing breakfast and packing things I had forgotten the night before. The cats saw the overnight bag and immediately knew what that meant. Corey planted herself on top of the bag, hoping that this would somehow prevent my departure. She did this every time and it never worked. I had to give her credit for her persistence. Tasha just stuck to me like glue, nearly tripping me several times. She kept looking up at me with those saucer eyes that screamed out "don't go." Oh, the incredible guilt they could inspire. Damn them, anyway!

The shuttle showed up on time and I was whisked away to the Kingston Airport. I could tell that many of my fellow travelers were destined for vacation spots, as they chattered excitedly in little clusters. I wished that I was on my way to some exotic venue, rather than in the midst of a daunting murder investigation, one that could dramatically affect my future.

As we zoomed down the freeway, I realized that I hadn't even devised any plan for my investigation in Springfield. I didn't even know where I should start. I had many possibilities. I could search through records at the vital statistics office, or I could run a check for vehicle ownership through the Pennsylvania motor vehicles division. That would turn up an address for…for who? All I had was Chris's name. Chris hadn't lived in Pennsylvania for years. I didn't know the names of any family members, if there were any still in Pennsylvania. If there ever were. *Oh god…maybe this is an ill-conceived idea.* I didn't even know where to begin.

I was in a deep funk for the remainder of the ride to the airport. I found my departure gate and paced back and forth nervously, nearly leaving the airport for home several times. But something was pulling me to Springfield. If I didn't go, I knew I'd regret it. So, when it was time, I dutifully boarded the flight to Newberry, Pennsylvania, which is the closest metropolitan area to Springfield. I'd gotten some information off the Internet early that morning about both towns. Apparently, Newberry is about the same size as Kingston, and Springfield is one of several bedroom communities, located about 25 miles to the south. I'd have to rent a car at the airport and try not to get lost. That was always a challenge.

With the time change and the layover, it would be late evening before I arrived in Newberry, and even later when I finally got settled into a motel room in Springfield. I hated wasting a whole day on traveling. I hoped it was worth it.

During the excruciatingly long flight, somewhere between the ubiquitous peanuts and the smallest chicken breast known to man, an idea occurred to me. I remembered reading on the Internet that

Springfield has only one high school. I could start there. Maybe someone in the school office could confirm that Chris went to high school there, and maybe I could get an address and proceed from there. It was worth a shot, anyway. It sure beat thumbing through musty old records and dealing with motor vehicle department bureaucrats. At least I had a goal now, a plan of some sort, doubtful as it may be.

I had the misfortune of being wedged between a bird-like woman with horrible breath who insisted on talking to me the whole time, and a troll-like creature with the worst toupee I'd ever seen. It was like a bad wreck; you don't want to look because you know it's awful, but you can't help yourself. My eyes were drawn to that furry mat of material perched atop the troll's head. I had to keep looking at it to make sure I wasn't seeing things. It looked like a badger crawled on top of his head and died there. Did this guy really think he was fooling anybody with that ridiculous thing? Troll man caught me staring at it a couple of times. It was simply mesmerizing in its hideousness.

When we finally landed, I was happy that I didn't have to wait with the mob of people to retrieve my luggage. I made my way over to the car rental booth and rented a sensible mid-size. I got directions to Springfield and headed down the highway. It was a straight shot, which was good because I was too tired to follow complicated directions. I stopped at the first decent place I saw and rented a room. I doubted Springfield had any gay nightlife, so I settled for HBO. Before long, I was in dreamland.

I awoke refreshed early the next morning. After devouring a big stack of pancakes and some bacon, I decided it was time to embark upon my mission. I asked the waitress for directions to the Springfield High School and got moving. The part of town I was staying in was strictly middle class, but the other side of town was anything but. It was like something off of *Dynasty*. I'd never seen so many BMWs in one block anyplace else.

The high school was located in a lush wooded area and was much nicer than any public school I'd ever seen. But then, I guess the Dynasty side of town could afford it. I parked in a visitor's spot and found the admissions office with relative ease. I spotted a kindly looking soul at the end of the counter and plastered on my best "you can trust me, I'm not a maniac" face.

"Hi, I was wondering if you could help me out just a little bit." The kindly look was replaced by a cold, blank stare. I cleared my throat and continued. "You see, I'm a private investigator from Oregon, and I just need for you to confirm that someone named Chris St. James graduated from this school in 1968 or '69."

A long pause of deafening silence. "You must be joking."

Uh oh. This was going to be harder than I thought. "Look, I know about all of the privacy and security issues. But Ms. St. James is dead, murdered, and I'm trying to find out who did it. So you see, while I can appreciate any rules you might have about giving out such information, the seriousness of the situation requires that you do so. Wouldn't you agree?" Oh geez.

Another long pause. "It's not that, although we do have such rules. It's just that we don't have access to records that old in the computer system. Records that old are archived, and I think you have to submit a written request to get a record that old. I suspect it would take a few days for the request to be processed, and then you might not get the record due to the privacy and security issues you just mentioned."

Oh great. A wonderful start to the boondoggle. My helpful cohort started to turn away, but then turned back and said, "What is it you need to know, anyway?"

"I'm just trying to get some background information on Chris St. James, the victim. I think she grew up here, but I'm not sure. If I could at least find out if she went to school here, that would be a start."

She scrunched up her face and replied, "Well, we do have a copy of every yearbook down in the library. Maybe you could find out if this Chris person went to school here by checking the 1968 and '69 yearbooks."

Not bad for a crusty old cohort. "That's not a bad idea. I'll try that." She pointed me in the direction of the library and I quickly located the yearbooks. I pulled out the '68 and '69 yearbooks and found a quiet corner in which to plant myself. I opened up the 1968 Springfield High School Yearbook first and searched the index for a student named St. James. Would it be under "Sa" (for Saint) or "St."? It didn't matter; there was no St. James listed under either spelling. I crossed my fingers and opened up the 1969 yearbook. Again, nothing. Great. I traveled all the way to the East Coast between a troll and a bird lady for nothing.

Wait. Maybe I was missing something. What was the name of the family in that newspaper clipping that Sandy found? It started with an "H"…what was it? Oh yeah, it was Hollingsworth. Sandy thought maybe Chris and this Hollingsworth person had been friends. Maybe I could at least get a line on that theory. I again crossed my fingers and opened up the 1969 yearbook. Paydirt! The index listed a Jamison Hollingsworth III. Sandy didn't know the young man's first name, but this could be him. Maybe St. James moved before graduation, and that's why her picture wasn't in the yearbook.

Omigod! I made a mental note to have my vision checked. It couldn't be…but yes. There was no mistaking that face. Her picture *was* in the yearbook, only she's not a she…she's a he. Jamison Hollingsworth III and Chris St. James were the same person! Chris had one of those faces that was handsome as a man and attractive as a woman. Her face didn't look that much different either way. This was a big part of the puzzle. I was sure of it. Those threats made sense now. The doll with the female parts cut away…the note that said "freak," and all the references to secrets. Maybe someone was blackmailing St. James. Maybe someone found out about this just like I did. And maybe St. James got tired of paying. Or maybe someone close to her…someone like Sandy…had discovered the truth and was not happy with it. Too many "maybes" for my taste.

At that moment, a frail, soft-spoken voice startled me out of my concentration. "Oh my, Jamison Hollingsworth. What a sweet boy, and such a tragedy." The voice belonged to a supremely stereotypical librarian, with the obligatory bun of white hair, a dress buttoned up securely under her chin, an old cameo pin, and a giant wad of tissue tucked halfway in her dress sleeve.

"A tragedy?"

"Oh yes, dear. Jamison loved to fly planes. Went out every weekend to fly. One Saturday night he went out and never came back. His plane crashed into the ocean and he was never found. So sad for his family. He was an only child, you know. And that poor Holly Travis. She was pregnant with Jamison's child, which was a scandal in itself back then. They planned to get married, and then tragedy struck."

"Did Holly have a boy or a girl?"

"Neither one, I'm afraid. She was so distraught over losing Jamison that she had a miscarriage not long after he died."

"I don't suppose Ms. Travis still lives around here?"

The old librarian furrowed her brow momentarily, and then brightened as synapses began firing. "I believe she lives over in Burton, which is about 65 miles east of here. She became a nurse and I think she works in that big hospital over there."

"Did she ever marry?"

"Not that I know of. She dearly loved Jamison, which was understandable. He was such a sweet boy."

"What about Jamison's family? Do they live around here?"

"The Hollingsworth family?" The old librarian laughed as though I had told a good one. The she pulled out the giant wad of tissue and dabbed at her eyes. When she had composed herself, she continued. "You're not from around here, are you, dearie? The Hollingsworth family owns this town, in a manner of speaking. They are richer than God. Pardon my blasphemy. They own most of the industry here, and much of the industry in the surrounding towns. Different things: textiles, mills, factories. You name it, they own it. So yes, they still live right here in Springfield."

My heart began racing. "Whereabouts do they live?"

"Well, dearie, you can't just go over to their house, you know."

"Why not?"

"They live in a heavily guarded compound. You have to have an appointment to see them, and not just anybody gets an appointment. No offense, dearie. Then you have to pass through this elaborate security check. It's ridiculous if you ask me."

"Have there been some kind of threats on their lives, or something?"

"No. They're just afraid that the 'little people' slaving away in their factories and mills will someday revolt and attack the palace, I suppose. They think the whole town is envious of what they have. I feel sorry for them, really."

I made a copy of Jamison's yearbook picture and persuaded the old woman to give me directions to the Hollingsworth compound anyway. I had an idea that just might work.

Opulence and Omniscience

After a few wrong turns, I finally located the Hollingsworth compound. And that was a good word for it. It really was a guarded compound. I thought maybe the old lady had been exaggerating somewhat. I approached the guard booth at the front gate and a guard flew at me waving his arms about wildly. "Stop! Turn around. You're going the wrong way."

"Well, obviously I have to stop. There's a gate in front of me. And how do you know where I'm going?"

The Hitler Youth eyed me suspiciously and stated in an authoritarian tone, "I know that you're not going in there." He gestured toward the compound. "There are no scheduled appointments this morning. *No* one gets in without an appointment. So just move along."

Such an anal retentive young man. If he wasn't careful, he'd have a nasty case of irritable bowel syndrome in no time. "Well, I admit that I don't have an appointment. However, if you would just contact Mr. or Mrs. Hollingsworth and tell them that I was acquainted with their daughter, I think they'll want to see me."

The Gestapo Patrol looked at me with contempt. "Are you some kind of nut case? They don't have a daughter, and their only son was tragically killed years ago. So whatever kind of game you're playing, you'll have to play it somewhere else. Move it!"

I sighed and said, "You know, this would go a lot more smoothly if you would just cooperate a little bit. I'd hate for you to lose your job over this."

The guard laughed and asked in a superior tone, "What are you talking about?"

Finally, I had his attention. "I have something of a delicate nature to discuss with Mr. and Mrs. Hollingsworth. But if I don't get to discuss it with them, I'm going to march down to the local newspaper and discuss the matter with a reporter. Your name will probably come up. Your employer will not be happy with your failure to handle this matter in an efficient, discreet way. Just get on your little walkie-talkie and tell them what I told you to say. What have you got to lose? If I'm a nut case, you'll simply be a bit embarrassed at taking me seriously. But if I'm on the up and up, you could lose your job."

The Aryan national thought this over and then disappeared into the guard shack. I could hear muffled voices. After a couple of minutes, the guard emerged and said, in a defeated tone, "I've been instructed to send you in." First, I was searched for weapons, as was my vehicle. Eventually, the massive iron gates opened and I scooted inside the compound, feeling like one of the select few. When I arrived at the circular drive in front of the palatial estate, I was greeted by a uniformed servant who instructed me to follow him. He took my keys and tossed them to another service person, who promptly removed the eyesore from its prominent location.

Words cannot describe the interior of the Hollingsworth palace. There were Oriental rugs, Tiffany lamps, Fabergé eggs, original works of art, and expensive antiques everywhere. It was incredible. It looked more like a museum than a home. I was escorted into the study and instructed to wait. There were leather-bound first edition books as far as the eye could see. The old librarian was right. These people really were richer than God!

In a few minutes, a stern, dapper, distinguished looking man joined me. He took a seat on the leather couch and eyed me with contempt. He looked me up and down and finally said, "Well, how much do you want?"

I had no idea what he was talking about, and I just stood there silent for a few moments, unsure how to respond. Finally, I said, "I beg your pardon?"

"Look, Miss, I'm a busy man and I don't have time to play games. Just name your price and we can be done with this. But understand that this is a one-time deal. Don't expect to come back for seconds."

"Are you under the impression that I'm trying to extort money from you?"

"Well, that is why you're here, isn't it?"

"No. I'm here because I want some information."

"Information?"

"Yes. You are Mr. Hollingsworth, aren't you?"

"Yes, and you are?"

"J. Z. Mackenzie. I'm a private investigator from Oregon. You do know that Chris was murdered, don't you?"

He let out a heavy sigh and replied, "Yes, I know. Means nothing to me, really."

"Chris was your…daughter. How can her death mean nothing to you?"

He got up and paced about the room. In a cold voice he replied, "I didn't have a daughter. My son, Jamison, for all intents and purposes, died in 1976."

I looked at him with disbelief. "I'm investigating Chris's murder, and I think her past may have something to do with it. I need to know everything you can tell me about her 'death' in 1976, the relationship with Holly Travis, and Jamison's transformation into Chris."

He spun around on me angrily. "Why should I help you?"

"Well, a few moments ago, you were willing to pay me to keep my mouth shut. I'm assuming you'd be willing to give me information to shut me up, right?"

He glanced down at the floor briefly. "If this is part of an investigation, it won't be secret for long."

"Maybe not, but you never know. All of this may have nothing to do with Chris's murder. It's too early to tell at this point."

He walked over to the bar and poured himself a shot of scotch. "I need a drink. You want something?"

"No, I'm fine, thanks." I sat down on the leather sofa and he joined me. After taking a generous slug of the scotch, he said, "Where to begin? Jamison was a good kid when he was growing up. Never had many problems with him. Things began to change when he got into his teens. He became moody and withdrawn. Once, I caught him dressed up in his mother's clothes. I was outraged. He said it was for some costume party, but I didn't believe him."

Another gulp of scotch. "Things got progressively worse. Oh, he did all right in school, and he seemed to have lots of friends. But at home, he acted out some."

"Did you ever get counseling for him?"

He looked at me with a mixture of confusion and anger. "Hell no! The Hollingsworth family takes care of its own problems. That's the way it's always been. Anyway, I sat him down one day and demanded to know what was bothering him, why he was so depressed and distant all the time. At first, he wouldn't tell me. Then, he said he felt like he was a mistake. I asked him to explain and he looked embarrassed. He finally told me that he thought he was supposed to be a girl. I was mad, madder than I've ever been. I beat that boy until he was almost unconscious. I told him to get those fool ideas out of his head right now."

He got up and walked over to the window and looked out over his vast domain. He finally turned around and continued. "I didn't hear another peep about it for quite a while. After he finished high school, he got into drugs. He was wasting his life, just partying and sleeping mostly, and having sex with every woman in town. He met a woman that he seemed to care for."

"Holly Travis?"

"Yes, Holly. She seemed to settle him down some. I was pleased with that, even though she was all wrong for Jamison. She was from a poor family, and it showed. She had no class. But I thought if she could keep him in line for a while, I'd keep my mouth shut about the relationship. She even talked him into going to college. He majored in history and got excellent grades. When he graduated, I assumed he'd want to get involved with one of the family businesses. But none of that interested him. Again, he fell into a deep depression."

He poured himself another shot of scotch and paced the floor. "He came over here one day and announced to me and his mother that he was going to have a sex change operation. I thought I was going to have a heart attack. We started fighting, physically, and I realized that I could no longer beat some sense into my son. He told us to get used to the idea because he was going to begin making the arrangements. A few days later, I called him over here. I told him that his mother and I had discussed the situation, and we'd come up with a proposition. I told him that we'd pay for the operation and give him a generous sum of money if he would move away and never have anything to do with this family again. I explained how we could fake his death so that no questions would be asked."

"What happened? Did Jamison jump out of the plane at the last minute?"

"Yes. We chose a secluded patch of ocean, a dark, foggy night, and we had Jamison jump out of the plane just before it plunged into the ocean. Very risky. A boat was waiting for him a short distance away. He left that night to embark on his new life."

"He left for Oregon?"

"No. He went to Europe to have the surgery done. After a brief convalescence, he went to Oregon, where he decided to attend law school, as you know."

"How does something like that work? I mean, the law school would ask for college transcripts, and those would be under a different name."

He laughed in a smug manner and said, "Do you have any idea how much money I have, Ms. Mackenzie?" I shook my head. "Enough to deal with petty details like that. If the government can create new identities for people, don't you think a private citizen with enough money can do the same? That was no problem, I assure you."

"Did you stay in touch with Jamison…I mean, Chris?"

"Absolutely not! As I said, my son was dead. We did keep tabs on…him, though. I knew where he was and what he was doing. But I had no contact with him."

"Your wife went along with this?"

"My wife does as she is told. She wasn't for the scheme, if that's what you mean. But then, she had no choice in the matter."

"I'm assuming that Holly didn't approve of the idea."

Another hearty laugh. "Do you honestly believe that we would let that white trash in on our scheme? She knew nothing of this. As far as she knew, Jamison died in that airplane crash."

"But she was pregnant with his child. Didn't that mean anything to you, or to Jamison?"

"Oh, Jamison wanted to tell Holly and wanted that baby more than anything. But I forbade it. I told him that I'd cut him off without a cent if he so much as breathed a word of it to that whore. I was relieved when she lost that child. I didn't need any white trash version of Jamison around. And we'd have no ties to that woman with the child gone. It was a blessing."

Oh my god! I couldn't believe the callousness of this man's words. To hate his own flesh and blood so much. It was simply unbelievable. I wanted to smack him or yell at him. The only thing that kept me from letting loose on this neanderthal was the possibility that I might need more information from him in the future.

"So Holly never learned the truth?"

"No, she never did, and I hope you're not going to enlighten her."

"No, I have no intention of doing so. I hope that someday you'll see fit to tell her. She deserves to know the truth."

An evil gleam sprang into his eyes and he bellowed, "I owe her NOTHING! She was never good enough for Jamison. She got what she deserved."

A long moment of silence. "She lives in Burton now, right?"

"Yes. She's a nurse and works at the hospital there." He scrunched up his face and asked, "How did you figure this out, anyway? We did such a brilliant job of covering our tracks for so long."

"Chris let the name of her hometown slip to someone. And the woman Chris lived with found a newspaper clipping about the plane crash with the name Hollingsworth in the caption. I just went to the high school in town, and when I didn't find the name St. James listed, I looked under Hollingsworth, and there she was. I knew immediately it was the same person."

He snorted and said, "Lucky guess. And that's another thing— why would a man have a sex change and then carry on with women? It makes no sense at all. I always knew that lifestyle would get him killed."

Steady, J.Z. I rose from the couch and thanked him for his time. As I was leaving, he asked "Did you know...Chris?"

"Only by reputation. She was one of the best trial attorneys in the country."

"As Jamison Hollingsworth, that would have meant something. But as the freak he'd become, it meant nothing. Less than nothing."

I shook my head and walked out. No wonder St. James had so many problems relating to people, and no wonder she kept all of this a secret. The one time she confided in someone, she was beaten to a pulp. That would surely discourage a person from opening up.

I retrieved my rented vehicle and high-tailed it out of there. On the way past the guard shack, I was treated to another look of contempt. Boy, these people sure were full of themselves.

I drove back to the motel and immediately called Slick. She set the phone down and I could hear her rummaging around in her mass of papers for something—probably an ashtray. When she finally come back on the line I said, "Slick, I have some, uh, news that I think might be relevant to the investigation. I don't really know how to say it, so I'll just blurt it out. Chris St. James used to be a man."

A loud kathunk reverberated in my ear. And then silence. "Slick, are you there? Slick?"

"I send you out to Pennsylvania to do a little investigative work and what do you do? You fall off the wagon. Kid, I'm disappointed in you."

"Slick, I haven't been drinking. It's a long story, but believe me, it's true." I explained to her how I discovered that St. James and Jamison Hollingsworth were the same person, and then I gave her a rundown of my conversation with Chris's father.

"Holy shit! Well, that explains the threats. I'd have to say that whoever sent those threats is the killer. Wouldn't you agree?"

"Probably. But who, besides Chris's parents, knew about Chris's past? I admit that her father is a cold son of a bitch, but I don't think he murdered Chris."

"You found out easy enough. If you found out, someone else could have. Not that I'm denigrating your investigative skills, kid."

"Yeah, that's true; someone else could have found out. It's looking more and more like blackmail to me. Maybe one of the many enemies Chris had did a little digging into her past and stumbled onto this. They could have used the secret to torture her and extract money at the same time. Or maybe it was *all* about money. Maybe the mob found out and they were using it to lure her back into the fold."

"But why kill the goose that's laying the golden eggs?"

"Maybe the goose got tired of laying golden eggs."

"Maybe. But maybe it wasn't about money at all. Maybe it was personal."

"Personal?"

"Yeah. How would you feel if you found out that the person you've been with for years has been lying to you?"

"You mean Sandy, huh? I could see why she'd be mad enough to leave, but murder? That's pretty far-fetched, isn't it?"

"I don't know, kid. I've seen murders committed with far less motive. Maybe it was personal to someone else."

"Who? Her parents hated the idea, but they helped her start a new life. Why would they kill her? There's no motive."

"Maybe Chris was tired of all the lies. Maybe she decided to come out, so to speak. Wouldn't that piss off Mommy and Daddy?"

"I guess. But still, murder? Maybe, but I don't know."

Slick and I chatted for a while longer, and I told her about my plans to interview Holly Travis. She brought me up to speed on the litigation and we said our goodbyes. I called Information for a Holly Travis in Burton and I also got the number for the hospital. Ms. Travis wasn't home, so I called the hospital. I was told that Ms. Travis works the 3 p.m. to 11 p.m. shift. I really didn't want to talk to her at the hospital. The privacy of her home would be better. I'd try her at home later.

But first things first: it was lunchtime, and I was craving something spicy. I drove around town until I found an inviting Mexican restaurant. My mouth started to water the moment I entered the restaurant with the wonderful aroma of food, glorious food, hanging in the air. I ordered a tamale and a chicken enchilada with plenty of black beans and rice. I slathered it all with hot salsa and guacamole and I was in spicy heaven. I'd probably regret it later, but right now, it was fabulous. Sam hated the fact that I could eat anything and not gain an ounce. What could I say? It was the luck of the draw from the gene pool…and I won. When I finished my meal, I kept nibbling at what was left of the chips and salsa, even though I was stuffed to the gills. I decided it was prudent to leave before I ordered more chips and salsa in a moment of weakness, of which I have many.

I tried Ms. Travis's number again from the pay phone near the restrooms. She was home and agreed to meet with me, though reluctantly. She couldn't meet with me today, as she had several errands to run before work, but we scheduled a meeting for tomorrow at 10 a.m. and she gave me directions to her place. *Oh well, looks like I have to spend another night in good old Springfield.* I went back to the hotel and called Cecelia to let her know that I wouldn't be home until tomorrow night. I then called the airport and booked a reservation for an afternoon flight back home. That would give me plenty of time to meet with Holly Travis and make it to the airport. I didn't want to rush the interview with her, though I didn't know exactly what she could tell me that would be useful. You never know.

I also remembered that I promised to call Sam. That would mean lots of questions, and I really didn't feel like answering a bunch of questions. I felt like taking a nap. But, being the good and loyal friend that I am, I called her and gave her the lowdown. I had to rip the phone away from my ear as Sam squealed with excitement. "OH MY GOD! This is incredible. Do you think Sandy has any idea about Chris's background?"

"If she does, she didn't tell me about it. So either she's in the dark or she's hiding the fact that she knows."

"Why would she do something like that?"

"Well, Sam, if she hacked Chris's head off, she'd probably avoid helping us out with the investigation, don't you think?"

"Don't be ridiculous! Like I've said all along, Sandy is not a killer. I think it's the parents, definitely."

"Two days ago, you were sure that it was the mob. Now you think it's the parents. Maybe it was the gardener…maybe he got carried away with the hedge trimmer. Or maybe it was an overzealous Avon lady or magazine salesman. Or an Amway salesman. I hear those people really take selling seriously."

Sam was silent, except for a little whimper. "Hey, I was only trying to help. That's all."

Heavy sigh. "I'm sorry. I've just never had so many 'maybes' in a case before. It's got me a little bummed. Maybe Holly Travis will have something to tell me that will push me in the right direction."

That was all we discussed about the case. Sam talked about business and about Nealy's new projects, but I was only half listening. This case had me tensed up, and not even food was helping. Things were serious.

I spent the rest of the evening writing down possible motives and suspects. It didn't get me anywhere, but at least it felt like I was doing something solid. I went for a walk, ate a deli sandwich and fell asleep early. I knew tomorrow was going to be a long day.

The Widow Who Wasn't

I left the motel early, having already settled the bill and packed up my modest amount of stuff. I scarfed down a couple of breakfast burritos on the way to Burton, and when I arrived in the city, I was pleasantly surprised. It was a pretty good-sized town, but it had a real small town charm and feel to it. Everything, that is, except the hospital. It was massive and located just south of downtown. It was one huge nucleus of buildings with several out-croppings at various locations. When I realized that this was a university hospital, that made sense. They're always huge, for some reason.

The residential parts of town that I drove through were immaculate. The lawns were emerald green and well-manicured, and many were dotted with giant shade trees that looked as though they had been around forever. Most of the homes were not expensive-looking, but were well-maintained and had a certain old world charm to them. It was all very nice, but after a while, I felt like I was driving through Stepford, since everything had a certain sameness to it.

Everything except the little armpit of town where Holly Travis lived, that is. She lived in a rundown mobile home court where everything was beat up and worn out; even the stray cats looked rusted. The place had an aura of poverty and depression, with a liberal sprinkling of hopelessness. Holly's place was located at the far edge of the grim little court, and looked like it had once been a shade of aqua. Now it was faded by age, the elements, and despair. I'd remember this place next time I complained about my home.

I knocked on the door and a haggard, disheveled woman answered the door. "Hi, I'm J.Z. Mackenzie. I have an appointment with Holly Travis."

That's me. Come on in. Just ignore the mess." Holy crap! This woman couldn't be Holly Travis. She looked like she was in her 60's. I assumed that Holly and Jamison were about the same age, which should put Holly in her late 40's. This woman looked old, drawn and defeated. She was dressed in one of those ratty house dresses that everybody's grandma wears, and her long brown hair was oily and unkempt. She had on big plastic frame glasses that were right out of the 70's. She was tall and didn't look frail, just kind of used up and burned out.

And her home, oh my god. It was a disaster area, and it reeked of old food and mildew. There were piles of shit everywhere, everything from dirty clothes to moldy food containers. Once or twice, I thought I saw something crawling around amidst the clutter. I tried not to look too hard. I just didn't want to know.

"Just clear yourself a place to sit. Here, let me take that old pizza box." As she got close to me, I detected the distinct odor of whiskey. That explained a lot. I was surprised she could still hold down a job. I wouldn't want her for my nurse. Between the booze and the millions of germs she was carrying around, she was a medical disaster waiting to happen.

When we were both seated I said, "I appreciate you taking the time to speak with me."

"What's this about, anyway? I mean, I know you want to talk about Jamison, I just don't know why."

Oh boy. Think fast. "Well, that's kind of difficult to explain, and due to issues of confidentiality, I can't really go into that. Let's just say that I'm investigating a murder and I have reason to believe that what happened to Jamison has some bearing on the case." I flashed her a sincere look.

She looked skeptical. "That doesn't make any sense at all, but it doesn't matter. I'll answer your questions anyway."

"Thanks. First, how 'bout some background information? Did you and Jamison graduate from high school the same year?" I thought this was much nicer than asking her how old she is.

"Yes, 1969. We knew each other in high school, but we didn't start seeing each other until later. In fact, it was almost two years after high school that we got together."

"What brought you two together?"

"We'd run into each other at parties. It was a gradual thing. But when it finally happened, there was no stopping us." She got a faraway look in her eyes, as though she was reliving the great romance of her life. "We were perfect for each other, and we were so much in love. It was incredible. I'd never felt anything like it before. It was good for both of us, because we wanted to make a life together. That meant we had to set some goals. So, I persuaded Jamison to go to college, something he'd been resisting."

"Why didn't he want to go to college?"

"I think it was just because his parents wanted him to. He didn't really get along with them, especially his dad. He took every opportunity to rebel against his father. I think that's why he chose to major in history—he knew that his father would think it was useless. Anyway, he studied hard and we saw each other every moment that we could."

"So you weren't living together during this time?"

"No, we couldn't. Even though Jamison rebelled against his parents, he wasn't a fool. He took their money every chance he got. They wouldn't pay for his college unless he was living at home. I think it was just a way for them to keep me and Jamison apart as much as they could. But what could I do? I wanted him to get a degree, so I went along with it."

"So what happened after Jamison graduated?"

Holly sighed and looked down at the floor for several moments. "I don't know what happened. Jamison grew distant and started partying again. It was like he was trying to blot something out of his consciousness. But I didn't give up. How could I? I loved him, and we planned to get married."

"So Jamison didn't get a job after graduation?"

"No. He just kind of languished for that year following graduation. Then…well, you know."

"It's still difficult for you to talk about his death?"

Her eyes welled up with tears, which she swiped away with the back of her hand. "Yes, it is. I never loved anybody after Jamison."

"I hate to bring this up, but how far along were you when Jamison died?"

She looked startled. "How did you know about that?"

"I spoke with Mr. Hollingsworth yesterday." I didn't want to finger the kindly old librarian as a gossip. And I suspected there was no love lost between Holly and Hollingsworth.

"Oh, that old fart. Figures. I was four months along when Jamison was killed. Two months later, I lost the baby. It was a difficult time for me, to say the least. I lost the only two people who ever mattered to me, and I lost one before I ever met him. I never quite recovered."

"So you never had any kids?"

A look of absolute heartbreak spread across her face and I immediately regretted asking that question. When she composed herself, she replied, "I couldn't. There were some complications with the miscarriage. I couldn't have children after that. Maybe I never would have. But not having kids and never being able to have kids are two different things. I would have liked to have the option."

"When did you decide to get into nursing?"

"It was a few years after losing Jamison and the baby. I had gone from one dead end job to another and finally I got my act together enough to go to nursing school. It seemed to help take my mind off of the grief somewhat."

"If it's not too difficult, tell me about the night Jamison died."

She wrung her hands and stared at a spot on the floor for a while. Finally, she was able to speak. "He loved to fly more than anything. He said it made him forget about all the problems on the ground. I rarely went with him because it frightened me. We'd spent the day together that Saturday. Went on a picnic and for a long bike ride. I thought we were going to spend the evening together too, but Jamison said he was going flying. I was mad, and I've always regretted that my last words to him were somewhat harsh."

Her eyes misted over and she dabbed at them with a tissue. "I was watching TV that night with my sister. I remember having an odd feeling that night, a feeling of doom, like something bad was going to happen. The next day, I slept late. My sister woke me up and told me that Jamison's plane had crashed, and that he hadn't been found. I knew right away that he was dead. I just sensed it. They never found his body, you know."

"Yes, I know. So you never held out any hope that he was still alive?"

"No, none. I knew he was gone from my life."

We discussed her job, the town, and similar topics. By then I was ready to escape the heavy layer of oppression blanketing that trailer. It was incredibly sad: the woman hadn't moved beyond the loss she suffered so many years ago. It was as though she died right along with Jamison and the baby. Nothing was more depressing than a wasted life, once full of promise and endless possibilities.

I drove away from the town as fast as I could, hoping to outrun any creepy crawlers that might have followed me out of that trailer, as well as the utter despair that lingered there. A shiver ran down my spine as the hopelessness of her words echoed inside my head.

I made it to the airport well ahead of schedule, and tried in vain to shake the mantle of depression that had settled upon me. The old saying, "'Tis better to have loved and lost than never to have loved at all' rang hollow. I tried to sleep on the flight home, but my sleep was punctuated by garish images of grief, poverty and loss. I'd be glad to finally get home and be surrounded by familiar things and people who loved me. All in all, I was pretty lucky.

Dropping a Bomb

I slept late with the kitties the next day. They vacillated between being happy to see me and being mad at me for going away. The three of us lounged in bed, me deep in thought and them napping off and on, purring loudly. I knew that I'd have to go see Sandy today and tell her what I had discovered on my trip. If she didn't know, it was going to be an incredible shock for her. I didn't relish telling her, but I had to see her face when she found out. I hoped that her response would give me some clue as to whether she already knew about St. James.

The three of us eventually crawled out of bed and treated ourselves to waffles and tuna pâte. I didn't try any of the pâte, and the girls weren't thrilled with the waffles either. It was one of the few things that I had learned how to cook over the years. After breakfast, I called Slick to make sure she was going to be in and told her I'd be there later.

The files on Slick's desk had either grown or sprouted offspring. I don't know how she ever finds anything in the mess. At least there were no creepy crawlies like there had been in Holly's place. Ugh!

"Hey, kid! Good to have you back. How did the interview with Travis go?"

"Fine. But man, was it ever depressing." I explained the condition of both Holly and her surroundings, and gave her a rundown of our conversation.

"Sounds like her life just fell apart after Jamison's death and the loss of the little one."

"Her life did more than fall apart. It completely disintegrated. She's nothing but a shell of a person, a poster girl for the walking wounded."

"That kind of grief could drive a person to do a lot of crazy things, including murder."

"Sure, but she thinks Jamison died in that plane crash."

"Yes, but as I pointed out, she, or someone else, could have found out the truth just like you. I agree that blackmail is a promising angle, but I think we have to consider Ms. Travis a suspect."

"I agree a hundred percent. I haven't ruled out anyone yet."

"Including Sandy?"

Another wave of guilt and a heavy sigh. "Yeah, including Sandy. I'm not looking forward to telling her about all of this. Do you want to come with me?"

Slick hacked for a few moments, and between puffs of smoke said, "Absolutely not! You can give me a report as to her reaction when you tell her. I don't care to be a witness to that. If she doesn't know, the news will no doubt make her very uncomfortable. The fewer people there, the better. Be gentle."

"Coward."

"Ass."

With those words of encouragement, I exited Slick's office. On the way out of the building, I turned to Irma and asked, "Hey, Irma, what's a hairy iota, anyway?"

Irma turned several shades of red, each a little deeper and more vibrant than the last. She cleared her voice and replied, "It's nothin' you need to be concerned with, little missy. God knows I was never concerned with it. Now get on out of here. Don't you have work to do?"

I laughed and went on my way. As my thoughts returned to the task at hand, I stopped laughing. By the time I got to the jail, I had managed to work myself into a ball of nerves. It was readily apparent to Sandy. "What's wrong, J.Z.?" There were dark circles under her eyes and all of the bubbly energy that used to be apparent on her face was gone. It had been replaced by intense anxiety.

I stammered and hemmed and hawed for a while, and paced madly back and forth. "I have something to tell you, and it's not going to be easy for you to hear. I don't quite know how to say it."

"Well, don't keep me guessing. Just tell me, whatever it is."

I paused and looked deep into Sandy's eyes. "Sandy…oh god…how do I say this? The thing is…you see…Chris used to be a man."

The color drained from her face and she shot out of her chair, which tipped backwards on the hard concrete. A guard came running, but I waved him away. "What? What are you talking about, J.Z.?"

"It's true. Chris used to be Jamison Hollingsworth III. He grew up in Pennsylvania, the only son of a prominent family. He had issues with his gender from a very early age. After college he decided that he wanted to have a sex change operation. His rich family couldn't bear the thought of that, so they faked his death in a plane crash. That's the newspaper clipping you found. He had the operation and moved to Oregon as Chris St. James."

Sandy sat in stunned silence and stared at me as though I had gone stark raving mad. "That just can't be. No, it isn't true. I lived with Chris for years. Don't you think I'd know something like that?"

I pulled out a photograph of Jamison that Holly had given me and I slid it across the table. The horror on Sandy's face intensified, and the denial seemed to melt away. If this was all an act, it was a damn good one. "Oh, my god. I can't believe this is happening. It's all so incredible."

"Did you ever have any inkling about this, a hint of any sort?"

Sandy shook her head and said, "No, none whatsoever. I guess it makes sense, though, in an odd sort of way."

"What do you mean?"

"Well, all the sexual issues Chris had. I'm no psychologist, but this had to be at the root of a lot of those problems."

Sandy may not be a psychologist, but I knew someone who was, someone who was also a damn fine grill master. "I'd guess that you're right. But like you, I have very little understanding of clinical human psychology."

In a slightly trembling voice, she asked, "How did you find out?"

I explained how I stumbled upon this bombshell, and I also told her about the two interviews in Pennsylvania. When I was done, it was apparent that Sandy didn't want to talk anymore, and I didn't blame her. If I were in her place, I'd want some time to think, too. I left her with her troubled thoughts.

Since my day was already ruined by the pain I had just inflicted on another human being, I decided I might as well really foul it up. So I drove over to the law offices of Cooper, Langley, Hayden, and Dowd to see my old friend, Camilla Bitchburger. I'd given her more time to come up with some names than I had promised. She'd better have something good for me. I was in no mood to play games with her.

Ann Boyd was speaking with the receptionist as I went in. She turned and beamed at me. "J.Z., I was just thinking about you."

"Were you picturing me in something seductive? I'm flattered, Ann, but I told you it would never work between us. Besides, I'm saving myself for Cameron Diaz." The receptionist blanched, but Ann laughed and guided me back to her work area.

"You are positively evil, you know that? Scaring our little innocent receptionist like that."

"I couldn't help it. Sometimes these evil urges just get the better of me, I guess."

"Speaking of evil, you're just in time if you want to speak with the Big B. She just got back from a court appearance. From the way she's acting, I'd say it didn't go too well."

"Oh, good. I can kick her while she's down. And by the way, if you hear screaming coming from her office, just ignore it."

I stood in Bitchburger's doorway as she yelled at someone on the phone. When she slammed the phone down, I said, "There's a new book out on office etiquette. I'll get you a copy." I walked in and closed the door.

Bitchburger sighed and shook her head. "You're the last thing I need today. Can't we do this some other time?"

"No. You've already had more than enough time. Give me some names."

Bitchburger pulled out a sheet of paper and handed it to me. It contained most of the names that Kara had suggested, and one other. "Wally Paris? Who's that?"

"He used to be a cop here in town. A detective, I think. He was a good cop, by all accounts. He got really involved in this one murder case, a little too involved. He was doing what cops aren't supposed to do—taking it personally. The victim was a teenage girl…I think 15. Paris had a daughter that age, and I guess that's why he took this case to heart. Anyway, I can't remember exactly what happened. But Paris messed up something in the investigation somehow. I think he exceeded the scope of the search warrant, and the evidence that he found, the only solid evidence, got tossed out on a motion to suppress filed by Chris. Without that evidence, there was nothing to tie the suspect, Manny Jarvis, to the crime. Jarvis was set free, and within a week, he'd killed another young girl. Paris lost it. He blamed himself for the murder. He tried to commit suicide by slashing his wrists, but his wife found him. He lost his job, of course. I don't think he's held down a job since. He's in and out of looney bins. Still lives in town, I think."

"You've been uncharacteristically helpful, Camilla. Let's get together sometime for a quiet evening, just the two of us." I winked at her.

"Fuck you."

"As tempting as that offer is, I'll have to pass. I haven't had all of the shots that the Centers for Disease Control recommends for intimate encounters with the Bitchburger."

"God, you're an asshole! Why do you hate me so much? Are you jealous, is that it?"

I laughed heartily. "Jealous? Jealous of what? You want to know why I can't stand you? I'll tell you. You're a disgrace to the legal profession. You're lazy, dishonest, and always looking to blame someone else for your mistakes. And if all of that wasn't enough, you're the kind of heterosexual woman that no lesbian could ever like."

"What?"

"You need a man to be complete. Actually, lots of men. You see no value in women and in the strong friendships that can be forged between women. You don't even see value in yourself, except in what you can do for a man. You have unbelievably low self-esteem, which is probably why you act the way you do. That, in a nutshell, is why I can't stand you."

"You can't stand me because I like men?"

I clenched my fists and shook them. "Oh, christ, you've missed my whole point! Never mind!" I stormed out of her office, slamming the door on the way out. I waved at Ann, who was busy working on pleadings that had to go out shortly. I was still shaking when I reached my van. That woman could really get to me. I was glad that I no longer had to see her everyday. No wonder I had ulcers the size of boulders when I was working with that beast.

My cell phone rang as I was pulling out of the parking lot. "What?"

"Well, aren't we in a chipper mood?" It was Slick. If I didn't recognize her voice, there was no mistaking that hack.

"Sorry. My day has been pretty shitty so far. What's up?"

"I forgot to tell you when you were here earlier. We can go over and look at the crime scene later this evening. Let me check my calendar. Yes, at 6:00. A uniformed officer will let us in and remain at the scene until we're done. You up for that?"

"Sure. I'll pick you up around 5:30."

"Sounds good. By the way, remember those hairs that were found near St. James at the scene?"

"Yeah. Long hairs, right?"

"Yep, they're not Sandy's. The lab results just came back. The hairs are brown, but belong to someone else. We have to keep in mind that the hairs may not necessarily belong to the killer."

"Interesting. Hey, did the cops ever find that newspaper clipping and pictures that Sandy told us about?"

"No, nothing like that was found. Maybe Chris got rid of them."

"Maybe. I guess they're not crucial now. I'm assuming the pictures were of Chris's parents and Holly. Chris cut herself out of the picture with her parents."

"Probably so. How did it go with Sandy?"

I groaned and replied, "About as well as could be expected. She was shocked, and it looked like genuine shock to me."

"That's good. I mean…you know what I mean."

"Yeah. I've got a call to make. I'll see you at 5:30."

I called information and got Barry Cole's office number. I had some questions to ask him about St. James. I needed to have a better understanding of what she was going through. He said he was free any time the next day late afternoon. I agreed to swing by his place in the afternoon or evening. Before he hung up, he told me to bring an appetite. That was never a problem. I reminded myself to check the Alka-Seltzer supply, though.

Since I had some time to kill, I thought I'd try to locate Michelle Knight, the assistant district attorney who left the practice of law rather than face disciplinary proceedings for allegedly destroying evidence. I had a Kingston phone book in my van, and I quickly located a listing for Ms. Knight at the Overland Insurance Company on the corner of Elm and 23rd streets. I was there in no time, and after a short wait, Ms.

Knight appeared in the waiting area. It was apparent from the fake smile plastered on her face that she thought I was a potential customer. After introductions were made, she escorted me to her office.

"Ms. Mackenzie, I commend you on selecting Overland Insurance Company to handle your insurance-related questions. I hope that I can be of service to you today. Now, how can I assist you?"

Good thing I'm not diabetic, because I just had a giant dose of sugar-coated shit. "Well, actually, I'm not here to purchase any insurance." The fake smile quickly vanished, to be replaced by a look of annoyance.

"All solicitations must go through the district manager, and she's not in today."

"I'm not selling anything, either. If you'll just allow me to explain, I promise not to take up much of your time. I'm a private investigator, and I'm working on a case, the murder of Chris St. James."

Michelle Knight began laughing hysterically, and when she realized that I was mortified by her response, she composed herself and explained, "I always told that bitch she'd get what was coming to her, and it looks like she finally did."

"That's a bit harsh, don't you think?"

"Harsh? Are you kidding? She was an A-1 bitch. I'm just sorry someone beat me to the punch."

"And your assessment of Ms. St. James's character is based on the fact that she brought to the court's attention your improprieties?"

Knight cocked an eyebrow and looked at me with disdain. "Those allegations were never proven."

"So you're telling me that after spending three hellish years in law school and going deeply in debt, you willingly left the practice of law due to some false charges leveled by Chris St. James."

Again I was treated to the cocked eyebrow and look of disdain, this time with a little anger thrown in. "I chose not to fight the charges, yes. I'll leave it at that. The point is, St. James was known to bend the rules herself. It was like the pot calling the kettle black."

"Be that as it may, my point is that you developed a deep animosity for Ms. St. James as a result. Isn't that correct?"

Knight snickered and replied, "If you're asking whether I hated the bitch because of what she did to me, you're right. I did. But so what. What's your point?"

"Did you hate her enough to kill her?"

She flashed me a sly smile and admitted, "Yeah, I think I did. I even thought about it once or twice." She stared up the ceiling, a devilish grin spreading across her features, obviously fantasizing about it right now. In a few moments, Knight returned to reality and continued. "I mean, I lost everything because of her. Wouldn't you want to make someone like that pay? But like I said, someone beat me to it."

"Do you have an alibi for that night?"

"I was home."

"Was anyone with you?"

"No, I was alone. I spent the whole night reading."

Knight didn't strike me as the bookish type, even though she had two advanced degrees. She probably read romance novels, the kind that featured Fabio on the covers. "I see. Did you have any interaction or contact with Ms. St. James after you left the practice of law?"

"Hell no! Why would I want to have contact with her?"

"I'm merely asking questions. But I also feel the need to point something out to you, Ms. Knight."

"Oh yeah, what's that?"

"You lost your job because of something *you* did. You destroyed evidence. Whether or not Ms. St. James bent the rules is beside the point. I used to be an attorney, and I worked for a firm where I was surrounded by attorneys who wouldn't recognize an ethical canon if it fell out of the sky, landed on their face, and wiggled. It doesn't matter if you're surrounded by people who break the rules on a daily basis. You still have your own duties and obligations to the court, duties that you failed to uphold. That's why you lost your job."

I waltzed out of there without giving her a chance to respond, her jaw hanging open. I don't know what came over me. I usually try to be diplomatic with witnesses and suspects, since I might have to talk with them again. I definitely wasn't going to be granted another audience with Michelle Knight. I guess it was just the Bitchburger syndrome that got to me: Knight was blaming someone else for her own screwup. Didn't anybody take responsibility for their own actions anymore?

It was now late afternoon and I realized that the source of my bitchiness might be low blood sugar, as I hadn't eaten any lunch yet. As I was waiting in the drive-thru line at Taco Bob's, I called Slick again. "Hey, sorry to bother you. But I was just wondering when we're going to get a look at St. James's financials."

"Should be within the next day or so. You're thinking about the blackmail angle?"

"Yeah. I mean, it should be easy enough to see if St. James was making large monthly outlays of cash to one source."

"Well, in most cases, yes. But according to Sandy, Chris made large payments to several sources each month. Some were for investment purposes, some were to various charitable organizations, and so on."

"I'm surprised Sandy had any knowledge of St. James's financial affairs."

"Me too, so I asked. Sandy admitted that she had sneaked a look at St. James's ledger the time she scoured her office and found the newspaper clipping and pictures. Some of the entries she recognized, but some she didn't. It may take weeks for a forensic accountant to sit down with St. James's books and determine where the money was going. St. James was one sharp cookie. If someone was blackmailing her, she was smart enough to cover the tracks."

"You're thinking that one of the sources she was paying might have been some kind of dummy company, set up for the payment of hush money?"

"It's definitely possible, but we won't know for a while, I'm afraid. I'll let you know when her financials arrive. But right now, I've got to meet with a client. Later, kid."

As I munched on my tacos and burrito, I wondered why nothing was ever easy. Why couldn't the bad guys be kind enough to leave us a little trail of crumbs to follow? In truth, there were tiny crumbs, but they went in a million different directions. They didn't lead down one well-defined path. I felt like I kept getting sidetracked and going down dead ends. But the truth was somewhere in those crumbs, and I was determined to find it, no matter what.

I finished my lunch parked under a big shade tree on the edge of the city. I must have dozed off because when I awoke, with crusted drool on the corner of my mouth, I was almost late for my appointment with Slick. I hightailed it over to her office, where I found Slick tapping her foot in the parking lot. Patience has never been one of Slick's virtues. "You're three minutes late. What happened to you? And what's that white shit on the corner of your mouth?"

Oh goddess on high, please grant me the patience to refrain from hitting this old lady. "Three minutes? You're whining over three minutes?

Give me a break. And the white shit on the corner of my mouth is Grade A cocaine, my friend. Nothing like tacos and cocaine for lunch, you know."

"That's not funny. You shouldn't even joke about something like that. Your body is a temple." As she uttered these words, Slick took a long drag on her cigarette and hacked up part of a lung.

I laughed and said, "Well, your temple's on fire, old woman."

"Just drive, smart ass."

So I did, and we made it to St. James's place with time to spare. Our friendly neighborhood cop escort had not yet arrived. While we waited, Slick turned to me and said, "I just talked to the D.A. and it looks like the tire track found in St. James's driveway is a perfect match for Sandy's."

"Well, that's no surprise. Sandy was here, and she admitted that she took off in a big hurry."

"If only she would have called the cops from the scene."

"They may have still fingered her for the murder."

"Sure, but at least we would have one consistent statement. As it is now, we have to explain to a jury why Sandy lied to the cops. Juries hate lies. They find out someone lied, and they will assign a malicious motive to it more often than not. I've seen it happen, and that part worries me."

"But wouldn't most people freak out if they found someone they knew lying in a pool of blood with their head nearly chopped off?"

"Yes, but that kind of horror and panic is extremely difficult to reconstruct for a jury."

"Well, they don't call you 'Slick' for nothin', you know."

At that moment, a shiny police cruiser pulled up alongside us and out popped Officer Cathy. I made the introductions and we all scooted under the yellow crime scene tape. Cathy unlocked the door to the sprawling mansion and we all went inside. Cathy looked around, whistled, and said, "Man oh man, what a place." After she'd gotten an eyeful, Cathy turned to me and said, "Look, I'm gonna wait out front. When you guys are done, just give me a holler and I'll come lock up."

We thanked her and Slick pulled out the grisly crime scene photographs. Now I knew why Barry had tossed his cookies that night. The area where the crime occurred was a large, formal living room, just off the entryway to the home. The room contained two large sofas, four wingback chairs, a coffee table, and several end tables arranged in a conversational circle. At the far end of the grouping, opposite the entryway, was a fireplace, and adjoining that wall was a bank of ceiling-to-floor windows, covered by heavy drapery. On the same wall as the fireplace was a modern bar area, and it was just in front of this where the chalk outline of St. James's body was located. The amount of blood, now an ugly rust color, was unbelievable. It stood out starkly against the cream-colored carpet.

The body was positioned with St. James's head pointed in the direction of the bar, arms over her head. It looked as though she was heading for, or at least facing the bar when she was attacked. The attack must have occurred from behind, because it would be impossible to do that much damage any other way. When St. James was found, she was lying face down on the floor.

Slick had spread out the crime scene photos across one of the sofas. She looked at them carefully and then studied the outline. "Okay. So we know that there were no signs of forced entry. Let's assume that St. James let this person in, which would suggest that she knew the person."

"Do you think that's a valid assumption, though? I mean, if Sandy is right and Chris knew who was making the threats, and if we assume that the person making the threats was the killer, why would she let this person into her home willingly?"

"If you ever had dealings with St. James, you wouldn't have to ask that question."

"Well, enlighten me, O Great One."

"St. James wasn't the sort to back down. She would meet challenges and threats head on. She was no doubt scared at times, like all of us, but she would never show it. It doesn't strike me as odd that she'd let this person into her home. Maybe she thought it would be her opportunity to end the threats once and for all."

"Well, she succeeded there."

Slick groaned and continued. "Anyway, she lets this person in, and maybe she's heading to the bar to fix some drinks. You know, to maybe ease the tension and defuse the situation as much as possible."

"Or, she already knew it was a mistake to let this person in and she was heading to the bar on the pretense of making a drink. But in reality, she was intending to retrieve the 9mm she kept behind the bar. See? That's on the list of items the cops took from the scene. One 9mm from behind the bar."

Slick looked at the list in my hand and sighed. "Yes, that's possible. Or maybe she was intending to hit the panic button for the alarm that's also located behind the bar." Slick examined the bar area and the panic button.

I thumbed through some of the other papers that Slick had brought with her to the scene. I had already read the coroner's report, but I paged through it until I located the passage I was looking for. "The coroner's report concludes that the wound was inflicted from left to right, which would mean that the killer is right-handed, if we assume that the attack occurred from behind. And we're probably looking for someone tall, since St. James was tall. And someone strong."

"I don't know if I'd go along with that last part."

"You don't think it takes strength to nearly chop someone's head off?"

"Not if rage is involved. I've defended people, guilty people, who committed crimes that you would think were beyond their physical capabilities. But when people get angry enough, they're capable of most anything."

I knew she was right. I'd seen instances like Slick described in my line of work as well. "Did St. James always answer her own door? I would think someone of her means would have an entire staff of domestic help."

"She had a gardener who was full-time, and she had a maid come in twice a week. She apparently did all of her own cooking. I think she enjoyed her privacy more than she enjoyed being pampered."

We studied the area for a while longer, and took a look in St. James's home office. It looked like the cops took the computer hard drive into evidence. "Have you gotten any report on what's been found on St. James's computer yet?"

"I'll be getting copies of the few files St. James had stored on her computer. It's mostly just mundane correspondence."

"What do you mean 'the few files'?"

"I mean she had only a few files saved."

"I find that hard to believe. I mean, wouldn't she use her computer to draft opening and closing arguments, and make trial outlines, and stuff like that?"

"Sandy told me that St. James had an amazing memory. She hardly ever wrote anything down, and she rarely used the computer. If she did have to make notes, she preferred good old-fashioned pen and paper."

We gathered up our things and walked out front to examine the tire marks. It was quite apparent that Sandy had left in a big hurry, assuming these were her tire tracks. She couldn't remember whether she peeled out when she left or not. She couldn't remember much about that evening, except all the blood. I guess that was understandable. When we were finished, I looked at Cathy and said, "Well, Deputy Dawg, I guess we're all finished here. Hey, I wanna hear about the love connection with Antonio. No holding back, either."

Cathy blushed and said, "A lady can't reveal everything."

"Yeah, but who said anything about a lady?"

Cathy stuck her tongue out at me in true ladylike fashion, and Slick and I piled back into the van and headed down the road. We rode back to Slick's office in silence, each of us pondering the many "maybes" associated with this case.

Getting to
Know You

When I got home late that evening, I thumbed through my Kingston phone directory for a Blaine Darrow, one of the names St. James's former secretary mentioned to me. He was the one whose wife was murdered and the kids sodomized, and St. James managed to get a not guilty verdict for the perpetrator. I didn't find a listing. When I got a chance, I'd run a criminal check on Darrow as well as a standard credit check, and one of those would provide a current address. I'd also run a check to see if Darrow was currently involved in any litigation, just for shits and giggles.

I got a good night's rest and fired up my computer first thing. Darrow had been charged with stalking St. James on two occasions, as Kara had indicated. He pled guilty the first time and was given probation. On the second offense, he did some jail time and was ordered to take some anger management classes. This had been several months ago. Maybe those classes had worked, or maybe Darrow just got sneakier. He had no other criminal record. I could find no indication of any pending civil litigation.

His credit check revealed that he had declared bankruptcy a few months after losing his wife. Kara indicated that he had lost his job. The mortgage on his home was foreclosed and his car was repossessed. He'd lost everything. But then a few short months ago, Darrow had purchased another home, estimated value of $273,000. I saw no security interests listed, which must mean that Darrow owned the house outright. How could that be? How could someone who had hit the skids turn everything around so fast? Maybe with blackmail money? Hmmm…I'd have to talk with Mr. Darrow. This looked interesting. His address was listed as 4577 Hill Street in Balentine, which was about 20 miles this side of Kingston.

I called information and got a number. I crossed my fingers a dialed. Someone answered on the third ring. "Hi. Sorry to disturb you, Mr. Darrow. I'm a private investigator, and I'm looking into the murder of Chris St. James. I was wondering if you might meet with me later today to discuss Ms. St. James?"

A long, stony silence. "You think I killed her?"

"I never said that."

"Why else would you want to talk to me?"

"I'm just trying to get a feel for what kind of person she was, and I know you had dealings with her, that's all." *Oh dear, I'm going to have to work on those lies.*

"You ain't no cop. Why should I talk to *you?*"

"Well, I'm glad you asked that question, Mr. Darrow." Oh, great. Now I sounded like a phone solicitor. "You see, as it stands right now, the cops are focusing on just one suspect, as you no doubt know."

"Yeah, it was the bitch's lesbo lover."

Hold your temper, J.Z. "Anyway, that could change at any moment."

"What do you mean?"

"Well, if I have to file a report that says you refused to speak with me, the cops might get very interested in you, especially considering your stalking charges. If, however, I file a report that shows that you fully cooperated, the cops probably won't want to question you. There would be no need." I didn't tell him that any reports I generated would be protected by attorney-client privilege, since I was working for an attorney in this matter. He didn't ask.

"Are you tryin' to threaten me?"

"No, no. On the contrary, I'm looking out for your best interests, Mr. Darrow. What do you say? Will you meet with me?"

I could hear him sighing, trying to think of a way out of this, one that wouldn't make him look like he had something to hide. After a while, he said, "If it don't take too long, I guess. You just make sure that your report says I fully cooperated. You hear?"

"Yes, I understand." We arranged a time and when I hung up the phone, I did a little victory dance around my office. The kitties, who were sitting next to each other in the doorway, stared blankly at me, then looked at each other, no doubt wondering about my sanity. "Oh, as if the two of you don't have your little idiosyncracies…please. Besides, a little insanity never hurt anyone."

I calmed down and gave the kitties treats to reassure them that I hadn't gone round the bend just yet. They seemed mollified but unconvinced. I dined on a hearty breakfast of Lucky Charms and a buttermilk scone. I would probably need all the luck I could manufacture today. I got ready in a hurry, and I'm ashamed to admit that I was reduced to using the "smell test" to locate a suitable shirt, since I had neglected my laundry responsibilities. I found an acceptable candidate, and promised myself that I would pay more attention to my domestic duties in the future. I knew this was a lie, but the empty promise somehow made me feel better. Kind of like sorting through stacks of bills and putting them in order according to urgency. It feels useful, even if you have no money to pay any of them.

I was on the road in no time, all the while thinking about the brutality of the crime. I shivered as the crime scene photo images flashed thorough my mind. It was clear that whoever did this was enraged. Could a person capable of such evil appear normal to everyone around them? Or was it likely that this kind of rage was part of a pattern for the person? Maybe I'd add this to the list of things to ask Barry Cole about.

With my mind occupied by such thoughts, I almost passed the small town of Balantine. It was a quaint, quiet town, perhaps a retirement community. I found Hill Street with no trouble. It was a tree-lined street, with the homes set back from the roadway. Darrow's place was on the left side of the street, with a long, winding driveway leading to the big house. It was nothing like St. James's place, but it was quite nice, by far the most expensive home in this small town.

I knocked on the door and within moments, a tall, gangly man with long brown hair opened the door. "I'm Darrow. Are you Mackenzie?"

"Yes, and I want to thank you for taking the time to see me today."

He eyed me suspiciously but opened the door for me to enter. "Have a seat anywhere you like."

Darrow was not a tidy housekeeper, but at least he did a better job than Holly Travis. "Thanks. Why don't we start with you telling me what you thought of Chris St. James?"

Darrow looked at me the same way my cats had earlier in the day, as though I'd gone off my rocker. "Are you shittin' me? I hated that bitch. Everyone knows that. That animal, Manfred Jakes, gutted my wife right there in front of my kids. They still have nightmares, and probably will for the rest of their lives. But that wasn't enough for the sick bastard. Then he messed with both my kids, and they'll probably never be normal now. And that bitch St. James convinced a jury that Jakes was innocent. Can you believe it?" Darrow shook his head, the pain, loss, and guilt evident in his hardened features.

"How did she do that?"

"Oh, she had some fancy-schmancy experts come in and testify about the evidence, how it was mishandled and all. Then she started bad-mouthing Kitty."

"What do you mean?"

Darrow blushed and looked down at the floor. "Well, it was no secret that Kitty and I had our share of problems. Most folks do if they're married long enough. I was working extra hours and Kitty...well, she strayed. I found out about it, and we fought over it something fierce. St. James hinted that maybe I was somehow involved. Maybe I just lost it over this fling she was having, and I hired someone to do that to her. Then she hinted that maybe this guy she was involved with was mad 'cause Kitty wouldn't leave me for him. Some of this bullshit must have made sense to the jury. But that's all it was—bullshit."

"So you stalked St. James, to get even."

He snarled and said, "Hell, there was no way I could get *even* with St. James, no matter what I did. But yeah, I was royally pissed. I followed her around and scared her. It didn't mean nothin'. I never hurt her. I did threaten her a few times, but that was all."

"You left some of those threats in her mailbox, right?" Just a hunch.

Darrow again looked at me like I was out of my gourd. "What? No, I never did nothin' like that. I made some phone calls to her and said some things to her, but I never left anything for her. It wasn't me."

"Do you have an alibi for the evening of May 12th, the night St. James was killed?"

"I didn't kill the bitch! If I'd wanted to kill her, she would have been dead a long time ago."

"You didn't answer my question, Mr. Darrow."

He scrunched up his face, deep in thought, if that was possible for him. "I think I was driving back from seein' my kids that night. Yeah, that's right. I didn't get home until around 9 or so. So I guess I don't really have an alibi."

"Where are your kids?"

A look of guilt snuck across his face, and he turned somewhat ashen. "They're livin' with my folks over in Jackson. They have to get regular counseling and go to a special school. They're real messed up, thanks to that animal. I just don't have what it takes to raise 'em."

Jackson was over in eastern Oregon, about a six hour drive from Balantine. "What time did you leave your kids that day?"

"We had an early lunch together, and I took off about 12:30. I'd spent a couple days with them and I needed to get home."

"But surely it didn't take you that long to drive home."

Darrow's eyes darted around the room. "I stopped off and had a couple drinks and a bite to eat."

"Where?"

He flashed me a look of anger and replied, "I don't remember where, dammit. Just some little hole in the wall place. How should I know the name of it?"

I sensed he was lying about something. Surely he would at least remember the name of the town he stopped in. It wasn't that long ago. If he left Jackson at 12:30, that could put him in Kingston by 6:30, in plenty of time to commit the murder. "You don't even remember the name of the town where you stopped that night?"

Darrow was quickly becoming annoyed with me. "I said no, I don't remember."

"Ok, no need to get upset with me. I'm just trying to sort a few things out. Let's move on to something else. Is it true that you lost your job after your wife was killed?"

"Yeah. I used to work for a siding company, J & H Siding over in Kingston. But I just couldn't manage to even get out of bed in the mornings after all of this happened. So, I got fired. I didn't blame them; I would have fired me, too."

I looked around his place and said, "Well, it looks as though you're doing okay now."

"In some ways, yeah."

"If you don't mind me asking, where did you get the money for this place? Did Kitty have a life insurance policy or something?"

He snorted and said, "No, nothing like that. Even with me working overtime, we were just barely making ends meet. We couldn't afford no life insurance. My cousin, Jimmy Hurkel, died a while back and left me some money."

"Were you two close?"

"Not really. He just didn't have any family. He was a little guy growing up, and I kind of looked out for him. I guess he remembered that."

"Did you deal with an attorney in that matter?"

He took out his wallet and fished around in it for a few moments. "Yeah, here's his card. Some feller name of Shane Thomas over in Kingston was my cousin's lawyer. He was the one that called me to let me know I had inherited some money."

"That must have been exciting. How much did he leave you?"

Darrow's eyes darted around again. "I ain't allowed to say, on account of that bein' one of the conditions of the inheritance."

"I've never heard of anything like that."

"Me neither, but it's true. Nobody even knew Jimmy had any money. He was kind of squirrelly that way, livin' like a hermit and all. He didn't like other people knowin' his business when he was alive, and I guess that just kind of carried over into his death."

"Well, I don't understand. You already have the money, right? So what could possibly happen if you disclosed the details?"

Darrow looked annoyed and replied in a stern tone, "I said I ain't allowed to talk about it, none of it. Period."

"I see. Well, let me ask you one final question, Mr. Darrow, if I might. Did you hate Ms. St. James enough to kill her?" It's not like I ever expected a suspect to respond in the affirmative and then confess spontaneously. But sometimes the response was telling, and that's why I asked the question.

A look of hatred passed through Darrow's eyes and he nodded

his head. "I did hate her that much. She took everything from me...and my kids. Yep, I hated that woman. But I didn't kill her."

The look in his eyes made me shiver—pure, unadulterated hatred. It was almost devilish. Hatred could be a powerful emotion, powerful enough to drive a person to kill. Did it drive Darrow to kill? I wondered.

I thanked him again and said goodbye. I pulled over at a rest stop a few miles down the road. I looked up the number for Shane Thomas and dialed. A very nasal, anal-retentive receptionist reluctantly put me through to Mr. Thomas. I explained to him who I was and the nature of the investigation. Then I asked him how much money Jimmy Hurkel had left his cousin, Mr. Darrow. "Ms. Mackenzie, you know I can't disclose that information. Even putting aside the attorney-client privilege, Mr. Hurkel directed that Mr. Darrow keep all such information secret."

"But surely you can appreciate my predicament."

"Certainly, but I can't just disregard ethical rules due to your predicament. Surely *you* can appreciate that."

I could. Finally, a lawyer at least somewhat acquainted with the rules of ethics. I was astounded and awed. I thanked Mr. Thomas for his time and got back on the road. Well, Darrow had inherited some money from his cousin, that much was clear. But enough to buy a brand new house? And enough to pay for a special school and counseling for his kids? That was a lot of dough. Darrow was hiding something about the night of the murder, that was also quite clear. But what? This man had enough animosity for St. James to do the dirty deed. I knew that much from our brief visit. But did he do it? And why would he wait so long to do it? More stuff to quiz Barry Cole about.

When I got to Kingston, I stopped by the big industrial complex adjoining the courthouse. The largest of these buildings housed the district attorneys, including the oft-humiliated Will Beaton. Thanks to a gun-wielding maniac, the offices of the district attorneys were enclosed in bullet-proof Plexiglass. A visitor had to pass through a metal detector and be buzzed through to the offices. When I gained admission, I stopped at the receptionist's desk to ask if Will Beaton was in. She said he had court in a few minutes, so I scurried down the hall to catch him before he left.

His door was open and he was reading something on his computer screen. I cleared my throat and he looked up, startled. Perhaps I caught him playing solitaire, or looking at porn sites on the Internet. In an annoyed voice, he said, "Yes, can I help you, Miss?"

Beaton was a nerdy looking fellow in his late 30's. His suit was rumpled and his hair was sticking out in different directions, as though he had just taken a nap. He wore huge metal frame glasses, the kind that went out with bell bottoms. He was an utterly forgettable man. "I'm sorry to disturb you, Mr. Beaton, but I'm investigating the death of Chris St. James, and I was wondering if you'd spare me a few moments of your time."

He made a "shooing" motion with his right hand and said, "I'm not handling that case. I think Amy Witherspoon is assigned to that one. Down the hall."

"Yes, I'm aware of that. I'm just trying to get some background information on the victim, and I understand that you and St. James were pitted against each other on several occasions."

He slowly raised his eyes from the computer screen and looked at me over the frames of his big, clunky glasses. "I see." A sly smile spread across his lips. "I suppose you think I'm a suspect, eh?"

"Mr. Beaton, a man of your experience in the criminal justice system knows that everyone is a suspect at first." Stroke, stroke.

He beamed and said, "Certainly. I can understand why you would feel the need to question me. I did have a few run-ins with Ms. St. James. She didn't like me, and it showed."

"Why didn't she like you?"

"I don't know. We just clashed for some reason."

"I hear she…um…showed you up in court a few times. Is that right?"

Beaton blanched and cleared his throat. "Well, I wouldn't say that, exactly. I mean, she tried to do that."

"Could you give me an example?"

"Well, if she was better acquainted with a piece of evidence, for example, she would make it sound like I didn't know what I was talking about. But the thing is, she had the luxury of being better acquainted with the evidence. Here she was, firmly ensconced in the most prestigious law firm around, with law clerks, paralegals, associates, and assistants all waiting to do her bidding. She had unlimited funds to work with, and could hire all the experts she wanted. Sure, she would know the evidence better than me. I've got a budget to operate within, and a very limited support staff. I've got a caseload that would choke a horse, and I'm supposed to turn these cases over quickly. I don't have the leisure to consider all the intricacies of every bit of evidence. But, of course, a jury doesn't understand that."

"Did this anger you?"

He smiled and replied, "Hell yes, but not enough to kill her, if that's what you're asking. Besides, we hadn't met up in the courtroom for quite some time. I'm handling mostly consumer fraud cases now."

"If you don't mind my asking, where were you on the night of May 12th?"

"Not convinced yet, huh? I was in Reno with my wife. We stayed at Fitzgerald's. Feel free to check it out."

"I will. Thanks for your time, Mr. Beaton."

As promised, I promptly called Fitzgerald's in Reno to see if Beaton had stayed there on May 12th. He and his lovely wife had indeed been there on that night. It looked like Beaton had an alibi, and he didn't seem particularly upset with St. James, even though he had been her whipping boy. I'd have to ask Slick about Beaton, and Knight, for that matter. She was probably well acquainted with both of them.

I called Barry Cole to see if he was home yet. He was, and I was thankful, since I had forgotten to eat lunch once again. I could almost smell the wonderful aromas rolling out of Barry Cole's grill.

Breasts
& Psychobabble

Barry didn't disappoint. When I arrived, my nose told me that Barry was in the backyard, slaving over a hot grill. I peeked over the fence and asked, "What's cookin'?"

Barry turned around from his place at the grill and smiled. "Come on in, J.Z. We won't have to wait long to sample my special grilled chicken breasts. I've also got some corn on the cob cooking in their husks here on the grill, and some big bakers."

I began salivating as the aromas wafted toward me. My eyes glazed over and I could hardly move. Barney barked and I came back to reality. "Oh, my god, that smells wonderful! What kind of sauce are you grilling those breasts in?"

Barry was mopping more sauce on the chicken as he spoke. "It's a mixture of barbecue sauce, a fruit paste of sorts, blended from apricots and peaches, a bit of minced serrano chilies, and the most important ingredient: Southern Comfort."

"Oh, I know it well, the last ingredient, that is."

Barry laughed and said, "You're not alone. But not to worry, the grilling cooks out all the alcohol. Mmmm, it does smell pretty good if I do say so myself."

Barney barked in agreement and looked at Barry with pleading eyes. Barry patted the dog's head and said, "Soon, my friend. Soon."

Soon, indeed. The chicken looked nearly done, and it was tantalizingly covered in a thick orange sauce with chunks of fruit and bits of chilies. I was getting woozy and light-headed looking at all that wonderful food. Barry closed the grill and guided me over to the picnic table. He poured us some lemonade and said, "You indicated that you need some expertise in the area of human psychology. I don't know if I'd go so far as to call myself an *expert*, but I'm certainly willing to assist you in any way possible, especially if it will help Sandy. What is it you need to know?"

"Well, several things really. I should start by explaining what I recently found out about Chris St. James. It's a doozy, and Doc, I don't have to remind you that all of this is very sensitive information."

"I understand. I won't tell a soul. Go on."

I sighed and wondered how I could put it delicately. When no inspiration came, I blurted out, "Chris St. James used to be a man."

Barry smiled and nodded his head, not at all shocked. "Well, of course, that makes so much sense. That explains a lot."

Confused, I asked, "How do you mean?"

"Well, remember when I said that something was 'off' with Chris? This is it! Now, don't get me wrong. I'm not disparaging transsexuals in any way. On the contrary, I believe that there are a certain percentage of people who are born with a gender identity in their brain that doesn't match their physical gender. There are a lot of theories for that, but that's another issue altogether. But you see, when people are socialized to be one gender, like Chris was socialized to be a male, it's not so easy to become a woman. I mean, the operation is simple enough. But undoing all of that socialization is another matter entirely. Even though Chris was, presumably, born believing she should have been a female, she was forced to live as a man. You can't just have an operation and make all of that go away, which is why transsexuals have a very difficult time of it after having the operation."

Barry paused for a few moments, deep in thought, then continued. "And this explains why Chris felt the need to smash her opposition into the ground. She wasn't at all comfortable with who she was, and perhaps even felt inadequate as a woman. And as you've probably observed in life, people who feel inadequate act just the opposite. They treat everyone as inferiors to cover up their own perceived inadequacies."

I immediately thought of Bitchburger. I then told Barry about what Chris had gone through with her father, and how she was forced to leave home and cut all ties. I filled him in on the relationship with Holly Travis, and I also mentioned that Chris and Sandy had "difficulties" in their relationship, sexually speaking, though I didn't go into detail. Barry nodded vigorously and said, "Well, no wonder Chris had such a difficult time confiding in others, and no wonder she didn't trust anyone. It makes perfect sense now. And the sexual problems, well, there's a huge variable there. Many transsexuals go on to have active sex lives. But some have serious difficulties, and, as you can imagine, these difficulties are pronounced when the transsexual is also a homosexual."

"I was hoping you'd enlighten me in that area."

"Oh, yes, it's fascinating." Barry's features lit up like a Christmas tree and he grew very animated. He was clearly in his element. "Let's take the food off the grill first and we can talk while we're eating."

"You'll get no argument from me there." I went inside to retrieve plates and silverware while Barry took the goodies off the grill. I went back in to find butter for the baked potatoes and corn on the cob. Within seconds, we were shoveling the food in with a fervor. "Hey, won't your wife be upset that you're dining with another woman?"

Barry laughed and a stray kernel of buttery corn slid down his chin. "My wife doesn't have a jealous bone in her body."

"Well, if I was straight and you were my husband, I'd be watching you like a guard dog, especially since you can cook like this."

Again the infectious laugh. "She used to, but after all these years, she knows I'm not going anywhere. Elizabeth is a good woman. I hope you can meet her sometime."

"What does she do?"

"She's a doctor, a surgeon, and a very gifted one I might add. I don't see as much of her as I would like, but we make the time we have together count. But enough of this mushy stuff. Back to our previous discussion. As I was saying, if a transsexual is also a homosexual…let me back up for a moment. A certain percentage of the population is homosexual. That's well-documented. So, it's not surprising that a certain percentage of transsexuals are homosexual. You see, people get confused when they talk about sexuality and gender as though they're the same thing. They're not, not at all. It's very simple, really.

Chris was born with a male body, believing she was female, but still attracted to women. Statistically speaking, it's not all that uncommon. But these people are persecuted. Those around them can't understand why someone would have a sex change operation and then lead a gay life. But the person was already gay long before they had the operation. Chris was at least lucky that no one around her knew."

"But someone found out. I'm convinced that this is connected with her murder. If someone found out that the person they loved was a transsexual, could that drive the person to commit murder?"

Between bites, Barry answered, "You mean Sandy. No, as I told you, I just don't see it. If you were asking me this hypothetically, and I didn't know the suspect you were referring to, I would probably say yes. I could see how a person could feel betrayed, and that betrayal might inspire violence of the magnitude seen in this case."

I shoveled in a big bite of baked potato loaded with sour cream and butter. "Now let me ask you this, from a hypothetical standpoint. Is it likely that a person could commit a crime involving extreme violence, and never have another violent outburst again? What I'm asking is this: could this crime be a one-time deal, or is the perpetrator someone who likely exhibits a pattern of violent outbursts?"

Barry wiped butter off his fingers and tossed Barney a hunk of meat. "Anger, violence, emotional outbursts…now you're getting into tricky areas. Nothing is cut and dried. That said, it's entirely possible that this is a one-time deal, as you referred to it. One thing I'm certain of is that the level of violence exhibited in Chris's murder was personal. Someone was outraged. She did something that some lunatic took very personally."

"Would it be possible for someone that enraged to refrain from acting on the rage right away? Could they, for example, wait several months, or even years, before acting on their rage?"

Barry frowned and thought for several moments before replying. "It's been known to happen, yes. It takes a lot of energy to sustain the same level of rage for a long period of time. Consequently, rage, like other strong emotions, ebbs and flows. Sometimes, a person who is enraged with someone else might almost forget about it, and then they see or hear something that sets them off all over again. So yes, it could be quite a while before any action is taken. But at the time the person acts, for whatever reason they have become enraged again, the rage is fresh in their minds, as though the precipitating act just occurred."

"This really is fascinating stuff. Maybe I'll have the attorney I'm working with put you on the payroll. You've been very helpful this evening."

"I'm glad to do it, J.Z. I like spending the evening with someone who truly appreciates my culinary skills."

"Well then, I'm your woman. Once again, this has been an amazing meal."

"Don't take off your feedbag just yet. I made key lime pie for dessert."

My eyes lit up and again, I felt a little woozy. "Oh, Barry, are you sure you're not a lesbian?"

We laughed and went inside to retrieve the pie. "Maybe I should have asked you this earlier, but what kind of shrink...I mean, psychologist, are you?"

Barry grew uncharacteristically silent for a few moments. In a hushed voice he said, "I used to have a very active practice. My cases ran the gamut, from troubled teens to obsessive compulsives. At some point, that barrier psychologists set up between themselves and their patients fell apart for me. It's not that psychologists are cold. It's just that we need to protect ourselves. We need to separate ourselves from all that grief and misery, or we're no good to our patients. Anyway, I was no longer able to do that."

"Why do you think that happened?"

"I don't know. I'd just gone through a pretty difficult time. My best friend killed himself, and I didn't even see it coming. I wondered what kind of psychologist I was if I couldn't even see what was going on with my best friend. I blamed myself for his death. And I guess subconsciously, I made the decision to 'tune in,' as it were, to my patients, so that I didn't let anyone slip through the cracks like I had Dan, my friend. Of course, that wasn't a wise move. I couldn't handle the burden of all that misery for long, and I eventually had what is known in the biz as a nervous breakdown." Barry looked down at the floor in embarrassment. After a few strained moments he continued. "I didn't go back to my practice. I turned it over to a psychologist friend. Now, I volunteer at a couple of local organizations. I counsel kids in crisis, mostly from low income homes. Some are dealing with abuse, others drugs or abandonment. Still others are dealing with sexuality issues." Barry looked at me and mumbled, "Now you know *my* deep, dark secret."

"That's the best you can do, Barry? That's nothin'. I can top that with any one of my drinking stories." I proceeded to tell Barry about the time I got shit-faced and loudly proclaimed my love for a complete stranger at a party. Her boyfriend was not amused. The next day I woke up with a bad haircut and a moustache and goatee drawn in permanent marker. I had no clue what had happened the night before. I later learned that I passed out at the party and the angry boyfriend got out the scissors and marker and went to town.

He laughed until I thought his sides would split. "That's rich, but at least you never did anything to jeopardize your career." It was then that I filled him in on my former career and the Bitchburger fiasco.

Again he laughed heartily. "Okay, I stand corrected. Enough reminiscing. Let's eat some pie." We dug into the pie greedily, though I was uncertain how we managed to wolf down another bite after that huge meal. As we were finishing up, a beautiful woman with long flowing hair meandered into the kitchen, obviously exhausted from the strains of the day. Barry embraced the woman, gave her a peck on the cheek, and introduced us.

"It's nice to meet you, Ms. Cole. Barry told me what a wonderful woman you are, and I was hoping to get the chance to meet you."

She smiled, beamed at Barry, and said, "Please, call me Elizabeth. And let me offer you a bit of advice: don't believe everything Barry tells you. He's been known to lay it on a little thick at times. But he does make a mean key lime pie, doesn't he?"

"As far as I'm concerned, he makes a mean everything. You're a lucky woman."

Elizabeth flashed me another smile and said, "Yeah, I think I'll keep him."

Since they were making googly eyes at each other, I took that as my cue to leave. "Well, I've got some work to get to, so I'll get out of your hair. It was nice meeting you, Elizabeth, and I hope to see you again." She returned the sentiment and Barry insisted on sending me on my way with a care package of chicken and pie. He walked me out to my van and I said, "Elizabeth is lovely. You make a nice couple."

"Thanks. Look, I hope you don't think any less of me now that you know my background. I'm happy to answer any other questions you might have about this case in the future, simply because I want to help Sandy. She's a good person. And by the way, I think you and Sandy make a nice couple."

"How did you know?"

"Just a hunch, that's all."

"Well, that's another story. But as far as your help, I appreciate it, and I know Sandy will too. Please don't ever feel that I think less of you now. That's ridiculous. In fact, I may think more of you because it takes a lot of courage to admit something like that. I've had my share of dark moments, too. Everyone has. It's just that most people don't own up to them. Besides, what's important is that you're doing good work now, work that is helping others. You're a nice guy, Barry. But more importantly, you're one helluva chef."

Barry smiled and gave me a bear hug. He waved at me from the driveway as I was pulling away. I think I'd just bonded for life with that big lug of a guy over key lime pie. I guess as bondings go, that wasn't a bad way to do it. I hoped Sam wouldn't be jealous.

East Coast Ties and West Coast Lies

I thought it might be wise to check in with Slick and bring her up to date on my most recent interviews, as well as Barry's take on things. I called her from my cell phone to make sure that she was still in the office, which she was, grouchy as ever. As I pulled into the parking lot, I saw Irma leaving the office for the day. I grinned and asked, "Hot date, Irma?"

She frowned and replied, "Not unless you think havin' your hemorrhoids scraped is a hot date, and if you do, I feel powerful sorry for you, missy."

It's not often that I'm rendered speechless. But, there I was, standing in the middle of the parking lot, with no idea how I should reply. Nothing came to me, so I just walked away. As I was shuffling into Slick's office, I couldn't help but wonder if a hemorrhoid scraping was what it sounded like. Was the goal of such a procedure to scrape something off of the hemorrhoid (ugh!), or to actually scrape the rhoid for some purpose, perhaps to make it smaller? Ouch! Having an inquisitive mind often has its drawbacks.

Slick was in her office with her feet propped up on her desk, reading some legal treatise. "What's a hemorrhoid scraping, anyway?"

"That's the sound your ass makes when it hits the chair. How the hell should I know what a hemorrhoid scraping is, and where do you come up with these ridiculous questions?"

"Well, I just saw Irma…"

"Oh, Irma…please, don't get me started. That woman is gonna be the death of me yet. You know that she volunteered me to be a guest speaker at some local gathering of Republican women. Now what the hell am I going to say to a bunch of tight-assed, gun-totin', radical right-wingers?"

"Well, Slick, I think that might be a bit of a generalization, but…"

"Ok, ok. But what am I gonna do?"

"Call and cancel if you don't want to do it."

An evil gleam appeared in Slick's eyes. "On the other hand, I would have a captive audience of conservatives. Think of the havoc I could wreck with my fiery, liberal rhetoric. Why, I could…"

"Slick, I don't mean to interrupt your delusions of grandeur, but could we talk about the case for a few minutes?"

Slick floated back down to Earth and reluctantly dug out a legal pad on which to make notes. "Sure, kid. Fire away."

"Well, within the past couple of days, I've spoken with three possible suspects, two of whom are pretty interesting. I also enlisted the help of St. James's neighbor, Barry Cole. He was the one who found the body. He's a psychologist, and I ran a few things by him for his input. He's been very helpful. Anyway, you probably know two of the people I spoke with: Will Beaton and Michelle Knight."

Slick crowed and slapped her pencil down on the desk. "Beaton…what an incompetent ninny! Every time I want a laugh, I pull out one of his motion responses. Lordy, that fool couldn't write a coherent sentence to save his soul. And what a perv! He's put the moves on every female attorney I can think of, even Chris St. James."

"So that's why she hated him, huh?"

"Well, that and the fact that he was incompetent. She had no tolerance for incompetence."

"Beaton has an alibi for the night of the murder, and I didn't get the sense that he was that annoyed with St. James's attempts to humiliate him."

"Beaton doesn't have the balls to kill anyone, that's for sure. But Michelle Knight, now she's a different story."

"Yeah, she admitted that she hated St. James enough to kill her, and she doesn't have an alibi for that night."

Slick stared at the ceiling and scrunched up her face in thought.

"I've no doubt that Knight hated Chris, and maybe she even fantasized and doing away with her. But thinking about killing someone and actually doing it are very different things. Plus, by all accounts, Knight has been very busy since she left the practice, getting her insurance license, finding a job, going to training classes, and building up a clientele. Do you think she could do all that and dig into Chris's background at the same time? I mean, we are still assuming that the person who killed Chris was the same one who threatened her, aren't we?"

"Absolutely. But I got the feeling that Michelle Knight is a very resourceful woman. I think she could keep a lot of balls in the air at the same time and not drop any of them. Correct me if I'm wrong."

"No, you're right about that, I admit. But, I guess I'm having a little trouble picturing Knight as a cold-blooded killer. I just can't see it."

"Well, that's not a particularly logical conclusion. While I can't say that I have any strong feeling one way or the other about Knight, I think she's a very viable suspect."

"Oh, I agree, despite my inability to picture her as a killer. So who's the third person you interviewed?"

I filled Slick in on Blaine Darrow's background and gave her a rundown of the interview. "I'd have to say that he's a strong suspect. He has no alibi and he got very nervous and shifty when I started asking him where he stopped for a bite to eat on the night of the murder. Plus, it's clear that he inherited some money from his cousin, but I can't confirm how much. It's entirely possible that some of that money came from blackmailing Chris. Of the three, he clearly has the strongest motive. I mean, he lost everything, and he blamed Chris for it. I could see the hatred still burning in his eyes. It was eerie, Slick." We were silent for a few moments, and then I remembered something else. "Oh, and he has long brown hair, too."

"So does half the county, kid. We don't know that those hairs belonged to the killer. At any rate, I agree that Darrow is, thus far, our strongest suspect. But let's not forget our Pennsylvania suspects: Mr. Hollingsworth and Ms. Travis."

"Right, but I like Darrow at this point. I'd see Travis as a more viable suspect if she knew anything about Chris's new life. But as far as I can see, she had no way of knowing."

"I'm just saying, let's not count them out just yet. Anyway, what did this shrink have to add to the mix?"

I told her about my lengthy conversation with Barry, leaving out the part about the nervous breakdown. I figured Barry told me that in confidence, and I didn't see any reason to pass the information along to Slick. When I had finished filling her in, Slick was oddly silent, and she was staring at a spot on the wall, as if entranced. "Slick?"

"Huh? Oh, sorry. When you were telling me what Dr. Cole had to say about transsexuals, I…um, I started feeling a little guilty for not reaching out to Chris St. James. I knew she didn't have any friends, but I never went out of my way to talk to her, or to ask her to lunch, like I do with a lot of the criminal defense attorneys here in town."

"Slick, I don't think a couple of ham on rye sandwiches would have fostered any bond between you and St. James. Chris pushed anyone who tried to get close away, including Sandy."

"I know, but I'd like to be able to say that I tried." Lest anyone think she's an old softie, Slick cleared her throat and put on her best all-business face. "Well, let me bring you up to speed on what I know. The coroner has confirmed that the time of death was between 6 and 8 p.m., so the original estimate was right on the money. Chris's financial records are in the hands of our forensic accountant as we speak. I took a look at them, and nothing jumped out and bit me on the ass, but feel free to have a look if you like. The accountant is John Blalock and he's just around the corner. Still waiting for the computer files, but those should be here shortly. I'm working on a very comprehensive motion to suppress right now, hoping that I can get some of the evidence tossed out. I think there may be some Miranda issues, at the very least. I'll keep you apprised of my progress on the motion. Other than that, we're still exchanging discovery."

I said goodbye and started on my long trek back home. On the way, I decided it might be a good idea to talk to St. James's former gardener. He wasn't there at the time of the murder, but he may have noticed someone lurking around the place, or he may have overheard St. James mention the name of the person threatening her. It was worth a shot anyway. I'd give him a call in the morning.

I was dead tired when I got home and went straight to bed with the kitties. I fell fast asleep in no time. However, I wasn't so tired that I didn't hear the sound of breaking glass downstairs at just after 2 a.m.

I bolted out of bed, and Corey and Tasha looked like your standard Halloween cats: backs arched, ample fur standing on end. I grabbed my 9mm out of the nightstand and waited quietly to see if I could detect other sounds that would help me locate the intruder. I heard nothing. Slowly, I crept down the stairs, my heart pounding and beads of cold perspiration rolling down my back. Again, I waited at the bottom of the stairs for any sounds. I heard something in the kitchen, but I couldn't make out what it was. I crept slowly in that direction, and when I got to the doorway, I could see a figure moving. "Freeze! Don't move a muscle or I'll splatter your brains all over the place. I mean it." With my right hand holding the pistol, I inched forward and used my left hand to flick on the light switch.

There was Ethel in her nightgown, standing over a shattered coffee mug. She was crying, but through her tears she said, "Earl and I had a big fight, Helga. I just came over for some coffee. I'm sorry I broke your coffee cup. I'll clean it up."

As the tension left my body, my limbs began to feel rubbery. The back of my t-shirt was wet, and I was getting chilled. "It's okay, Ethel. You sit down, and I'll clean up the mess." Since I was wide awake now, I offered to make us some coffee and Ethel proceeded to tell me about her "fight" with Earl. Apparently, Ethel told Cecelia that she could go to the prom with Juan Esteban. Earl was furious, not because he had any particular animosity for Hispanics, but because he was always concerned with what other people might think. Earl forbade Cecelia to go to the prom with Juan. Knowing that Earl was wrong, Ethel told Earl that she would not have conjugal relations with him until he changed his "fool" mind. This sent Earl, a rather frisky devil, over the edge. When she was done relating the details to me, Ethel looked at me and said, with tears in her eyes, "You think I'm right, don't you, Helga?"

"Well, sure. I think Cecelia should be able to go to the prom with whoever she chooses, and I hear that Juan is a sweet boy. But maybe your tactics are a little harsh."

Ethel cackled through her tears and said, "Oh, believe me, Helga, the only way to get through to Earl is to hit him where it hurts. Mark my words, by tomorrow, he'll be singin' a whole different tune."

"I guess you know best."

At that moment, a frantic Cecelia knocked on the back door. I motioned her in and she rushed over and hugged Ethel. Cecelia started crying and said, "I got up to go to the bathroom, and I noticed Mama wasn't in her room. I got so worried, and then I noticed your lights on. I was hoping she was here." Cecelia turned to me and continued, "I'm so sorry about this."

"Don't worry about it. We've been drinking coffee and reminiscing."

"I guess I'm gonna have to check into some kind of security system to let me know when she leaves the house in the middle of the night. She's a giant pain in the rear, but I love her, and I'd hate for anything to happen to her. C'mon, Mama, let's get you back in bed." Cecelia hugged me and thanked me profusely.

"Hey, Cecelia? Did you go to the prom with Juan Esteban?"

Cecelia blushed and a grin spread across her face. "Oh my gosh, I haven't thought about that in years! Yes, I went with Juan. He was a handsome boy, and so polite. Daddy was dead set against the idea at first. But something happened to change his mind real fast. He even drove us to the prom."

Something happened, all right. I locked up and smiled to myself. I crawled back into bed with the kitties, and after what seemed like a lot of tossing and turning, we were all fast asleep once again. We received no further night visitors, unless you count the phantom visitors Corey frequently receives, the ones that make her paws twitch and her whiskers wiggle.

I awoke the next morning feeling less than refreshed. The nighttime visitor had taken her toll, or, more likely, the initial tension she inspired kept me from getting a restful night's sleep. It would probably take two doses of espresso to get me going today. After fortifying myself with pancakes and caffeine, I flipped through my notes to locate the name of St. James's former gardener. I guessed he was Sandy's gardener now, though I didn't know if he was still taking care of the place. I got his number through directory assistance and phoned him. "Hello. Is this Alvin Butterworth?"

"Yes. Who's calling?"

"This is J.Z. Mackenzie and I'm looking into the murder of your former employer, Chris St. James. I was wondering if you'd be willing to speak with me today?"

"Miss Sandy didn't do it. I don't know what I can tell you that will be of any use, but if it will help Miss Sandy, I'm glad to do it."

He indicated that he would be home all day and that I could drop by anytime. He said he was still looking after the place, but only once a week now. Since I had to make the trek to Kingston, I might as well see if I could line up some other interviews for the day. I thumbed through my notes from the meeting with Kara Welsh for possible candidates. I still hadn't interviewed Bill and Jackie Freeman, the couple who lost their daughter, son-in-law, and four grandkids to a drunk driver, for whom St. James managed to obtain a favorable verdict. Kara told me they lived in Copperville, which is about midway between Cloverdale and Kingston. I located a Bill Freeman in the phone book and dialed the number. A raspy voice answered the phone. After confirming that the voice belonged to Mr. Freeman, I told him who I was and what I was investigating. In a gruff voice, he said, "Nobody should be going to jail for that *crime*. Instead, somebody should be gettin' a medal for doin' away with that piece of trash."

"Yes, well…my goal is to ensure that the guilty person goes to jail for this crime, and I'm sure that an upstanding citizen like yourself would want to assist in that endeavor. Right?"

Freeman hooted and replied, "Nobody did that for my daughter and her family. I sure as shit ain't gonna help anybody else! Besides, there's no 'justice' in the so-called justice system. It's all a waste of time. I ain't interested in helping you. Don't call me again!" With that, Freeman slammed down the phone. I guess that was that.

I went upstairs to get dressed and when I was almost done, the phone rang. It was Jackie Freeman. "Is this the private investigator?"

"Yes, it is."

"You sure got Bill all riled up. He went outside to tend to the livestock. We have one of those new-fangled Caller ID boxes, and I used it to find your number. Look, I've made peace with what happened to us, but Bill never will. If I can answer some questions for you, I will. I don't want someone going to jail who isn't guilty. I'm going shopping in Kingston today. I can meet you somewhere to talk if you like."

"That would be great. I'll buy you lunch at Chez Meatball on Market Street. Say 1:30?"

"That's fine. I'll see you there."

I thanked her and hung up the phone. Now I would have to hustle to make it to Kingston by 1:30, especially since I wanted to generate a few reports off the computer before I left. I ran the usual checks on the Freemans: credit, criminal and civil litigation, though I felt somewhat guilty since Ms. Freeman had been so nice to me. There were no criminal charges against either of them, and no credit problems. They were, however, involved in a civil action against Buddy Dukes, the drunk driver who wiped out their family. I wasn't particularly interested in that and I'd stay away from the topic unless Jackie Freeman brought it up.

I hurriedly finished getting ready, said goodbye to my furry friends, and flew out the door. If I stepped on it, I'd make it just in time. As luck would have it, the patron goddesses of speed and convenient parking were with me. I made it there with five minutes to spare and as I was pulling up to the restaurant, a car was just leaving one of the few parking spots in front of the Italian eatery. *I must be living right.* Maybe it was all the patience I showed for Ethel, or the extra treats I gave to Corey and Tasha.

I had neglected to ask Ms. Freeman what she looked like, and I quickly regretted this oversight since the place was packed. I spotted a woman at a table for two near the rear of the restaurant and she seemed to be scanning the place, apparently looking for someone. I approached and asked "Are you Jackie Freeman?"

"Yes. J.Z. Mackenzie?" She was a frail, conservative-looking woman in her early 60's, attired in a simple summer dress with a pastel print. She wore thick glasses that made her eyes look huge.

"That's me. I hope you haven't been waiting long."

"Oh, no. I just got here, and I started looking at the menu. I love Italian food, but Bill can't tolerate it." She leaned close to me and whispered, "It gives him gas."

"I see. Well, everything here is great. I think I'll have the three cheese ravioli and a salad. How 'bout you?"

Jackie scanned the menu intently and finally decided. "I believe I'd like the lasagna and a bowl of minestrone."

We placed our orders and munched on garlic bread. As soon as it seemed polite to begin the questioning, I said, "Tell me about your ordeal with Dukes. What I'm particularly interested in is your impression of how St. James handled the case."

"I don't know how this will help you catch a murderer, but all right. You probably already know what happened to my…daughter and her family. I'd rather not rehash that. I didn't really understand all the legal wrangling, but if I recall, St. James managed to get some of the evidence…oh, darn it, what's the word?"

"Suppressed?"

"Yes, that's it—suppressed. I think it might have been some statements Dukes made after the accident, and the breath test results, or something along those lines, that were…suppressed. Anyway, since the district attorney trying the case couldn't mention those things to the jury, Dukes didn't get convicted. He got off scot-free."

Jackie went silent, so I tried to prod her along. "Could you describe Bill's reaction?"

"We were both outraged, naturally. But like I said, after a while I made peace with it. You have to, or you're consumed with rage and hatred. I can't say I'll ever forgive Mr. Dukes, but I don't waste my time hating the man. He just isn't worth that kind of energy. But Bill…well, that's another matter. He's a different man now, completely consumed by feelings of guilt, hatred, and dark emotions. He's very moody and difficult to get along with. Not like the Bill I married at all."

"You said he's consumed with guilt. Why guilt?"

Jackie looked down at her lap and when she looked at me again, I could see she was close to tears. "Because the night it happened, my daughter, Delia, and her family were driving home from our house after visiting for the day. They wanted to leave earlier to get the kids home to bed, but Bill insisted that they stay and finish watching the movie. He blamed himself—said that if it wasn't for him, they would have been safely home long before Dukes got out on the highway."

"That must be a terrible burden for him to live with. But tell me, did you or Bill have any feelings of animosity for St. James as a result of the verdict?"

"Sure, lots of animosity. We even sent her a threatening note. Just to put a scare into her, you know. But after a time, I realized that she was just doing her job, and I let go of those feelings."

"But Bill didn't?"

"Oh, no. He wouldn't let go. When he heard that St. James was murdered, he was happy as a lark. Happiest I've seen him in a long while. I thought it was shameful taking such pleasure in someone else's pain. In fact, I remember him saying 'One down, one to go' right after her death."

"Meaning Dukes?"

"Yep. Bill's suing Mr. Dukes. I guess technically we both are, but I don't want any part of it. It's his way of tormenting the man. I wish he'd just move on with life and let the past go."

Our soup and salad came and we took a breather from the conversation to enjoy the first course. Jackie was a sweet woman, gentle and naïve in some ways. It was clear that she didn't understand that I was questioning her to determine if she, or more likely, Bill, had any involvement in St. James's death, and I felt guilty for taking advantage of her naïveté. When we'd polished off the first course and our dishes had been whisked away, Jackie continued. "I apologize for the way Bill treated you on the phone this morning. He was very rude."

"That's ok. Don't worry about it."

"No, it's not ok, and it's not something the Bill I married would have done. He was such a gentle, happy, good-natured man until this happened. I met Bill when we were both quite young. He came out here to earn enough money to start a ranch. That had always been his dream. He had an uncle who lived out here and promised to give Bill a job."

"Where did Bill move from?"

"Greensboro, Pennsylvania. He grew up there."

A cold shiver ran down my spine. "Is that anywhere near Springfield, Pennsylvania?"

"Why, yes. It's just a hop, skip and a jump from Greensboro. Are you from there?"

My heart was racing. "No…I have some friends there. Has Bill been back to Pennsylvania since your daughter's accident?"

"How did you know that? Bill's made a couple trips back there since then. His brother, Jim Ed, fell ill and Bill had to help out with Jim Ed's business. I had to stay here and take care of the ranch. Then, about six months ago, he went back to help move his ma into a retirement home. That stubborn old biddy is almost 90 years old, and thinks she can still take care of herself. It's easy to see where Bill gets his stubborn streak."

"Did Bill act…funny when he came back from this last trip? Or did he mention finding out something while he was away?"

Suddenly, a light clicked on inside Jackie's white-haired head. "Say, what's this all got to do with St. James, anyway? You don't think my Bill had anything to do with her death, do you?"

Luckily, I was given a few moments to think of an answer, as our food appeared and the waiter offered us Parmesan cheese and more bread. When he finally left, I said, "No, of course not. It's just that St. James was also from Pennsylvania, and Bill may have stumbled across some information about her, the same information that the killer stumbled across." What a lame explanation. This was never going to work.

Jackie crinkled her nose, as if getting a whiff of shit, and said, "Oh, ok then. I just want you to understand that my Bill would never do such a thing. But anyway, no, I don't remember him acting funny, and if he inadvertently found out something important, he didn't tell me anything about it."

"Now, Ms. Freeman…"

"Please, call me Jackie."

"Okay, Jackie. I believe you when you say that Bill didn't murder Chris St. James. I really do. I mean, a woman couldn't be married to a man her whole life, and not know if he killed someone. Am I right?"

"Absolutely."

"But, you know how pesky the police can be, and they certainly don't appreciate women's intuition. They'll want to know where Bill was on the night of the murder, May 12th. Do you remember where he was?"

She looked down momentarily and mumbled, "He was gone."

"Gone?"

"Yes. Like I said, Bill's not the same man. Every once in a while, he takes off on a bender and doesn't come home for a day or two. Bill left the afternoon of the 12th and I didn't see him until the following evening. I'm tryin' to get him some help, but he's fightin' me every step of the way."

"I understand. So, you have no idea where Bill was during that time?"

"No, can't say that I do. Sorry."

I tried to talk her into staying for dessert, but she wanted to get back to her shopping. I felt bad about tricking her into setting her husband up as a prime suspect in St. James's murder. As I nibbled at the exquisite cherry cheesecake in front of me, I pondered what Jackie had told me. Was it possible that Bill Freeman set out to dig up some dirt on St. James, and he stumbled across the same information I had recently discovered? How would he have learned where Chris was from?

I supposed that Chris might have let the name of her hometown slip to more than one person. Did his remark "One down, and one to go" after Chris's death signify involvement on his part, or simply glee and wishful thinking? It's clear that Bill Freeman had the motive and opportunity to do the dirty deed, but did he? More questions to answer.

I located Alvin Butterworth's modest home on the edge of town. He was sitting in a rocking chair on the front porch reading the newspaper as I pulled up. He had white hair, but it was difficult to estimate his age, since he was a sturdy, muscular man. His skin was tanned and somewhat leathery. We exchanged pleasantries and he offered me a cold drink. When we were both settled in, I asked, "In the weeks and days before the murder, did you notice any strange vehicles in the neighborhood, or any strangers hanging around?"

He thought for a few moments before responding. "No. But then, I can't say that I paid a lot of attention to the various comings and goings in the neighborhood. Maintaining that huge yard, the shrubbery, trees, and flowering plants was hard work. I really didn't have time to keep tabs on people. St. James was nice enough, but she could be demanding at times. I pretty much kept my nose to the grindstone, if you know what I mean."

"Sure. Were you on friendly terms with St. James? I mean, did she talk to you at all?"

"Well now, I was hired help, and that was always clear to me. It was different with Miss Sandy. She would come outside and carry on a conversation with me once in a while. But not St. James. She was all business. Now, don't get me wrong, I'm not speaking ill of the dead. For the most part, she left me alone and let me do my job, and she paid me good money. You can't tell it by looking at this old shack, but I've got a tidy sum of money saved up thanks to her. I could have retired a long time ago, but I enjoy working outdoors. Keeps me young."

And will probably give you skin cancer, but I kept that to myself. "Did you ever overhear any conversations in which St. James seemed upset, or scared?"

He frowned at me and asked, "What are you implying? Do you think I eavesdropped on my employer? Is that it?"

"No, I didn't say that. Of course you wouldn't *intentionally* listen to one of St. James's conversations. But maybe you just happened to be somewhere, and you couldn't help but overhear part of a conversation."

"Like I said, I was always busy trimming, mowing, fertilizing, or planting something. I didn't have time to be listening in on other people's conversations. I never even went inside that house. I used the little gardener's shack out back. I kept my supplies there, and it had a little refrigerator where I could keep my lunch and cold drinks. It even had a little bathroom. So I had no need to even go near the house, which suited me just fine."

He seemed a little defensive and I wondered why. When in doubt, ask. "If you don't mind me saying, you seem a little angry. Did I say something that offended you?"

He shook his head and looked at me. "No, no. Nothin' like that. I've just got some things, on my mind, that's all."

I finished my drink and went on my way. That was odd. Something was definitely troubling the man. I had no reason to suspect that he was involved in the murder of his employer, but maybe he knew something, something that he didn't want to share.

The Free Press & Preservative-Free Foods

I stopped by Slick's office and filled her in on the day's events before leaving town. She seemed excited when I told her about Bill Freeman's trips to Pennsylvania, though we both agreed that it could be a coincidence. But still, it was something.

I spent a quiet evening with the kitties and got a good night's rest, which was welcome after last night's adrenaline rush. Not that all adrenaline rushes in the middle of the night are bad, mind you. When I awoke the next morning, I called Matt Chambers at the local newspaper, *The Cloverdale Courier*. Matt used to be a big-time reporter in New York City. He began his career in Washington, D.C., where he accidentally uncovered a rather sordid affair between a well-known former senator and a dominatrix. The dominatrix would dress the senator up in a diaper and spank him until he told her government secrets, which, unbeknownst to the senator, the dominatrix would sell to the highest bidder.

Matt was a young reporter when he uncovered this story, and he was catapulted from a nobody to the most sought-after reporter in the country. He felt rather guilty about the instant fame, since he had merely stumbled onto the story, but he rode the wave of fame, nonetheless. He was lured to New York City by a salary offer that seemed astronomical to him at the time. There, Matt went on to prove himself a capable, tenacious reporter, perhaps too tenacious. One day, he woke up, looked at himself in the mirror, and didn't like what he saw: somebody who would intrude upon another person's grief and suffering just to get a story. So Matt packed up his stuff and left New York City, eventually landing in our little town, writing about such scintillating topics as the county fair, the annual spelling bee, and Nate Garston's appearance on the TV show *Cops* when he visited Seattle last year.

Matt was an interesting guy with a million stories to tell. He and I probably would be friends, rather than just acquaintances, except for two issues. First, he was an incredibly frenetic person, which I found both annoying and exhausting. He always seemed to be doing several things at once, a throwback, I guess, to his days as an ace reporter in the big city. Second, he was hopelessly in love with Sam, and every time I saw Matt, he asked a plethora of questions about her.

I guess I was partly to blame. I'd thrown the two of them together at a party, thinking that this was a friendship match made in heaven: a reporter who has the scoop on everybody who's anybody, and a hopeless gossip. Sam prefers to be called an "informed" citizen, rather than a gossip, however. Anyway, I introduced them at this party, neglecting, of course, to say "Matt, meet my lesbian friend, Sam," or some such nonsense. There was really no way for him to know. Nealy was out of town on a photo shoot, and Sam forgot to wear her shirt that says "I dig chicks." Frankly, Matt wouldn't have picked up on even the most blatant hints. One look at Sam and he was gone, completely ga-ga over this adorable redhead. He spent the rest of the evening following her around like a puppy dog, laughing at even her most inane comments. It was truly pathetic, and obvious to everyone there, except Sam, that we had a little problem brewing.

The little problem reached a full boil three days later when Matt showed up on my doorstep and announced that he was in love with Sam and fully intended to make her his wife. Unbeknownst to Matt, Sam and Nealy were sitting in the next room, and the rather abrupt announcement of Sam's impending nuptials took Nealy somewhat by surprise, understandably. This is the only occasion on which I've seen Nealy, our subdued, quiet, Ninja-like Nealy, become loquacious and extremely animated. I think she even used some words that I didn't recognize (not an easy feat), and suggested that Matt do some things that, to my knowledge, are not humanly possible. Though I admit that my knowledge of male physiology is quite limited. If I hadn't stepped between them, we would have had an estrogen/testosterone explosion. Any reasonable person would have immediately realized the hopelessness of pursuing such an ill-fated romance. But no one has ever accused Matt of being reasonable.

Matt wasn't in the office yet, but his pre-recorded message indicated that he expected to be in by 10 a.m. That gave me just enough time to eat a quick breakfast, shower, and dress. I arrived at the *Courier* offices just after 10, and I saw Matt happily tapping out a story on his computer. He saw me and motioned me back to his desk. "Workin' on a story about local graft and corruption?"

Matt laughed and replied, "Close, but no cigar. It's a story about Fred Zellwiger's claim that the arthritis in his big toe is a predictor of downturns in the stock market."

I looked at Matt blankly, expecting him to laugh and tell me it was a joke, but he didn't. "You're serious, aren't you?"

"Yep."

Trying to suppress a laugh, I asked, "You don't really believe that, do you?"

"No, but half the county does. So, I figured it deserved a write-up. In case you're interested, Fred's toe is feeling good this week."

"Thanks, but I'm not really interested in Fred's big toe."

"I didn't think so. What brings you down here, besides my handsome face and charming manner?"

"I'm interested in the series of articles you did on the mob not too long before you left New York. I need to pick your brain, if that's ok."

"Pick away." Matt was still typing, and at the same time, he was madly tapping his left foot, bobbing his head to some tune only he could hear, and eating a jelly donut. Just watching him made me tired.

"Well, you've heard about the murder of Chris St. James, no doubt. I've learned recently that she was doing some legal work for the mob in Los Angeles. I guess things went smoothly at first. Then, she was asked to do things that required her to bend the ethical rules more than she liked, so she balked and refused to do any more work for them. The mob wanted her back badly, and I guess they were trying to strong-arm her into coming back to the dark side before she was killed.

There's been some suggestion that the mob may be behind her death. What do you think?" I relayed the details of St. James's murder to Matt, as well as other pertinent information.

Matt thought for a few moments before replying, but was still typing, eating and tapping. "This isn't the 1950's, J.Z. Don't get me wrong, mob executions still happen occasionally. But they're usually designed to make some kind of statement. I can't see the mob taking the time to whack some attorney who just decided she didn't want to play ball anymore. Let's face it, attorneys are a dime a dozen. Why, we've got three law schools right here in Oregon, churning out a bumper crop of baby legal beagles each year."

"Yes, but these new lawyers can't offer the mob the kind of skill and expertise that St. James could offer them."

"That's true. But I doubt that it was her skill they were interested in. St. James was the kind of big gun you could bring into the courtroom and make the other side quake in their boots. I'm sure she was able to cut some sweet deals for them just on her reputation alone. Plus, she lent the mob a certain air of credibility. I think that's why they wanted her so badly. The mob has a lot of capable attorneys on their payroll, but not many who are well known and widely respected. So, I'm not surprised that the mob would use strong-arm tactics to try to get St. James back. But kill her? No, I don't think so."

"What makes you so sure?"

"Well, the point of my series of articles about the mob was to show that the modern mob is different from the mob of yore. I'm not saying that today's mob is a kinder, gentler one. But, I am saying that today's mob has learned the value of keeping a low profile, when possible. They're not going to execute someone unless they feel there are no other options. You see, every time they create waves, the feds, due to public pressure, start sniffing around. Inevitably, the feds will dig up some tax fraud, or similar charges, and the mob is back in court. If they lay low, the feds leave them alone and everybody's happy. St. James's decision to stop working for the mob simply wasn't important enough for the mob to create waves. Instead, they'd simply find some other well-known, respected attorney to do their bidding. This might take time, but so what."

Matt finished typing and sent his article to the printer. He poured us both a cup of coffee, which he clearly didn't need, and sat back down at his desk. After taking a big gulp of caffeine, he began tapping out a rhythm with his pencil. "Besides, the way she was killed—it's all wrong for a mob hit. They don't decapitate people, they shoot 'em. I once did a series of articles on criminal profiling. I got to go to Quantico and I talked to some of the best FBI profilers in the business. From what I learned, I can tell you that the person who did this to St. James did it for very personal reasons. This wasn't about some business relationship gone bad. This was about somebody who felt incredibly wronged by St. James."

"That's what I've felt all along, but I wanted to run it past you to get your take on things. I appreciate your time, Matt."

He was now tapping his fingers on his desktop and scribbling some notes on an article. He looked up from his work for a moment and said, "No problem. By the way, how's Sam?"

I flashed him a disapproving look, the kind that used to work so well for my mom. "Matt, we've been over this before. Sam's a lesbian, and she's very happy with Nealy. Even if she wasn't happy with Nealy, she wouldn't be interested in you. It's nothing personal, really, just the little matter of your gender."

"I take issue with the use of the term 'little' in reference to my gender." For a moment, Matt ceased all his harried activity and looked at me with cow eyes. "I can't help it, you know. I…I love her."

I shook my head and replied, "Matt, you're a great guy. You should try focusing your attention on an attainable goal. How 'bout Sally Houghton? She's cute, bright, energetic and cheerful. And most importantly, she's straight, and she's not paired up with anyone yet."

Matt chuckled and said, "Yes, I know. There's a reason she's not paired up with anyone."

"Oh?"

"She has genital warts."

"You're making that up."

"No, I'm not! Why do you think all the guys in town avoid her like the plague? And didn't you hear about that slick Baptist preacher over in Grove County leaving town in a hurry?"

"No."

Matt looked at me in amazement. "You really are out of the loop, aren't you? That old fart preacher's pecker was so covered in warts it was almost unrecognizable. He tried to convince his wife that the warts were sent by the Devil, because he was doing such a bang-up job for the Lord. He was doin' a bang-up job, all right, but I don't think the Lord was involved. His wife didn't fall for it, and, in fact, went after the wart-ridden pecker with a pair of scissors. The preacher took off and hasn't been heard from since."

"Ok, so maybe Sally Houghton isn't a wise choice. But…"

Matt put his hand on my shoulder and said, "I know, I know. I appreciate your concern. But I'm not giving up hope just yet."

"You're wasting your time."

"Yeah, but it's my time to waste."

I thanked Matt again for his time and left him to his work, while I returned home to do the same. Poor Matt. I hope he doesn't waste his whole life pining over Sam. Maybe the right woman would calm some of his frenetic energy, or at least redirect it into something useful, like sex.

I sensed that Matt's conclusions about the mob were correct, especially since his conclusions reaffirmed my own instincts. A mob hit was a possibility, but it was a long shot, as Matt indicated. I'd keep the theory on the back burner, but focus on more likely scenarios. Speaking of more likely scenarios, it was about time for me to have a talk with Daryl Torrington, brother of the notorious serial killer, Wilson Torrington. Kara Welsh indicated in our conversation that Daryl Torrington had vowed revenge against St. James because she failed to summon up her usual legal legerdemain on behalf of his brother. Kara thought Daryl, who himself had a criminal history, was employed by a construction company in Lincoln, a small town just east of Cloverdale.

Luckily, there were only two construction companies in Lincoln and I hit pay dirt on my second call. I learned that Daryl Torrington was still employed by the Lederlee Construction Company, but the secretary wouldn't give me his home number. In a sweet but hesitant voice, she asked, "Honey, why do you want to talk to Daryl, anyway?"

"I'm a private investigator and I'm looking into a murder. I just need to ask Mr. Torrington a few questions."

"Well, if I was you, I wouldn't try to meet him alone. He has a bad temper, and he wouldn't be workin' here except that his sister, a real sweet girl, is married to Mr. Lederlee, the owner. Daryl is a dangerous man, and I understand he's an ex-con."

"Well, I appreciate your concern for my safety, but I really do need to speak with him."

"You could go talk to him at the job site."

"Will Daryl's boss let him stop work to talk to me?"

I heard a little giggle on the other end of the line. "He will if I tell him to. Daryl's foreman, Joey Deitz, is my son. I'll call and arrange it. They're working over on Kepplinger Street on that new apartment building. They should be there until four or so."

"Hey, thanks. I appreciate that. You've been very helpful."

"My pleasure. Say, you sound about my son Joey's age. He's single, you know."

"I'll keep that in mind."

I had Sam trying to fix me up with every woman she meets, and now Joey Deitz's mom was trying to fix me up with her son. When would it end? Speaking of Sam, I knew I was in trouble. She'd left me several angry messages since my return from Pennsylvania. She was peeved that I hadn't stopped by or called to chat with her, and, no doubt, bring her up to date on the investigation. I felt a little guilty, but I had been getting home late every night from Kingston, and there was just no time. Since it looked like my day was going to be spent in Cloverdale, I thought I'd better try to smooth Sam's rumpled feathers while I had a chance.

While I was still thinking about it, I called Sam at work to see if she was free for lunch. She was, though I detected a "you should have called sooner" edge to her voice. We agreed to meet for lunch at The Psychedelic Alfalfa Sprout, a local restaurant owned and managed by vegetarian, lesbian, modern-day hippies. The atmosphere was…different, but the food was fabulous and always fresh.

That left me just enough time to run criminal background reports on both Daryl and Wilson Torrington. I also ran a credit report on Daryl, just in case. I thought the printer would never stop spewing out paper; the respective criminal histories of the Brothers Torrington went on and on. It was simply amazing. Wilson had, indeed, been a very bad boy. He had been convicted of eight counts of murder in the first degree (this was the trial that St. James lost), rape, armed robbery, assault, and burglary. While Daryl hadn't been convicted of any murders, his criminal history was, nonetheless, quite colorful. Daryl had a history of assault, armed robbery, DUI, burglary, criminal mischief, menacing, criminal harassment, and…extortion. That last little bit of information piqued my interest. Here was a guy well versed in the art of blackmail, not to mention harassment and menacing, a lovely delinquent Triple Crown.

Daryl's credit report, on the other hand, turned up nothing of interest. As I was reviewing the mundane report, I was trying, in vain, to remember details of Wilson Torrington's killing spree. I remembered that he killed eight women in southern Oregon, but I couldn't remember the time frame, or how he had killed them. I didn't know if it was important, but I hopped on the Internet and searched for articles on Wilson Torrington. My search returned several hits and I clicked on one. As I scanned the article, the details came rushing back. Torrington had slashed his victims with a large hunting knife, and the last victim, Sheila Patterson, was nearly…oh god…decapitated. I almost fell out of my chair! Did Daryl kill St. James in the same manner, as a sort of deranged homage to his brother? I felt sick, and I was beginning to think that Joey Deitz's mom was right—Daryl Torrington was a very dangerous man, whom I suddenly didn't want the pleasure of meeting.

I tried calling Slick, but she was in court. Damn! I wanted her input, and I wanted it now. What if Daryl was the killer? Sure, I'd be ok meeting with him in broad daylight with other people around. But what about later, when I was home, all alone, in the dark with my two defenseless kitties? What if he thought I was getting too close to the truth? *Calm down, Mackenzie. You're getting hysterical. You're a strong, capable woman, fully self-sufficient, and don't forget, you've got a gun!*

On jelly legs, I left to keep my lunch date with Sam. Sam was already seated inside the restaurant waiting for me, and immediately detected that something was wrong. "You're white as a ghost, J.Z. What's wrong?"

I gave her a quick rundown on the Brothers Torrington, as well as the latest on the investigation. When I finished, Sam looked like she had gone into a state of shock. "Earth to Sam. Hey, are you ok?"

"J.Z., you can't seriously be thinking about meeting with this animal."

At that moment, a plump waitress with a pink crew cut, nose ring, and tie-dyed t-shirt came to take our order. Even though we'd already been there for 15 minutes, this was incredibly fast service for this establishment. You never go to The Sprout, as we call it, if you're in a hurry, as The Sprouties (our affectionate name for the employees) have their own concept of time. I suspect there is some pharmaceutically-related reason for this laid-back attitude, which would also explain the pink hair.

I looked up from the menu and ordered. "Can I get the falafel that comes with the hummus?"

Our waitress, appropriately named Pinkie, looked at me with disapproval and replied, "Ma'am, you know our policy. You must say the proper name of the dish if you wish to order it. The names of the dishes have been developed by a leading lesbian psychologist, and are proven to be very beneficial to the female psyche when said aloud."

Heavy sigh and dramatic roll of the eyeballs. We go through this every time, more for principle than anything else. Because the food is so good, I always relent. "Ok, ok. I'd like the 'I used to feel awful until I tapped into the source of all my power and independence—my vagina' falafel." I said it as fast as I could, like a kid forced to apologize.

"There, now don't you feel better?"

"No. And don't you think it's a bit ironic, not to mention hypocritical, to force a customer to recite some independence mantra in order to be served?"

Pinkie looked at me in confusion, apparently failing to grasp the irony. Sam felt bad for the poor woman and jumped in with her order before Pinkie had a chance to respond to me. "I'll have the 'I used to be wrapped up in myself until I found the joy that only a woman-to-woman relationship can bring' spinach wrap."

As Pinkie was walking away from our table, I yelled, "Could I get a side of preservatives with that, please?" Pinkie looked at me with disgust and flashed Sam a look of genuine pity, apparently assuming that we were a couple.

Sam shook her head and said, "Why must you always taunt The Sprouties?" I started to answer, but Sam continued. "But more importantly, are you nuts? Do you have some kind of death wish or something? You're meeting a lunatic, possibly the killer, in order to inquire about any involvement on his part in the murder. If he is the killer, don't you think that's going to piss him off just a bit?"

"Well, Sam, I am investigating a murder, you know. Talking to murder suspects is my job in this case. Besides, plenty of other people will be around when I question Torrington. I'll be perfectly safe."

"You don't know that. The guy could snap at any moment and go postal on you."

"Sam, I know you're worried about me, and I appreciate that. But I have to do this, and there's no way around it."

Sam brightened and got a distinct gleam in her eyes. "I could go with you."

I suppressed a laugh out of respect for our friendship, and because Sam was holding a sharp knife at that particular moment. "Sure, I'll be Jill and you can be Sabrina. Maybe we can bring Nealy along to be Kelly. Nothing personal, Sam, but what good would it do to bring you along? If Torrington goes postal on me, what are you gonna do? Stab him with your lipstick?"

Sam's features caved in and she looked like she was going to cry. Wouldn't you know it? It was at that exact moment that Pinkie approached the table with our drinks. She offered Sam a tissue and looked at me with contempt for several seconds. Pinkie put her hand on Sam's shoulder and said in a soft voice, "Whatever this one here did to you, she ain't worth any tears. I can tell you that right now. You can do better, honey. In fact, I have a friend I can introduce you to any time. You just say the word."

The evil devil popped up on my shoulder and I just couldn't resist the temptation. "She's right, Sam. I'm just not good enough for you. You should go back to your husband and four kids. We've tried to make it work. You can't help it if you prefer sex with a man. It's nothing to be ashamed of."

Pinkie ripped her hand off of Sam's shoulder like it was on fire and promptly ran screaming into the back of the restaurant. Decontamination efforts were probably underway already. Sam tried not to, but she giggled anyway. "Damn you! You weren't supposed to make me laugh. I'm mad at you!"

I batted my eyelashes at Sam and said, "How could you stay mad at me?"

"Well, I'm not really mad—not exactly. It's just that…you're my best friend, dammit! And I love you. Yes, I know you can take care of yourself. But that doesn't mean that I don't worry about you. Please don't go talk to this Torrington character alone. Let me go with you. Please!"

Sam has this look of worried desperation that is simply irresistible. Her nose crinkles, her left eyebrow arches slightly, and this vein appears down the center of her forehead, a vein that would look hideous on anyone but Sam and Julia Roberts. Trust me, it's a look that's almost impossible to say no to. I gave up trying years ago. "All right, you win. But you have to promise me that you'll stay in the van."

"Well, how am I going to be of any use inside the van?"

If this had been any woman other than Sam, I would have had a snappy comeback. Instead, I said, "I'll park the van across the street from the construction site. You can watch the action through my binoculars. I'll make sure that Torrington and I are in full view of the van at all times. If he gets aggressive with me, you dial 9-1-1 immediately." Of course, I'd probably be dead by the time help arrived, but I didn't tell Sam that. I could tell by looking at her that she was hooked. Her "duties" sounded important enough for her to be reeled in. I just hoped that she wouldn't get overzealous in her assigned tasks.

Pinkie finally brought our food, looking a bit wan and overwrought. She smiled at me, her new favorite, and glared at Sam, the freak of nature. The food, as usual, was wonderful and completely satisfying. Sam and I shared a piece of gluten-free carob cake for dessert, which, thankfully, tasted much better than it sounded.

Once we were fully fortified, we set forth on our mission. I drove slowly so that I could reiterate the narrow scope of Sam's role in the task before us. She kept nodding her head at all the appropriate places, so I naturally thought she understood her role. As I parked across the street from the construction site, Sam made abundantly clear the utter folly of my thinking. With an absolutely serious expression on her face, she turned to me and asked, "So, where's my gun?"

We're No Angels

I rolled my eyes in disbelief, and managed, in a level voice, "Um, Sam, you don't get a gun. You get binoculars and a cell phone. That's it. No matter what happens, stay in the van at all times. If it looks like trouble, call the cops. You got that, Sabrina?" As I was exiting the van, I turned around and asked, "Did I say stay in the van?"

"Yes, Jill, several times, in fact."

I walked across the street to the construction site, nervously glancing over my shoulder while an impending sense of doom descended upon me. One of the workers directed me to Joey Dietz, a clean-shaven, muscular man with a baby face. No wonder his mom called him Joey. He could have been 12 or 45; it was impossible to tell. He saw me approaching and smiled. Had I been straight, I would have melted right on the spot. Someone should tell Joey's mom that he doesn't need any help in the romance department.

Joey held out his hand and said, "Hi, I'm Joey Deitz, and you must be J.Z. Mackenzie. My mom called about you."

"Nice to meet you, and by the way, your mom's a sweet lady."

He laughed and said, "Nice, but pushy at times, which I'm sure you noticed."

"No, not at all."

"Oh, come on, now. During your conversation with her, didn't she mention, at least once, that I'm single?"

"She might have said that."

"Yeah, that's what I thought. I'm sorry about that. I know she means well, but at times it can be embarrassing."

"Believe me, I know exactly what you mean."

"Well, I don't want to take up all your time yapping about my mom. You wait here and I'll go fetch Torrington for you." Joey moved a little closer and said in a low voice, "He's an ornery critter. When you talk to him, stay right out here where I can keep an eye on you. Don't let him intimidate you, and if he scares you, don't let him know it." With those words of wisdom, Joey hurried off to locate Torrington.

I glanced over my shoulder and waved at the van. The side windows were tinted, so I couldn't see Sam, but she could see me. With those zoom binoculars, she could probably see the pores of my skin. In a few moments, Joey returned with a huge, mean-looking man whom I assumed was Torrington. "Hi, Mr. Torrington. My name is J.Z. Mackenzie and I'm investigating the murder of Chris St. James." I stuck out my hand to shake Torrington's hand, but he just glared at me. "Ok then, let's get down to business. I understand that you weren't too happy with Ms. St. James's performance when she defended your brother on murder charges."

Torrington glared at me for several seconds before responding. "No shit, Sherlock! That bitch lost the fucking case! Who would be happy? Wilson's never gonna see the light of day."

"I understand you went so far as to vow revenge against St. James. Is that right?"

If looks could kill, I'd have been a pile of ashes right about then. I thought Torrington would never stop glaring at me. "Look, bitch, don't try to pin this thing on me. I didn't kill that cunt lawyer, and you're not gonna get me mixed up in this. I've had enough problems with the cops already."

"Mr. Torrington, you've got it all wrong. I'm merely trying to eliminate suspects. That's all."

"What are you talkin' about? The cops already have the murderer locked up in prison. Some stupid dyke who was doin' St. James."

At that point, I wished that I'd given Sam that gun she'd requested. "Yes, it's true that the cops are holding a suspect. But frankly, the cops only have circumstantial evidence tying the suspect to the crime. Their case is unraveling at the seams, and they know it. Any day now, the cops are gonna be out beating the bushes for St. James's enemies. You're right at the top of that list, and that's common knowledge. You're in this thing up to your neck whether you want to be or not. So, you might as well cooperate and get it over with." Liar, liar pants on fire.

"All right, all right. Yeah, I swore revenge on St. James, but that was just talk. I never followed through on it, and I sure as shit didn't kill her."

Out of the corner of my eye, I noticed that Sam had rolled down the window and had the binoculars trained right on us. She was sitting there in full view of the world watching everything through giant binoculars. What was she thinking? If this lunatic looked over and saw her, who knew what could happen. I moved to my right, and Torrington, as I hoped, shifted around so that his back was to the van. "Well, forgive me for pointing this out, but you do have a history of harassment and menacing, so it wouldn't be out of character for you to make good on your threat of revenge."

"Those charges were bogus. That stupid bitch I used to go out with called the cops on me every time she didn't get her way. Of course, the cops always believed her. It was all bullshit, man."

"How 'bout the blackmail charges?"

"We got us a fucking female Columbo here, don't we? That's ancient history, man. It was some scheme Wilson thought up. I used to do a little moonlighting with this other company. Couple of broads worked in the front office. Real prudes. Thought they was better than me. Neither of them would even give me the time of day. Wilson said I should get some cash from them if I couldn't get any pussy. So I told 'em that I was gonna tell their husbands I was sleeping with them both if they didn't each pony up a thousand dollars. Bitches went to the cops."

Right at that moment, I heard an extremely loud clunk coming from the direction of the van. I looked over and saw Sam getting out of the van to retrieve the binoculars she had dropped on the street. Unfortunately, Torrington had noticed too. His face got bright red and he swung around and with a demonic gleam in his eyes, Torrington yelled, "What the hell is that bitch doin' watching me? That's binoculars she's picking up! What the hell kind of scam are you trying to pull here?"

My brain cells went into overdrive, powered solely by my survival instincts. I saw Deitz out of the corner of my eye, and with my right hand I waved him off from behind. "I'm not pulling any scam. The truth is, that's my mentally challenged half-sister, Jamie. She's been tossed out of several institutions due to her violent and uncontrollable outbursts. I'm trying to find a home for her, but for now, I have no choice but to cart her around with me. Believe me, it's no fun. She drools all the time and breaks my equipment, as you can see. But what am I supposed to do? She's my sister, and I have to look out for her…like you look out for your brother."

This apparently struck a chord with him, as he calmed down and said, "Yeah, what are you gonna do? They're a pain in the ass, but they're family."

He started to turn around and glance at Sam. "No, don't look at her. She hates it when people look at her. It'll send her into one of her fits, and I'll have to give her an injection. It's not pretty: she shakes, foams at the mouth, and sometimes pees her pants."

"So what the hell else do you wanna know? Let's get this over with before Linda Blair goes apeshit on us."

"Good idea. At Wilson's trial, there was testimony that one of the victims was almost decapitated. That's quite similar to the way in which St. James was killed. That seems like a pretty big coincidence."

"So? Wilson was in jail when the bitch attorney was snuffed."

"Yes, I know."

Torrington squinted his eyes and fixed me with a steady, contemptuous gaze. "I'd do a lot of stuff for my brother, but not murder. Now, I admit I've had a few run-ins with the law, but nothin' like that. I've been known to get into fights, and I've whacked a few people upside the head when they needed it. But I ain't never killed nobody, and that includes that St. James bitch. I don't mind that she's dead, but I didn't have nothin' to do with it."

"Where were you on the night she was killed, May 12th?"

He thought for a few moments and then said, "I went for a ride on my Harley that night. I was gone for several hours. I stopped on some back road to have a couple shots of Yukon Jack."

"Did anybody see you?"

"No, asshole! That's the whole idea of goin' riding on the back roads. So that you don't run into anybody to hassle you. Now look, I gotta get back to work."

"Mr. Deitz is certainly lucky to have such a conscientious worker. But might I ask you one more question?"

"WHAT?"

"Is it possible that Wilson had something to do with this murder, maybe he hired someone to do it? And maybe he just didn't say anything to you about it."

"NO! Me and Wilson are tight. I'd know if he had a hand in this, and I'm tellin' you right now that he had nothin' at all to do with that bitch's murder."

Torrington stormed off and I could feel the heat of his anger all around me. I waved to Joey Deitz and walked across the street. Sam was sitting quietly in the front seat, looking sweet and innocent. I gave her my best 'I told you so' look, complete with the cocked head and hand on hip stance. Before I could say anything, she said in a low, plaintive voice, "I turned the key in the ignition just enough so that I could listen to the radio. I guess while I had the binoculars up to my eyes, I accidentally hit the window switch with my elbow and the window came down. I didn't even know it was down until I dropped the binoculars. I'm sorry."

I wanted to yell at her, but she looked so pitiful. "Forget about it. How are the binoculars, by the way?"

Sam handed them to me reluctantly. They were toast. They wouldn't even focus anymore. My super-duper telescoping, zoom, auto-focus, ultra-lightweight binoculars, which cost a small fortune were history. "I'll buy you a new pair."

It was a sincere offer, but Sam didn't know how much those babies cost. I knew she couldn't afford them any more than I could, but I could write them off as a business expense. "Naw, it's no big deal. I picked them up cheap at a flea market."

We sat in silence on the drive back to the bookstore where I dropped Sam off. As she slithered out of the van, Sam looked pathetic. Before she shut the van door, I said, "Hey, Nancy Drew, thanks for being worried about me."

Sam shook her head and said, "I could have gotten you killed, J.Z. I'm sorry. I should have trusted you to do your job."

Sam shuffled into the bookstore with her tail tucked between her legs. The great thing about Sam's episodes of depression is that they last for about ten minutes. I knew she'd be dancing around the store humming to herself in no time. She just couldn't help it—Sam was a naturally happy person.

I drove back home and dug out my Kingston phone book. There was a listing for a Wally Paris, the former cop Bitchburger told me about. A timid-sounding woman answered the phone and identified herself as Renee Paris. "Ms. Paris, my name is J.Z. Mackenzie and I'm a private investigator. I'm working on a case that your husband may be able to help me with. I was wondering if I might be able to stop by and see him sometime?"

There was an incredibly long pause on the other end of the line. Then I heard what sounded like crying, and finally a loud thunk. It sounded like Renee Paris had dropped the phone. A gruff female voice came on the line and demanded, "Who is this?"

I repeated the same spiel and was treated to another long pause. "Is this some kind of sick joke?"

"No. I'm a little confused. Is Mr. Paris there? Maybe it would be better if I just spoke to him directly."

"Now that would be a neat trick. He's dead!" The gruff woman slammed the phone down so hard the noise resonated in my ear. It figures—the one name Bitchburger gives me, and the guy is dead. That's par for the course where Bitchburger is concerned. I called Officer Cathy and she confirmed that Paris was dead, an apparent suicide. She also said that he had been in a nearby institution for quite some time, well before May 12th. So, Paris couldn't have had anything to do with St. James's murder.

I called Slick and arranged to meet with her for a powwow tomorrow afternoon. It was high time for us to narrow down our suspect list so that we could focus on the most likely ones. Slick sounded tired on the phone and I hoped she wasn't overdoing it. But knowing Slick, she was. If I ever got into trouble, she's the one I'd want in my corner.

I drove down to the courthouse to look at the full files on Daryl Torrington's menacing, harassment, and blackmail charges. The menacing and harassment charges were, as Torrington indicated, a result of complaints made by Torrington's then girlfriend, Jenny O'Halloran. However, according to the file, Torrington had left out a few salient details when he discussed the matter with me. The blackmail charges Torrington told me about coincided with what was in the court file. So at least Torrington wasn't a total liar.

That was enough detecting for one day. The kitties deserved an evening of attention and treats, and I deserved a dinner that didn't come in a bag. To Corey and Tasha's delight, we dined on grilled chicken and baked potatoes. They didn't care much for the baked potatoes, but they loved the sour cream. We spent the rest of the evening batting around their kitty toys and lounging on the couch. The interviews of the past few days kept running through my head. I had the distinct feeling that I had, indeed, already talked to Chris St. James's murderer, but I didn't know which suspect gave me that impression. My instincts are usually right, even if they are, at times, somewhat vague and undefined. Who amongst the motley crew I had spoken with committed this heinous crime? I hoped that Slick and I could at least narrow down the list of likely suspects.

The Usual Suspects

I awoke the next day feeling refreshed and much more capable of tackling the task ahead of me: identifying the murderer in the current list of suspects. I was looking forward to the meeting with Slick. I spent the morning reviewing my notes from the various interviews and thinking about all the possibilities. As I thought about each suspect in turn, I tried to clear my mind of all extraneous details so that I could get a good "feel" for that suspect, and perhaps some vibe as to guilt or innocence. Again, I had the feeling that the killer was among these suspects, but no *one* suspect left me with any distinct impression.

On the long drive to Kingston, I mentally replayed the interviews and went over the details again and again. I arrived at Slick's office right on time, where I found Slick and Irma engaged in a serious debate about the merits of denture adhesives. Here they were, two grown women, both intelligent, carrying on a heated debate over such a benign topic. I stared at them and said, "It's hard to believe that a sizeable percentage of Oregon citizens entrust the two of you with their legal matters."

Slick turned to me and asked, "Why? Because we get a little carried away in discussing matters of concern to women our age?"

"Denture adhesives? That's the biggest concern for women your age? Not world hunger, the spiraling cost of health care, poverty, race relations, or world peace? Denture adhesives? How 'bout sanitary undergarments for senior citizens? Where do you weigh in on those?"

They both shook their heads and stared at me in disgust. Since neither was inclined to answer my questions, I continued. "If you guys are gonna argue, at least argue about a worthwhile, meaningful topic."

They both laughed and gave me dumbfounded looks. Slick said, "Hell, J.Z., we weren't arguing. That was just a spirited debate. You'd know if were arguing, all right. We haven't argued since 1988, and I believe the police had to respond on that occasion." Irma nodded her head in agreement.

"You two are something else. Now, if I can pull you away from this riveting denture adhesive debate, Slick, it would be nice if we could get down to business on the little matter of a murder investigation."

Slick looked like she was going to say something, but Irma beat her to the punch. "Now look here, missy, when you get to be my age, you'll understand why denture adhesives are no laughing matter. I recently had a very traumatic experience involving a member of the opposite sex. We were engaged in conjugal relations, some would say of an unnatural sort. My dentures slipped, and well…let's just say that injuries were sustained to the other party which required prompt medical attention."

Slick and I stared at each other, and then at Irma, for several seconds with our mouths gaping. Slick finally turned to me and said, "Yeah, about that murder investigation…I think we should get busy." Slick grabbed me by the arm and hustled me down the hall. When we were out of earshot of Irma, Slick whispered, "I didn't see that one coming."

I winced and said, "Now I'm gonna have that mental image in my head for hours. I'm glad I didn't just eat."

We decided to use the conference room, since it was much larger and virtually clutter-free. I spread out my notes on the table and got comfortable. Once we were settled in, I said, "We've got a number of viable suspects, and I think at this point we need to narrow down the list so that I can really hone in on the best ones. I don't know how much stock you put in gut instinct, but I have a very strong impression that the killer is among our current list of suspects."

Slick shook her head and replied, "I put a great deal of stock in gut instinct. I have to. I rely on it in my job just like you do. We just have to be careful in our winnowing process. We don't want to exclude a suspect without having a strong basis for doing so. Let me also remind you that in the typical case, your job would not entail finding the murderer. That's what the cops are for. Instead, your job would be to gather information on likely suspects, so that we could show a jury that reasonable doubt exists. Now, I know that you have your own personal reasons for wanting to find the murderer, and our client agrees that you should pursue that task. But let's not forget that the ultimate goal here is to get a verdict returned in our favor. So, while we may exclude suspects because we don't believe they murdered St. James, those suspects may still be useful in terms of securing a favorable verdict. In other words, don't stop gathering other such useful information."

"Absolutely. I understand what you're saying and I agree. That said, let's jump in and discuss the suspects one by one. How do you feel about Hollingsworth?"

Slick scrunched up her brow and stared at the ceiling. "I just don't see a motive. I know we've discussed the possibility that maybe Chris decided to come out of the closet, so to speak, as far as her past was concerned, and maybe she informed her parents of these intentions. But that would have been totally out of character for her. She was a very private person by nature. And why would someone bother to have a sex change operation and then tell everyone about it? That kind of defeats the purpose, doesn't it? I could see why Chris would want to tell a few people close to her, maybe."

"Yeah, especially Sandy, in the hope that it would convince her to stay. If we're operating under the assumption that the person who left the threats is the murderer, Hollingsworth doesn't make sense. One of the notes left for Chris threatened to reveal Chris's secret, presumably her sex change. Revealing that would be the last thing Hollingsworth would do, or even think about doing."

"True. I feel strongly that the person who left the threats and the murderer are one in the same. The threat that mentioned Chris losing her head was too close to reality to be a coincidence."

Irma came in with a carafe of coffee for us. We paused and looked at her, hoping that no further details of her sex life would be forthcoming. None were. We breathed a collective sigh of relief as Irma left the room. "Oh, I forgot to tell you about Wally Paris, the former cop. He committed suicide recently, and was in an institution at the time of St. James's murder. Unless somebody was acting on Paris's behalf, and I doubt that, we can cross him off the suspect list."

Slick took a sip if Irma's sludge-like coffee and asked, "Well, what about the mob connection?"

"I have a friend, a reporter, who has quite a bit of knowledge about organized crime. He doesn't think that the mob would waste its time offing some attorney who didn't want to cooperate anymore. He also pointed out that the way in which St. James was killed was not indicative of a mob hit, and I have to agree. They know what they're doing, and are rarely this sloppy in the details."

"I agree with you about the typical m.o. of the mob. But, putting that issue aside for the moment, maybe we're characterizing the motive all wrong."

"How do you mean?"

"Maybe Chris threatened to go to the authorities regarding some mob activities that she learned about. Ethically, she could do that if she had learned of current mob activities which were illegal."

"Would that have been in character for St. James?"

Slick scratched her wrinkled forehead and replied, "No, I guess not. The only reason Chris said anything about Michelle Knight's ethical violations is because those violations affected her. Chris certainly wasn't any crusader for justice."

"Right. Plus, the mob wouldn't send a bunch of threats to an intended murder victim. Warnings, perhaps, but not threats. That's not the way the mob operates. I just can't see it."

"Agreed. What about Daryl Torrington, the suspect you interviewed yesterday?"

I gave Slick a quick rundown of my interview with Torrington, as well as the information I had gathered from the various reports I generated. "Well, he has no alibi for the night of the murder. And he is fiercely protective of his brother, Wilson, and it's possible that Daryl killed St. James out of some twisted sense of loyalty to his sibling. He has enough rage and anger inside of him to commit that kind of brutal crime. Torrington has a history of harassment and menacing, and a botched attempt at blackmail. Those threats definitely reflect Torrington's mentality."

"But?"

"Huh?"

"You don't sound convinced. I'm waiting for the 'but'."

"Oh no, I think Torrington's a strong suspect. The one thing that bothers me is that Daryl Torrington doesn't strike me as the brightest crayon in the box. I don't know if he'd have the smarts to figure out St. James's past. That's all."

Slick grinned at me and cackled, "What do you mean, Einstein? You did."

"Don't give up your day job, Slick."

Slick thought for a moment and then asked, "What color is Torrington's hair?"

I pictured Torrington in my mind and answered, "Brown. Long brown hair that he wears in a ponytail."

"That's something to keep in mind. Those hairs found near the body were long brown hairs. Like I said before though, those hairs may have been there for days. They don't necessarily belong to the killer."

"Right, but they could. That fact combined with the stuff we just mentioned makes Torrington a strong suspect. I can't get past the way in which St. James was killed, and the similarity to one of the murders committed by Wilson. So, if we're agreed, I'll place Daryl Torrington's name on our short list."

"Yes, I agree. How 'bout Bill Freeman?"

"Oh, yeah. He had a very strong motive to murder St. James, since she used her bag of tricks to get Buddy Dukes off the hook. I'm no psychologist, but I think Freeman focused so much rage on St. James as a way of diffusing the guilt he was feeling for the loss of his daughter and her family. He was gone that whole night of the murder."

"And don't forget the words he said to his wife: 'one down, one to go.' Plus, he had sent St. James a threatening note previously."

"What I find most compelling is the rage factor. This was a crime of pure, unadulterated rage, the kind that Freeman harbored for St. James."

"What was it that Dr. Cole said about this crime being personal?"

"He said that the killer is someone who feels as though St. James wronged them in some very personal way."

"That's Freeman, all right. Let's not forget the fact that Freeman recently traveled to Pennsylvania. It's quite possible that he came across the same information you did."

"But how would that happen?"

Slick was deep in thought for a couple of minutes and startled me when she spoke. "Wait a minute! Didn't you say that Freeman had gone back to Pennsylvania to help move his mother into a retirement home?"

"Yes. Why? Are you thinking of checking out the home for you and Irma?"

Slick frowned at me and said, "You are quite the little shit today. What I'm thinking is that when this rich high school kid gets killed in a flying accident, that's gonna be big news in all the small towns surrounding the kid's hometown. Right?"

"Sure, I suppose."

"Well, I helped my 93-year old aunt Emma move a couple years back. That woman had an entire room full of nothing but old newspaper clippings, photos, old magazines, and other similar junk. I'm guessing that Bill Freeman's mom is like every other old lady in America; she's a hopeless pack rat. So you know what that means, don't you?"

I stared at Slick and shook my head from side to side.

"I know I'm asking a lot, but try to keep up with me here, kid. Freeman goes to move his mom's stuff. A lot of her stuff consists of old newspaper clippings. If this kid crashing his plane was big news, as I suspect it was, old lady Freeman would have all the clippings associated with that accident. Maybe Freeman came across those clippings and recognized St. James the same way you did."

"Slick, it's possible, but your theory contains a lot of assumptions, which we have no way of validating. First, you're assuming that the crash story was news outside of Springfield. Second, you're assuming that old lady Freeman kept clippings of the story. Third, you're assuming that Bill Freeman found them. How can any of those assumptions be checked?"

Slick held up her hands and answered, "Simple. Ask old lady Freeman. Old ladies love to chat with just about anyone. She'd probably tell you her life story if you'd let her. Act casual and just bring the topic up innocently. You can do it."

I had a sinking feeling. "It's hard to act casual and innocent over the phone, Slick."

"Yes, I know."

I could see it coming, but that didn't make it any easier. "You want me to go all the way back to Pennsylvania to talk to some old lady, who may not even be coherent, about ancient newspaper clippings?"

"I'm sure you can find a way to make the trip more productive. Perhaps you can dig up other goodies on St. James."

I stared at Slick with a stone-faced expression for several moments. Finally, I just said, "Great. I can't wait. Maybe I can round out the trip with a visit to the Quakers, or the Pennsylvania Dutch. Yippee."

Slick ignored my sarcasm. "Good. Now that we have that settled, let's continue on with our list of suspects, shall we? We already excluded Will Beaton because he has an alibi, but what about Michelle Knight?"

"Well, she certainly hated St. James enough to kill her, and even admitted that. But it doesn't make any sense that Knight would kill St. James once she discovered her well-kept secret."

"Why not?"

"St. James humiliated Knight. If Knight had a chance to return the favor, don't you think she'd take it? If Knight had stumbled across the secret, she would have told everybody who would listen. Hell, she probably would have taken out an ad in the Bar journal. There's no way Knight would have just killed St. James. Nope, she would have watched St. James be humiliated and ridiculed, the same way she was, and Knight would have relished every minute of it."

"Yeah, that makes sense. She is a vindictive little bitch. And even though I think she's fully capable of murder, I just don't see her as a viable suspect in this case. Ok then, Knight is off the short list. What about Holly Travis?"

"Do you have some brilliant theory as to how Travis would learn that her former boyfriend didn't die, but instead was transformed into a female attorney in Oregon?"

Slick pondered this for some time, and finally said, "No, I can't say that I do. But for the sake of argument, let's assume she did. That mutilated Barbie doll, with the female parts hacked away, has some sexual implications, at least to my way of thinking. It strikes me as the kind of thing a betrayed or scorned lover would send to the person who betrayed them. And, don't forget the note that came with it. It said something like 'you can't fool everyone, *especially* not me,' meaning that the person who sent the note has some kind of special or personal knowledge about St. James."

"It could mean that. Or, it could just mean that St. James couldn't fool the person who sent the note because they had discovered the truth."

Slick shook head stubbornly. "I don't think so. But at any rate, wouldn't you agree that someone in Travis's situation, who discovered the truth, could be propelled into the kind of rage exhibited by this murder? I mean, the woman mourned this man for most of her life, lost her child, probably due to the grief that consumed her. She's now an alcoholic living in squalor, and has never loved anyone since."

"Yes, I'd have to agree that *if* Travis discovered the truth, she would probably be enraged enough to kill St. James in a vicious manner. Sure, she would feel completely betrayed."

"Right. And doesn't she have long brown hair?"

"Yes, she does."

"Is she right- or left-handed?"

I tried to get a clear mental picture of Holly Travis, but I didn't remember whether she was a southpaw or not. "I don't know."

"Well, maybe you can stop by and chat with her when you go back to Pennsylvania. While you're there, ask her to write down her phone number or something so you can see if she's left-handed. And ask to use her restroom and maybe you can find a stray hair lying about."

I crinkled my nose and said, "I probably won't have to look too hard. There's probably 3 or 4 inches of hair in the drain. But I think I'd better get a tetanus shot before I step foot into Travis's place again." This trip just kept sounding better and better: a 90 year-old woman, yellowed newspaper clippings, and hair-clogged drains. As David Letterman would say, "more fun than humans should be allowed to have."

"So then, Travis is a keeper. I guess the only one left to discuss is Blaine Darrow."

"Yeah, and he's definitely going on our short list. He was lying about something when I interviewed him. He's gotten a lot of money from somewhere, and I have no way of knowing how much of it he inherited. Some of it could be blackmail money. He has no alibi for the time of the murder, and it's quite clear that he really hated St. James with a passion, enough to kill her. You should have seen the look of evil in his eyes. It was frightening."

"I've no doubt that Darrow possesses the necessary rage to commit this crime, and yes, the financial aspects of his situation are suspicious. I think you also mentioned that he was especially nervous at certain points when you interviewed him."

"Yes, that's true. His eyes darted around like a caged animal. What concerns me the most is his inability to recall when and where he stopped on the way home from visiting his kids. You'd think he would remember the name of the place, or at least the town."

"Unless he didn't stop anywhere, and he's afraid you'll check."

"Yeah, that's what I'm thinking. So, what are we left with? We've got Darrow, Travis, Torrington, and Freeman on our narrowed-down list of suspects. I guess I'll start by flying back out to Pennsylvania to talk with Bill Freeman's mom, and chat with Holly Travis again. That sound ok?"

"Sounds great. Oh, I almost forgot to mention it, but I received St. James's computer files from her home today. They're in my office and you're free to take a peek, but I saw nothing of any interest at all. I should have a draft motion to suppress ready for you to take a look at when you get back from Pennsylvania. I planned to have it done by now, but I've gotten sidetracked by a number of other things this week. You know how it is."

"Yep, I do. Hey, have you seen Sandy lately?" I tried to sound nonchalant.

"I saw her a couple of days ago. I went over just to bring her up to speed on things. She asked about you. Maybe you should stop by and chat with her sometime. She could sure use it, kid."

I looked down at the floor and said, "It's too hard, Slick. I'm trying to protect myself, you know? If she is a killer, I don't want to get any closer to her than I already am."

"And if she's not?"

I didn't have an answer for that, and Slick knew it. I said goodbye to Slick and Irma and trekked back home to make flight arrangements. The whole way home, Slick's words reverberated in my ears.

Leavin' on a Jet Plane—Again

I managed to get a decent night's sleep, even with the kitties walking over my head all night long. There was another cat in the yard for part of the night, and that got them all stirred up, as it usually does. They both feel the need to crawl up to the window and press their noses against the glass in an effort to intimidate the audacious intruder. The fact that my head is located right beneath the window, and they therefore must walk over it to get to the window, is of no consequence to them. One must have priorities, after all.

Before crawling into bed, I'd made arrangements for flights to Pennsylvania, as well as the airport shuttle. I'd already packed my things, so it was just a matter of getting ready and having a quick bite to eat. I certainly didn't want to fill up when I had that wonderful airline cuisine to look forward to. I could already taste it. Which reminded me: I'd better change the cat box before leaving.

I'd forgotten to notify Cecelia and Ethel of cat duty, so I went over to their place to tape a note to the door. It was too early to wake them. As I was taping the note to the door, it flew open, startling me. It was Ethel, in a flannel nightgown, curlers and bonnet. Once I'd calmed down, I said, "You scared me, Ethel. It's still dark out. Why aren't you sleeping?"

"Sleep? Who can sleep at a time like this?" With that, Ethel jerked me inside the house and shut the door.

192 Margie S. Schweitzer

"A time like this? What do you mean?"

"Oh, Ruby Jean, it's so embarrassing. I don't know how to say it."

"Ethel, I'm your best friend. You can tell me anything."

A pained look spread across Ethel's face, and she finally muttered, "It's a sexual problem."

I didn't really want to hear this, but what choice did I have? "Go on."

Ethel wrung her hands and bowed her head in shame. "Oh, gracious. It's just that...well, um...I don't think Earl...likes me anymore."

"Don't be silly. Earl is crazy about you."

"He was. Now he just doesn't seem to be as interested in partaking in marital relations as he used to be."

"Well, that's normal. It doesn't mean that he likes you any less."

Ethel wrung her hands some more and furrowed her brow as if worried. "Oh, Ruby Jean, you don't know Earl. He's always been regular as clockwork. And now his interest has dropped off something fierce."

I didn't want to ask, but I sensed that she wanted me to for some reason. "Well, how much has the activity dropped off anyway?"

Ethel shook her head and clasped her hands, as if in prayer to the goddess of conjugal relations. In a low voice, Ethel muttered, "We only have relations now 9 or 10 times a week."

I gulped and asked, not without trepidation, "How often did you do it before?"

"Oh, at least twice a day. At least."

Poor Earl probably died from exhaustion. I looked at Ethel with renewed respect and said, "Maybe he's just tired. He's been working real hard lately. I bet that's it."

Ethel brightened and said, "Maybe you're right. Maybe I just need to take a more active role. Earl might be waiting for me to make the first move. I'm gonna try that right now, Ruby Jean." Ethel scooted off in the direction of the bedroom with an air of mirth and gaiety about her. I was left standing in the living room with my mouth open. I knew what was going to happen next, so I hightailed it out of there, making sure that the note was securely taped to the door on my way out. As I closed the door, I heard Cecelia scream and Ethel laugh. I tried to suppress a laugh, but my attempt was unsuccessful. I was still laughing when the shuttle picked me up right on time and whisked me off to the airport.

The ride was monotonous, and I alternately slept and read Joan Hess's latest adventures in Maggody. I thought about how to approach Bill Freeman's mother. Who could I say I was, and how could I discreetly and cleverly ask whether she had a pile of newspaper clippings when Bill helped her move? I'd think of something, I was sure, though I doubted that it would be very clever, or even believable. Maybe I just looked sweet and innocent. People rarely seemed to question the ridiculous explanations I often provided as a ruse. Hmmm…I'd have to ponder this further some other time.

The trip was uneventful except for the miniature sandwich I was served for lunch. I didn't know whether to eat it or send it to Ripley's. It was the smallest sandwich I had ever seen. I thought that perhaps it was an appetizer or something. When it became apparent that the sandwich was meant to be the full meal, I dug out the bag of honey-roasted peanuts I'd been given earlier. It contained a total of five peanuts, and as I scarfed them down, the guy next to me looked on enviously. What is it about an airplane that makes grown adults think that a teaspoon full of peanuts is some kind of treasure? I've seen seemingly rational, well-adjusted people lose it when told by the stewardess that there are no more peanuts.

When we landed, I raced to the car rental kiosk, where I was told that only full-sized cars remained available for rental. I rented a black Lincoln Continental, which felt like driving a tuna boat. I felt swallowed up inside that giant cage of steel. But thanks to directions from the car rental attendant, I easily found Greensboro, and hoped that it didn't contain too many retirement homes. I'd worry about that tomorrow. Tonight, it was time to find a decent, cheap motel and some real grub, preferably in non-airline portions. I was successful on both counts, and as I gobbled down my bacon cheeseburger and onion rings, I was treated to an orgasmic symphony from the adjoining room, which, thankfully, crescendoed as I polished off the last bites.

The next day, I scanned the local phone book, which listed two retirement homes. The first one I called, Shady Glen, had an Alberta Freeman. I drove to the home, which was only a few blocks away and was directed to unit 34. I knocked on the door and a genial-looking, white-haired woman answered the door. Since Jackie Freeman had described her mother-in-law as an "old biddy," this wasn't what I was expecting. Maybe it was just a mother-in-law thing. "Hi. Are you Alberta Freeman?"

"Why, yes, I am. How can I help you?"

Clipboard and pen in hand, I said, "My name is Audrey Valentine and I'm a graduate student at the University of Pennsylvania. I'm majoring in Gerontology and Sociology, and my summer project is to gather information on the demographics of senior citizens. I was wondering if you'd be willing to talk with me for a short while?" I had learned long ago the value of a clipboard. For some reason, it imparts an aura of credibility and legitimacy to the owner. I'm convinced that with a clipboard and an expression of self-importance, the places to which one can gain access are limitless.

Alberta nodded her head vigorously, smiled, and ushered me inside her apartment. For a retirement home, it was quite nice and had a pleasant atmosphere. Alberta's apartment contained the ubiquitous knick-knacks collected over the course of a lifetime, all proudly displayed on lace doilies. Alberta herself was adorned in a long skirt featuring a flower print, a polka-dot blouse, a plaid apron, stockings that stopped below her knees, white geriatric shoes, and an array of costume jewelry. She offered me some tea and cookies, which we enjoyed in her living room. Once we were settled in, and I had politely eaten two very stale oatmeal cookies, I explained, "My research project requires that I ask you a few general questions, and then we'll get to more specific ones later. Is that ok?"

"Sure, sweetie, that's fine. I don't get many visitors, so take your time."

I felt guilty for deceiving the lonely old lady, but then, at least I was providing her with some entertainment for the morning. I asked her a lot of random questions just for the sake of appearances, and then I got to the good stuff. "How many children do you have?"

"I have two good-for-nothin' sons that never come to see me, and one lives not far from here. Jim Ed and Bill are their names."

"Did you recently move here?"

"Yes, it's been about six months now."

"That's good. It would be real helpful for my project if you could tell me some things about the move, like who helped you, who packed your things, what kind of things were moved, and so forth."

"Bill and a couple of my neighbors helped me. Bill did most of the packing himself, and you can see right here what was moved."

"Certainly. Part of my project focuses on the kinds of things that senior citizens collect over the years. Now, do you collect newspaper clippings, magazine articles, or things like that?"

"Well, I have a few that I've kept as reminders or mementoes."

I munched on another stale cookie in an attempt to buy some time in which I could think of other approaches. "I interviewed a woman a couple of days ago that had a bunch of newspaper clippings. We looked at some of them. I remember one had to do with a young man named Hollingsworth. Do you remember him?"

"Jamison Hollingsworth?"

"That's the name."

"Sure, everyone knew him, or at least, knew of him. He was from the richest family around these parts. Got himself killed in an airplane accident years ago."

"Yes, that's right. I bet you have some newspaper clippings about that, don't you?"

Alberta took a sip of tea and said, "No, I doubt it. I only kept clippings about people I really know. I have an article about when my friend Lulu Banks went into the hospital for dehydration. Darn fool took a handful of stool softeners thinkin' they were vitamins. They had her propped up on the pot for days. I can probably find that article if you'd like to read it."

My hopes dashed, I meekly replied, "No, thanks, but it's nice of you to offer. That's about all I need for the survey. But I was wondering how long Bill stayed with you when he helped you move?"

"A few days. I don't remember exactly."

"Did he go to Springfield while he was here?"

"What's this got to do with your project?"

"Nothing. It's just that I have a friend who lives in Springfield, and I could have sworn that she mentioned someone named Bill Freeman to me. That's all."

"No, he was with me the whole time."

"My friend's name is Chris St. James. Did Bill mention her?" I hoped that Alberta did not know any of the players in Buddy Dukes's trial.

"No, doesn't sound familiar."

I had to eat three more stale oatmeal cookies and drink another cup of chamomile tea before I could escape. I felt sorry for Alberta Freeman, so lonely that she had to latch on to complete strangers for company. It was easy to see why senior citizens were perfect targets for scam artists.

I drove to Burton, planning to chat with Holly Travis, but she wasn't home. At least, she didn't answer the door, though her car was in the driveway. She didn't strike me as the type to go for a walk, but you never know. I recalled that she worked the 3 to 11 shift, so I'd try to catch her at work. I'd rather talk to her at home, but as Mick Jagger once said, you can't always get what you want. In the meantime, I'd have a bite to eat and think about where to go from here. Much to my surprise, I found a wonderful little Indian restaurant near the hospital, and lunch was buffet-style. What a spread! Everything from Chicken Vindaloo to curried rice and vegetables. After four helpings of the vast array of dishes, I felt a little guilty about the drop in profit that I was causing. I left a big tip, and I could almost feel the sigh of relief the owner breathed as I sauntered out of the restaurant, fuller than I could remember being in quite some time.

I wandered around the town for a while, since I still had some time to kill, and shortly after three, I headed for the hospital. After several inquiries, I located the floor where Holly Travis worked. I stopped at the desk and asked if I could speak to Holly. A stern looking, by-the-book type nurse advised me that Holly wasn't there. I looked at my watch and said, "But I thought she always works the 3 to 11 shift."

"She does, when she bothers to show up. Called in sick again."

That was odd. I'd already been by her house and there was no answer. Maybe she'd been sleeping, or too sick to get out of bed. As I was thinking these thoughts, another nurse sidled up next to me and said in hushed tones, "I couldn't help but overhear you asking about Holly."

I lied and said, "Yeah, I'm a friend of Holly's. I just need to talk to her about a few things."

The nurse looked me up and down and asked, "Are you a *good* friend of hers?"

Lies were getting easier and easier to tell in this line of work. At last, I had something in common with so many of the attorneys I used to work with. With nary a feeling of guilt, I responded, "Yeah, I am."

The nurse ushered me into a break room, which was currently deserted. She looked around nervously and said, "I'm not supposed to be on a break right now. I just started my shift. Forgive me, my name is Cheryl Steed, and I work with Holly." She offered her hand and I shook it and introduced myself with yet another alias. I waited to see what it was Ms. Steed wanted to tell me. "I'm real worried about Holly. She's missin' a lot of work, and I'm afraid she's gonna get herself fired if she doesn't clean up her act. Holly and I aren't close. She isn't really close to anyone here, but I still care about her. I think something's really bothering her, and that's why she's missin' work all the time."

"And you think I might know what's bothering her?"

Cheryl shook her head up and down and looked at me expectantly. I shrugged my shoulders and said, "Sorry, I don't have a clue. She doesn't really open up to me."

"Darn! I wish I knew what was bothering her so I could help. You know, she used to be such a reliable person, always on time and never called in sick. Then, about two months ago, she started acting real weird."

A shiver ran down my spine. If I remembered correctly, the threats had started about two months ago. "What happened two months ago to make Holly start acting weird?"

Cheryl stared off into space for a few moments, and then looked over at the TV in the corner. The proverbial light bulb went off, and she answered, "You know, I'd forgotten all about it until just now. We were in here one night about two months ago, takin' a little break. The TV was on, and we were chatting and kind of watching the news. All of a sudden, Holly turned white as a sheet. She was sittin' right in that chair." She pointed to a chair across the room and continued. "I thought she was having a heart attack or something. I asked if she was ok, and she didn't even hear me. She just sat there, staring at the TV. I looked at the TV, thinking maybe they'd just announced the end of the world or something. It was just some news show about the mob, and how some attorney had gotten some mob figure off the hook for something he did."

I almost wet my pants right there. "Was it a female attorney?"

Cheryl stared at me, with a confused expression on her face. "Yeah, I think so. Why?"

"It's not important."

"Anyway, Holly called in sick for several days in a row after that. Then, she asked if she could take some vacation time. She had a bunch saved up, since she never used it. Said she had no need to. Management

198 Margie S. Schweitzer

didn't like it, since you're supposed to schedule vacations way in advance, but they let her take it anyway. She only recently came back to work."

My head started to spin and I thought I was going to faint. I slumped into a nearby chair and Cheryl looked at me with a worried expression. "Oh god, now it's happening to you. Stay here, I'm gonna get you some water." Cheryl raced over to the sink and retrieved a glass of water for me. I thanked her and assured her that I was all right.

It all made perfect sense now. Travis had seen St. James on TV when she attracted national coverage during the last mob trial she had handled. Maybe that's why St. James stopped working for the mob: too much publicity. She probably feared that Travis would recognize her, and she was right. Travis had seen her, and then she went to Oregon and started the campaign of threats. Maybe she'd known all along that she was going to kill St. James, or maybe the idea just came to her. I imagined the rage Travis must have felt, seeing the palace St. James lived in, compared with her depressing little hovel. Knowing that she'd mourned someone who wasn't dead, and that she'd lost her child out of grief for a person who'd simply ran out on her. Yes, that would inspire enough rage to commit the viciousness evident in the St. James killing.

I had to go back to Travis's place, as crazy as that sounded. I had to confront her and hear her admit that she'd murdered St. James. I didn't have any great plan, since I wasn't in the least intimidated by the shriveled up shell of a woman I had met a few days before. Rage gave her the power to kill St. James. Against me, she wouldn't have the same advantage, or so I hoped.

I went downtown and bought a pair of cargo pants and the best miniature recorder I could find. I set the recorder for voice-activated mode and placed it inside the cargo pocket of my pants. I knew that a recorded confession of this sort wouldn't be admissible at a trial. But I hoped that if I could get Travis to admit what she'd done, Slick could convince the D.A. to drop the charges against Sandy. Sandy...she'd been innocent all along, just like she said. I owed her a big apology, and right now, I felt like I owed her what I was about to do. Maybe I should have called Slick first, but I knew she'd just try to talk me out of it. So instead, I drove over to Travis's place, switched on the recorder in my pocket, and bravely swaggered up to the door.

A Woman Scorned

I knocked on the door, but again, no answer. I tried the knob and discovered that the door was unlocked. I opened the door and slowly walked in. Once inside, I called Holly's name and looked around. No sign of her in the living room. As I turned to make my way down the hall, out of the corner of my eye, I saw a flash of metal. Before I could react, something hit me on the right side of my head and I collapsed.

I don't know how long I was unconscious, but when I awoke in a crumpled heap on the living room floor, the searing pain in my head sent waves of nausea through me. I groaned and tried to move, but the nausea grew worse. I felt the side of my head, which was wet and sticky with blood. My vision was somewhat blurry, but I could make out a figure on the other side of the room: it was Holly, aiming a gun in my direction. She snickered and said, "I've never been cold-cocked, but I'm told it hurts like hell."

I groaned and mumbled, "Your sources are correct."

"I just talked to Cheryl at the hospital. She said she was real worried about me, and so was my *friend* who was just there. I asked her what she told my *friend* and she repeated it all back to me. I knew it was you. I saw you here earlier today. So, I guess you know, huh?"

Through intense pain and ferocious nausea, I mumbled, "Know what?"

"Oh, a smart ass, huh? Don't toy with me! You know I killed Jamison…I mean St. James. No, dammit! He'll always be Jamison to me. My sweet Jamie."

I shut my eyes against the pain and asked, "You sent the threats too, didn't you?" I already knew the answer, but I wanted her to admit it on tape, on the off chance I got out of this alive.

Holly took a huge gulp of whiskey and answered, "Yep, that was me. Scared the shit out of him, too. I watched him open the box with the rat in it. You should have seen him jump!" She let out a loud cackle that sent ripples of pain through my throbbing head. "I didn't have any sort of plan. At first, I didn't plan to kill him. Hell, I even fantasized about us gettin' back together. Can you imagine? Man or woman, he was still my Jamie. But then, I thought about how he just left me, pregnant with his child. He left me to grieve over him. And god, I did that…all my life. At some point, I decided that I had to kill him. He couldn't live after what he'd done to me. He deserved to die."

I was barely clinging to consciousness, but I willed myself to hang on. "Did he just let you in that night?"

"Oh yeah. The idiot thought I was there to make nice. I showed up on his doorstep, all smiles and with a bottle of wine. He didn't know that I had a meat cleaver in that huge handbag I bought special for that night. He tried to explain what had happened in the past, how he had no choice but to leave me and his kid behind. He made it sound like he was doin' us a favor by deserting us. That fucking coward! At least he could have had the balls to own up to what he did." Holly laughed heartily and said, "Did you hear what I just said? Balls—get it? No wonder he didn't have any balls. They were lopped off!" Again, she laughed loudly at her little pun.

I tried to will away the pain, but it wasn't working. "So what happened?"

She stopped laughing and said, "Pretty obvious, isn't it? I told him all was forgiven, and then I apologized for the threats. I told him that I just wanted to scare him, to kind of get even. Then, I suggested we drink a toast to our newfound friendship. As Jamie got up and went toward the bar, I pulled out the cleaver and followed him. It was so easy. That cleaver was razor sharp and it cut right through him. I watched the life ooze out of him and then I left, but not before I wiped my prints off the handle of the meat cleaver. I was real careful not to touch anything while I was there. I was hoping that tramp that used to live with him would get nailed for the murder. That was just a bonus when it happened."

I was losing a lot of blood and I was growing woozier by the second. My thoughts were all running together and my vision was blurry. I tried to conserve energy by not moving and not asking any more questions. I had enough on tape. Travis took another gulp of whiskey and tossed the empty glass against the wall behind me, glass fragments showering me. "And now, honey, it's time to take care of the mess you've created."

I grunted and managed to force out some words. "I called the cops…both here and in Oregon. They know the whole story. Give it up."

"You're bluffing, you stupid bitch! The cops would have been here already if you'd called them."

"There was a hostage situation downtown. They'll be here. You might as well surrender."

"I don't think so." With these words, Travis got up, walked toward me and stared down at me for several seconds. Then, she walked behind me and placed the barrel of the gun at the base of my head.

My whole body went numb and I was shaking with fear. I didn't want to die. There were still plenty of restaurants that I hadn't eaten at yet, and probably some new Cameron Diaz movies in the works. I mustered enough energy to say, "Don't do it. You'll never get away with it, Holly."

A few seconds later, the gun exploded. For a moment, I thought I must be dead. But then, I heard a loud thud next to me. With great effort, I moved just enough to see Travis lying a few feet away on the floor, a gaping hole in the side of her head. I guessed she must have realized at the last moment that there was no way out of this mess for her, or maybe she wanted to join St. James and her child in the afterworld. At that moment, I lost my battle to retain consciousness.

I awoke some time later in the hospital. I learned that one of Travis's neighbors heard the gunshot and went to investigate. Upon entering Travis's place, he called the cops and an ambulance. I was thankful to this nameless, faceless stranger, but at the moment, pain was my predominant preoccupation. My angel of mercy, Nurse Nancy, was about to hook me up with some good drugs, but the cops arrived.

Damn! They always spoil a good time. I gave them a rundown of everything that had happened, both here and back home. By the looks on their faces, I think they doubted my veracity. At any rate, they left me to my much-needed pharmaceutical bliss, as provided by the ever-gracious Nurse Nancy.

When I awoke again, I didn't even know what day it was, and when I turned my head, I thought I was hallucinating. I blinked several times, and when the image didn't fade, I said, "Sam?"

Sam smiled and said, "Yes, it's me. How are you feeling?"

"A lot better, but my head still hurts a little. How did you know where I was?"

"We all got worried when you didn't check in. I called the attorney you were working with in Kingston, and she hadn't heard from you. She told me you were going to Greensboro and Burton. I got worried and started calling hospitals, and I found you here."

"How long have I been here?"

"A couple of days."

I told Sam the whole story. When I finished, I looked around the room in a panic and asked, "Where are my pants? The ones that had the recorder in them? Oh god, they didn't get tossed, did they?"

Nurse Nancy sauntered into the room and said, "Relax, Miss Marple, the recorder that was in your pants is in the drawer next to you." She saw my look of confusion and said, "I had to go through your wallet to figure out who you were. I came across your P.I. license."

I had Sam pull out the recorder so we could listen to the tape. I wanted to make sure that the recorder had picked up everything Travis had said. When it got to the part where Travis pulled the trigger, Sam jumped and looked like she was going to cry. She looked at me and said, "That could have been you."

"But it wasn't. I'm ok. You always said I have a hard head. I guess it's a good thing, huh?"

"It's not funny, J.Z. You could have been killed."

"I know, Sam. I did a stupid thing by going over there alone. I know that now. I just wasn't thinking at the time, I guess."

"Obviously. I hope you're better soon so that I can kill you for making me worry so much. I get some satisfaction by looking at your dashing new haircut. It serves you right."

"Huh?"

Sam retrieved a small mirror from her purse and shoved it at me. I reluctantly looked into it and surveyed the damage. I looked like some kind of punk rocker or a Sproutie with part of my head shaved. And the stitches, those were truly lovely, along with the giant welt. "I hope you brought one of my Atlanta Braves caps."

"Believe it or not, your vanity was not at the top of my list when I hopped on a plane to rush to your bedside as a best friend should."

I looked at Sam and said, "You really are a great friend, you know."

She kissed the undamaged side of my head and said, "I know."

I called Slick and told her everything that had happened. She, too, vowed to kill me once I was fully recovered. I had to pull the phone away from my ear when I told her how I'd gone to Travis's place alone after I knew she was the killer. I feigned drowsiness to get off the phone, and Slick promised to call the D.A. right away and fill her in on all the latest happenings. No doubt the D.A. would want to listen to the tape before making a decision on Sandy's release.

While I further recuperated the next day, Sam took care of several errands so that we could leave right away once I was released. She settled up my account at the motel and retrieved my things, located the rental car, and made airline reservations for us. I was glad she came, not so much for the errands, but just because she's Sam.

When we finally arrived home, Nealy met us at the airport. She hugged us both for several minutes, and finally she looked at me, hand on her hip, and shook her head from side to side. "That's all I'm gonna say. I'm a woman of few words, as you know, and I'm sure that you've already had an earful."

"Thanks, I appreciate that. And for being so kind and understanding, I'll share my happy pills with you."

It seemed like I was home in no time, the kitties ecstatic at my return, though they too seemed to be shaking their furry heads at me. Maybe it was just the happy pills. We all piled into bed together and immediately fell asleep. My furry friends snuggled close to me all night. I knew I was lucky to be alive, and lucky to have so many two- and four-legged friends who cared about me.

Lovers Reunited?

I hurried to get ready the next morning and drove to Kingston like a bat out of hell. Slick was waiting for me and we hightailed it over to the D.A.'s office, where we all listened to the tape. When Slick heard Travis's gunfire, she put her hand on my shoulder and looked down at the floor. I knew the crusty old bat had a soft spot for me. The D.A. agreed to drop the charges against Sandy, and indicated that it would take a couple of days to process all the paperwork.

As Slick and I were walking back to the van, she looked at me and said, "What's wrong? You don't look like someone who's just saved the day."

"Slick, it was dumb luck. I didn't even think Travis was a suspect. I only included her because you thought so. What kind of investigator does that make me?"

"Kid, if I had a nickel for every time I've won a case because of, as you call it, dumb luck, I'd have…well, a shitload of nickels. It doesn't matter. What matters is that you did it. You proved Sandy's innocence."

"Yeah, but…"

"No buts. Look, you were the one who got the idea to fly out to Pennsylvania in the first place. You found out about St. James's past. Without that link, we would be nowhere right now. So what if I had a feeling about Travis. I've lived a long time, kid. A lot longer than you.

I'm supposed to have better instincts. Deal with it, and accept the fact that you can't always do it on your own. You did good, and I'm proud of you."

"Thanks, Slick," I murmured, still not convinced.

"Don't mention it. Now, I've got a court appearance to make in a few minutes, so I'm gonna mosey on into the courthouse. Why don't you go on over to the pokey and tell Sandy the good news. Don't worry about me, I'll catch a ride back to my office."

"You sure?"

"Absolutely. Now get."

I did as instructed and walked down the street toward the correctional facility that housed Sandy, at least for a few more days. I walked with my head down, deep in thought, and was startled when a voice said, "Nice work, Mackenzie."

I looked up and saw Officer Cathy on the sidewalk in front of me. "What?"

"I heard about your trip out to Pennsylvania, and how you nabbed the St. James killer. Is the D.A. going to drop the charges?"

"Yeah, Slick and I just spoke with her."

Cathy studied my face and said, "You don't seem too happy for someone who just cracked a major case. What's wrong?"

I sighed and said, "Well, I didn't really 'crack' the case. I just kind of accidentally stumbled across the killer. So I'm feeling a bit inadequate just now."

Cathy shook her head up and down in agreement and said, "Yeah, I used to have the same problem."

"Used to?"

"Yep. Last year I was assigned to a big case. Some jerk was breaking into women's homes, raping them, and then burgling the place. None of the women could identify the creep. I thought I knew who was doing it and I investigated this guy for weeks. Then, I'm at a bar, off duty, and a fight breaks out. I haul the guy who started it down to the station, I run a check on him, and he's got some outstanding warrants for assault and other things. While I'm asking the guy about those crimes, he confesses to the rapes I've been investigating. Can you believe it? I felt like a complete fool. I even thought about quitting the force. But a few days later, a woman drops by the station and asks to speak with me. She's in tears. She's seen the rapist on the news and says that she's seen him hangin' around her place recently. She hugs me and thanks me for saving her from what the other women went through. I explained to her that I just kind of stumbled upon this guy. She looked at me with tears in her eyes and said 'Officer, it doesn't matter how you did it—the result is the same.' And you know what? She was right."

"I guess, but…"

"Listen, I have to work my ass off to solve some of the cases I'm assigned to. The way I figure it, these cases that we just kind of stumble into the answer are like rewards for all the work we put in on other cases. It's like that invisible hand theory from economics. Remember? Well, I think there's an invisible hand of justice that helps good cops and P.I.s out every now and then. Take the free pass and move along to the next case. That's what I say. Remember, our jobs aren't about egos, they're about results. You got results, didn't you?"

"Yes."

Cathy lifted up my hat to look at the wound on the side of my head. "And it looks like you're gonna have a scar to prove it. You proved you client's innocence and she's getting out of jail, Mackenzie. You did your job. So what if you didn't get to use your deductive powers of logic as much as you would have liked. You accomplished what you set out to do. You can't ask for more than that."

I smiled at Cathy and said, "You know, you're right. It doesn't happen often, but this time, you're absolutely right."

"I'd slug you if you didn't have an ugly head wound."

We said our goodbyes and I continued on to the jail and was escorted into a room where I waited for Sandy. In a few minutes, Sandy appeared. She looked better than she had on our previous visits. After pausing at the door, Sandy walked over to the table, sat down, and looked at me with great warmth for several moments. "I heard about what happened in Pennsylvania, with Chris's old girlfriend. You shouldn't have risked your life for me. But I certainly appreciate it. Slick told me about the tape, too. Did the D.A. listen to it yet?" I could see the look of hope and desperation in her eyes.

I nodded my head and said, "Yes, and she's agreed to drop the charges against you."

Sandy's upper body collapsed onto the table and she began sobbing. I knew they were tears of joy and great relief, so I just waited for

Sandy to regain her composure. When she did, she asked, "When do I get out of here?"

"It'll take two or three days, at least, to process all the necessary paperwork. Just be patient. It's almost over."

Sandy smiled warmly at me and said, "Thank you so much for everything you've done. I can't say that enough. You're the reason I'm getting out of here."

"I had some help from Slick. Don't forget about her."

"Yes, I know. I've already thanked her. You've both done such a wonderful job for me. I really appreciate it, J.Z."

"My pleasure, ma'am."

Sandy and I chatted for a while. I caught her up on current events and all the news pertaining to the Braves. I hated to leave, but she looked at ease when I left. I guess the promise of impending freedom was enough.

I went home and Sam and Nealy showed up to take me out to celebrate the outcome of the case. Sam was positively giddy at dinner, with thoughts of me being reunited with Sandy running through her devious little head, no doubt. At the first opportunity, Sam said, "I said all along that Sandy was innocent, didn't I?" Without allowing me to answer she continued. "Now that we have this little mess cleared up, it's time to get back to the important things. When are you and Sandy going out again?"

"Well, I don't know, Sam. I guess I'll have to call the warden and ask when I can come take my honey out for a little courtin' and sparkin'. I'm sure that the warden is a reasonable man, having needs of his own, and all. It'll probably be ok with him as long as I have Sandy back before lock-down."

Sam cocked her head at me and said, "Naturally, I know that you have to wait until she's released, smart ass."

"Well, I don't know exactly when that's going to happen. You know how slow the wheels of bureaucracy can turn. Why don't we just hold off on making any plans until Sandy's released. Ok?"

"You really spoil all my fun. You know that, don't you?"

"Yep. That's my one true purpose in life, Sam. And by the way, thanks for hauling your ass all the way out to Pennsylvania to be with me. It meant a lot to me." I winked at Sam, who promptly teared up.

"What are best friends for?"

I spent the next few days catching up on all the administrative stuff that I had let go by the wayside during the investigation. I had piles of unfiled letters, bills, and assorted junk. I had tons of telephone and e-mail messages to return. I spent most of the day on these mundane pursuits, trying not to think about Sandy's impending release. I was extremely excited, but I tried to keep it in perspective. I knew that Sandy would require a period of readjustment to the outside world. I needed to be sensitive to this and let her call all the shots for a while. If she needed time to herself at first, I could certainly understand that.

On the third day, I got a call from Slick. "I just wanted to let you know that Sandy was released a couple of hours ago. I arranged for transportation home for her. She should be home within an hour or so."

Despite my resolution to remain calm, my skin broke out in goose bumps, my throat got dry, my palms were wet, and I felt like I was having some kind of panic attack. I managed to stutter out a response. "Yeah, thanks. That's great news."

"You sound funny, kid. Are you coming down with something?"

Just a terminal case of lust and horniness, I thought. But I said, "No, I'm ok."

"It's been great working with you, kid. Let's hook up again real soon. Gotta go now. Talk to you later."

Slick hung up, but I didn't realize it until the phone started making that awful beeping noise it makes when you leave it off the hook. Sandy was coming home. I wanted to race over and see her. I wanted that more than anything. But I resolved to wait until tomorrow, and then, I'd only stop by for a few minutes to check in on her. Unless, of course, she wanted me to stay longer. I'd have to oblige, wouldn't I?

I had a difficult time sleeping that night, thinking about Sandy across town in her bed…alone. I was still tired the next morning, and a little surprised that Sandy hadn't called me yet to at least let me know she made it home safely. I waited until lunchtime, when I could wait no more. I grabbed some takeout from The Sprout and some lavender roses from the corner florist and drove over to Sandy's, more excited than I'd ever been. She answered the door and flashed me a surprised, somewhat guilty look. Sandy cleared her throat and said, "Oh, it's you, J.Z. I wasn't expecting you."

"Sorry. I guess I should have called first. I just wanted to see you."

"I wanted to see you, too."

I stood on the porch and waited for Sandy to invite me in. Finally, I said, "Can I come in? I brought some lunch for us." I held up the takeout containers.

"Oh. Sure. Come on in." Sandy thanked me for the flowers and took the food from me. We stood in awkward silence, and I noticed that Sandy wouldn't look at me.

"What is it?"

Sandy hesitated, then said, "Look, we need to talk." She led me into the living room, and I immediately noticed the suitcases sitting in the corner. A huge lump formed in my throat, and I could hardly breathe.

"Are you going somewhere for a couple of days to become re-acclimated with freedom?" I asked hopefully.

Sandy stared down at the floor and after a few moments said, "Not exactly."

"Sandy, you're scaring me. What's going on?"

She came toward me and brushed the side of my face with her hand. After kissing me on the forehead, Sandy said, "I don't mean to scare you. But I need some time to think about things."

I moved away from her slightly and asked, "Things?"

Sandy began pacing the floor, the same way she did the first night we met. She turned toward me and said, "You know I have feelings for you, and I sense that you have feelings for me too. But I just can't get past the fact that you thought I was capable of murder. More than that—you thought I was capable of killing someone I had once loved and spent years of my life with. I don't know if I can be with someone who could think that about me."

I felt like my legs were going to give out on me. This isn't exactly how I'd pictured our romantic, heartfelt reunion. "Sandy, I'm a private investigator. I have to consider all possible scenarios. I admit that I had doubts, but given the circumstances, you would have had the same doubts." The tone of desperation and pleading was evident in my voice.

"No, that's where you're wrong. I've had a lot of time to do nothing but think about things. I put myself in your position. And you know what? I wouldn't have doubted your innocence, not for a second. When we made love, it was like I could see inside your soul, see the very essence of you. I could see that you were good, through and through. I have to ask myself why you couldn't see that about me. Maybe it means that we're not supposed to be together. I don't know. I just need some time to think."

I fell onto the sofa in a defeated heap and just stared at the wall in front of me. I couldn't believe what I was hearing, and I didn't know how to respond. Sandy came and sat down next to me and took my hand in hers. She kissed my hand and brushed the hair away from my face. "J.Z., I don't know where we're going from here. I hope I can get past this, but I just don't know yet. I can't make you any promises right now."

I looked up at her with tears in my eyes. "Where will you go?"

"I don't know, as strange as that sounds. I thought I'd figure that out when I got to the airport."

"How long?"

She sighed and answered, "As long as it takes, baby. As long as it takes."

I looked at the packed bags and asked, "Weren't you even gonna tell me?"

She looked a bit guilty as she responded, "I was going to call you. I didn't want some big emotional scene. This is hard for me too. Looking at you now, all I want to do is stay."

"Then stay," I pleaded. I looked straight into those beautiful eyes, hoping to glimpse some magical and sudden change of heart.

Sandy kissed my cheek and whispered, "I can't." She got up, walked across the room and retrieved an envelope that was sitting on an end table. She held it up and said, "This is for you."

I got up, walked toward her and asked, "What is it?"

"Payment for services rendered, of course. I doubted that you'd ever send me a bill, so I just picked a number. That should be enough to cover your time, with a little extra for hazardous duty pay."

I held the envelope in a shaky hand and looked down at the floor, not wanting to look into her alluring eyes any more than necessary. Again, Sandy kissed my forehead. She picked up her bags and walked toward the door, glancing back at me before leaving. I watched her load the bags into her car and drive away. I stood there for the longest time, still feeling her presence all around me.

Epilogue

When I had the heart and energy to open the envelope Sandy had left for me, I discovered a check for $150,000. I was shocked beyond belief. I had to cash the check because I had turned away almost all my other work to focus on Sandy's case. But, I decided that I'd put the excess, which was most of the money, into an account until Sandy came back...*if* Sandy came back. Then, I'd try to give it back to her. I knew she had tons of money, especially since she inherited St. James's estate, but I didn't feel right about taking money that I hadn't earned.

Alvin Butterworth called me a few days after Sandy left town. He told me what was bothering him when he and I chatted: he went back to the St. James place to fetch some tools he needed for a project at home. As he was driving up the street, Sandy passed him in her car. She was driving fast and looked scared. Alvin thought Sandy was the killer, but he wanted to protect her.

I also learned why Blaine Darrow looked so cagey when I'd interviewed him, or at least, I was pretty sure. He was arrested recently in a raid on a brothel not too far from the town where his kids lived. I'm sure that's where he was the night of the murder, but he was too ashamed to admit it.

Life goes on. But not a day passes in which I don't think of Sandy several times. Sam was just as crushed by Sandy's departure as I was.

We eat a lot, in an effort to blot out the pain and disappointment, and I've spent a lot of time talking to Barry Cole. We've become good friends, and he's even trying to teach me to cook. Some people are eternal optimists.

About the Author

Margie lives in Salem, Oregon with her partner, Nancy, and their two cats, who bear a strong resemblance to the felines in this book. She has a B.S. in Communications and a J.D. from Willamette University College of Law. Together, Margie and Nancy own and operate JurisNotes.Com, an electronic publisher of intellectual property case summaries and other information. In her "spare" time, Margie enjoys camping, cooking, reading mysteries, and watching movies. She is currently working on the second mystery in the J.Z. Mackenzie series, *Death in a Lovely Shade*.

Other books by
Justice House
Publishing

___

Accidental Love, BL Miller

Accidental Love is a captivating story between Rose Grayson, a destitute, lonely, young woman, and Veronica Cartwright, head of a vast family empire and extraordinarily rich. What happens when love is based on deception? Can it survive discovering the truth? 0-9677687-1-3 $17.99

Above All, Honor, Radclyffe

Single-minded Secret Service Agent Cameron Roberts has one mission-to guard the daughter of the President of the United States at all cost. Her duty is her life, and is the only thing that keeps her from self-destructing under the unbearable weight of her own deep personal tragedy. She hasn't counted on the fact that Blair Powell, the beautiful, willful First Daughter, will do anything in her power to escape the watchful eyes of her protectors, including seducing the agent in charge. Both women struggle with long-hidden secrets and dark passions as they are forced to confront their growing attraction admist the escalating danger drawing ever closer to Blair.

From the dark shadows of rough trade bars in Greenwich Village to the elite gallaries of Soho. Cameron must balance duty with desire and, ultimately, she must chose between love and honor.   0-9708874-1-8 $17.99

Blood Scent, Patty G. Henderson

A story of obsession…
Love beyond the grave.

Blood Scent akes the popular trappings of vampirism, romance and the gothic; bringing them together in a modern tale of a young woman's journey into the dark side of her soul.

Set in fictional Bayton Isle, off the coast of Maine, Samantha Barnes, a successful cover artist for romance novels, must come to terms with her manic depressive past and her obsessive desire to find true love even if it leads her to the grave itself.

When Samantha suddenly finds herself attracted to a woman

with a mysterious and haunting past, she is whisked into a nightmare world of vampires, blood and murder. Thinking that she has finally found the perfect lover in Lara Karnov, the unholy pact she forges with the vampire nearly costs her the lives of those who love her most. Samantha slowly discovers that the infamous Karnov Family is a savvy group of vampires surviving for centuries on the blood of those who served them. By the time Samantha comes to realize the truth, the trail of blood has taken a deadly turn.

The Countess Lara Karnov brings to vampire lore a new and surprising twist in an ending that will haunt you long after you've put the book down.

Blood Scent delivers a bold and daring look into our own darkest fears.   0-9708874-4-2 $14.99

The Deal, Maggie Ryan

Laura Kasdan is cruising along as the News Director at the number one television station in Dallas. When a momentary lapse of control almost costs her a stellar career, she makes a deal to save her job and keep a promise and moves to a smaller station, where she meets a charismatic reporter who promises to turn her well-ordered world upside down.   0-9677687-7-2 $17.99

Of Drag Kings and the Wheel of Fate, Susan Smith

Elvis isn't dead, he's just in Buffalo—and he's a she. When Shakespearean scholar Rosalind meets Taryn, a young drag king, they invoke a karmic cycle that began with recorded history. Is their love strong enough to outwit fate and revise their destiny? *Of Drag Kings and the Wheel of Fate* is passion, mystery, and magic, just as you like it.   0-9677687-8-0 $17.99

Josie & Rebecca: The Western Chronicles,
BL Miller & Vada Foster

At the center of this story are two women; one a deadly gunslinger bitter from the injustices of her past, the other a gentle dreamer trying to escape the horrors of the present. Their destinies come together one fateful afternoon when the feared outlaw makes the choice to rescue a young woman in trouble. For her part, Josie Hunter considers the brief encounter at an end once the girl is safe, but Rebecca Cameron has other ideas....
0-9677687-3-X $17.99

Hurricane Watch, Melissa Good

Dar and Kerry are back and making their relationship permanent. But an ambitious new colleague threatens to divide them—and out them. He wants Dar's head and her job, and is willing to use Kerry to get it. Can their home life survive the office power play? 0-9677687-6-4 $17.99

Kona Dreams, Shari J. Berman,

Kona Dreams, the tale of a chance encounter between two mature women still looking for that special someone, unfolds on the beautiful Big Island of Hawaii. Freddie and Stephanie are in their sexual primes and self-aware enough to be able to laugh at themselves, but can they make an improbable relationship out of their newfound laughter and lust?

Freddie

Can love at first sight be trusted? Twice unlucky in love, Freddie is in Kona nursing the demise of her second marriage. Forlorn and frustrated among the honeymooning vacationers, she heads off the beaten path. When she sees Stephanie, her heart and soul turn somersaults. Life, as she has known it flips abruptly. Can she handle all of the acrobatics involved?

Stephanie

Healing from a break-up, Stephanie decides to console herself at the Kona Cantina. What she finds there looks like it could be the whole enchilada. Everything about Freddie is perfect, except Freddie's never been with a woman before! Freddie's excess baggage also includes a parade of visiting family members who add to the mayhem. Stephanie wants it all, but is that too much to expect from a straight tourist?

Lucifer Rising, Sharon Bowers

Lucifer Rising is a novel about love and fear. It is the story of fallen DEA angel Jude Lucien and the Miami Herald reporter determined to unearth Jude's secrets. When an apparently happenstance meeting introduces Jude to reporter Liz Gardener, the dark ex-agent is both intrigued and aroused by the young woman. A sniper shot intended for Jude strikes Liz, and the two women are thrown together in a race to discover who is intent on killing her. As their lives become more and more intertwined, Jude finds herself unexpected falling for the reporter, and Liz discovers that the agent-turned-drug-dealer is both more and less than she seems.

In eloquent language, author Sharon Bowers paints a dazzling portrait of a woman driven to the darkest extremes of the human condition-and the journey she makes to cross to the other side. 0-9677687-2-1 $17.99

Redemption, Susanne Beck

Redemption is the story of a young woman who finds out that the best things in life are often found in the last place you'd look for them. Angel is a small-town girl who finds herself trapped within her worst nightmare, a state penitentiary. She finds inner strength, maturity, friendship and love while at the same time giving to others something she thought she'd lost within herself: Hope. It is the story of how Angel rediscovers hope blazing within the piercing blue eyes of another inmate, Ice.   0-9677687-5-6 $17.99

Several Devils, K. Simpson

What do you do when you live in the most boring city in America, you hate your job, and you're celibate? Invoke a demon to shake things up, of course. Join Devlin Kerry on her devilishly funny deconstructive tour of guilt, fear, caffeine, and suburbia. 0-9677687-9-9 $14.99

Tristaine, Cate Culpepper

Tristaine focuses on the fierce love that develops among strong women facing a common evil. Jesstin is an Amazon from the village of Tristaine who has been imprisoned in the Clinic, a scientific research facility. Brenna, the young medic assigned to monitor Jess's health, becomes increasingly disturbed by the savage punishments her patient endures at the hands of the ambitious scientist Caster, and a bond grows between the two women. The struggle Brenna and Jess face in escaping the Clinic and Caster's determined pursuit deepens the connection between them. When they unite with three of Jess's Amazon sisters, the simple beauty of Tristaine's women-centered culture weaves through the plot, which moves toward a violent confrontation with Caster's posse.   0-9708874-0-X $14.99

Tropical Storm, Melissa Good

Tropical Storm... Enter the lives of two captivating characters and their world that hundreds of fans of Melissa Good's writing already know and love. Your heart will be touched by the realism of the story. Your senses will be affected by the electricity, your emotions caught up by the intensity. You will care about these characters before you are far into the story... and you will demand justice be done. 0-9677687-0-5 $17.99

Unexpected Sparks, G.L. Dartt

opens with a fatal fire for Sam Madison, Truro's local Lothario, as his insurance office burns to the ground. This arson and subsequent fires makes falling in love a little more complicated as Kate Shannon, forty years old, elegant and highly respected in the small Maritime town, finally surrenders to her growing feelings for twenty-six-year-old Nikki Harris, a country girl who has a habit of poking her nose in where it doesn't belong. Will discovering the unexpected sparks for each other blind these two very different women to the sparks set by an arsonist? Or will the new couple, working together, stop the killer before anything else goes up in flames?   0-9708874-7-7 $17.99

A Year in Paris, Malaurie Barber

When student Chloe Jones becomes an au pair, all she's looking for is an interesting year abroad in Paris, but she gets more than she bargained for in the mysterious Glairon family. While caring for sweet little Clement, Chloe begins to care a great deal for his beautiful but haunted half sister, Laurence. But not even the most romantic city in the world can help these two when the family's secrets threaten to destroy them all.   0-9708874-1-8 $17.99

Join the legacy of
Justice House Publishing

☐ **Above All, Honor**, Radclyffe
0-9708874-2-6 $17.99

☐ **Accidental Love**, BL Miller   0-9677687-1-3 $17.99

☐ **Blood Scent**, Patty G. Henderson
0-9708874-4-2 $14.99

☐ **The Deal**, Maggie Ryan   0-9677687-7-2 $17.99

☐ **Of Drag Kings and the Wheel of Fate**, Susan
Smith   0-9677687-8-0 $17.99

☐ **Hurricane Watch**, Melissa Good
0-9677687-6-4 $17.99
(Dar & Kerry Vol. 2, the sequel to **Tropical Storm**)

☐ **Josie & Rebecca: The Western Chronicles**,
BL Miller & Vada Foster   0-9677687-3-X $17.99

☐ **Kona Dreams**, Shari J. Berman   0-9708874-3-4 $17.99

☐ **Lucifer Rising,** Sharon Bowers   0-9677687-2-1 $17.99

☐ **Redemption**, Susanne Beck   0-9677687-5-6 $17.99

☐ **Several Devils**, K. Simpson   0-9677687-9-9 $14.99

☐ **Tristaine**, Cate Culpepper   0-9708874-0-X $14.99

☐ **Tropical Storm**, Melissa Good   0-9677687-0-5 $17.99

☐ **Unexpected Sparks**, GL Dartt   0-9708874-7-7 $17.99

☐ **A Year in Paris**, Malaurie Barber   0-9708874-4-2 $17.99

To order by mail send this page and a check or money order for the cover price(s) and $4.95 s/h for the first book (plus an additionall $1 per each additional title) to **Justice House Publishing (JHP), 3902 South 56th St, Tacoma, WA 98409**. Delivery can take up to 6 weeks.

Name: _____

Street Address: _____

_____

City/State/Zip: _____

_____

Country: _____

Phone: _____

Email: _____

I have enclosed a check or money order in the amount of

$ _____

Please be sure to check the books you would like to order on the other side of this page.

Visit us on-line at www.justicehouse.com

Order our books at your local bookstore.